PROJECT EMILY

a Haven Port Island story

DONNA LEE ANDERSON

BLUE FORGE PRESS
Port Orchard, Washington

Project Emily
Copyright 2019
by Donna Lee Anderson

First eBook Edition August 2021
First Print Edition August 2021

ISBN 978-1-59092-954-4

For information about film, reprint or other subsidiary rights, contact blueforgegroup@gmail.com

Blue Forge Press is the print division of the volunteer-run, federal 501(c)3 nonprofit company, Blue Forge Group, founded in 1989 and dedicated to bringing light to the shadows and voice to the silence. We strive to empower storytellers across all walks of life with our four divisions: Blue Forge Press, Blue Forge Films, Blue Forge Gaming, and Blue Forge Records. Find out more at www.BlueForgeGroup.org

Blue Forge Press
7419 Ebbert Drive Southeast
Port Orchard, Washington 98367
blueforgepress@gmail.com
360-550-2071 ph.txt

*In loving memory of
Donna Lee Anderson*

PROJECT EMILY

a Haven Port Island story

DONNA LEE ANDERSON

CHAPTER 1

Natalie Ann Greene, of the *don't forget the E on the end of Greene*, stood in front of her full length mirror by the front door. She patted her perfectly permed dyed black hair, and inspected her lips for smudges. *So many older women let their lipstick run up into those little cracks,* she thought, *and I'm certainly not going to be one of them. Besides, being eighty doesn't necessarily make me one of those older women.* Nor would she be one of the saggy hose bunch. She smoothed her navy blue skirt and inspected her stockings, also noting that her low heeled daytime pumps were properly polished. Next she checked the sleeves of her white blouse and the pocket of her dusty rose colored sweater, but no hanky. She went into the bedroom, opened the top drawer of the bureau and picked up one of her favorites, a soft white linen with a fine row of lavender crochet around the edge. She patted her lips and could smell the spicy scent of the sachet.

When she returned to her hallway door again, she heard voices she recognized coming from the hallway.

"Poor Emily," Doctor Pete said with a heavy voice and a sigh.

"Why poor Emily?" asked Sister Nora.

"I sure thought coming to work here would end her depression. Just being among these lively people and seeing some of their antics, I mean, how could anyone stay depressed?" He sighed again. "How long do you think she'll be on the evening shift?"

"Don't worry. We're already working on a schedule change." Then Sister Nora gave a small chuckle that was very familiar to all that knew her. "You know what I think she really needs..."

"What?"

"A special friend. Someone who would help her step out of her funk. Maybe a gentleman friend?" She chuckled again. "But I guess that's her business."

It was Dr. Pete's turn to laugh. "Now Sister, are you planning to start a dating service here? It just might be very lucrative."

"Oh, I don't think so. Just being the director of St. Francis seems like a full time job."

Natalie could hear them still chatting and laughing as they started away from her door and moved down the hall. She hadn't meant to eavesdrop, and she supposed she shouldn't have listened to their conversation, and she also supposed she should have moved away from her door, *however*, she reminded herself, *I only stayed listening so I'd know when I could leave my apartment without interrupting*. Then she decided it wasn't really a breach of etiquette... *Wasn't it almost an act of fate that I was the one to hear about Emily's need for a special someone in her life? And, this is just what I need... a project.*

Never one to stand on the sidelines when a situation needed a leader, Natalie, all five-foot-two inches of her, knew just how to put a plan into action and started to plan the details. *First I'll form committees,* she thought and smiled.

Natalie could have been "in charge of the world given the chance," at least that's what her daughter always said, and *in charge* is not only what she did, it was what she was. For the last fifty-plus years she'd been chairwoman of the Annual Garden Show, the Ladies Aid Annual Dinner Dances, the Girl Scout Council, all the fund raisers at the high school, and volunteered every summer to organize the All-Years-High-School Reunion here on Haven Port Island. However, now that she was retired and living at St. Francis there didn't seem to be that much need for her expertise. That is, not until today when she overhead Dr. Pete and Sister Nora

She didn't stop to wonder if Emily wanted to be handled by committees or ponder the fact that just because Emily had been a little depressed and had come here to work, didn't necessarily mean she wanted her life changed any further, but Natalie decided to move ahead with her plan. She would check with Emily later, but now, first things first.

Projects meant lists, and Natalie did lists very well too. She picked up her notebook from the table and turned to a fresh page. She wrote PROJECT: EMILY at the top. Under that she wrote:

NEEDS:

1. *Chairwoman*
2. *Leader for sub-committee—to contact prospective dates*
3. *Leader for a sub-committee—to check on Emily's response*
4. *Secretary—to take minutes at the meetings*

...because of course there would be meetings.

Next to number one she put her initials: N-A-G.

She would be the chairwoman because everyone always said "Natalie can get the job done" and it was true. Just look at all the scrapbooks she had full of her many successes.

As she left her apartment and started down the hall, notebook in hand, she had a smile on her lips, and her mind was already cranking out plans. She felt needed again.

The next step would be to interview and appoint people to head up these sub-committees.

Steven Xavier might be able to find gentlemen dates for Emily. Natalie had heard rumors he visited some of the ladies in their apartments in the evening, and that sometimes he stayed the whole night. *If he's still dating, he'll probably know other men that are too,* she thought, even at the age of seventy-nine. In front of number two on the list she mentally filled in SX, and changed the word sub-committee to Procurement Committee. *Now just where do you suppose he is?*

She found him in the dining room. "May I have a word?"

He looked up from his coffee cup. She wasn't his first pick for company but she'd be better than nothing. "Sure. Have a seat."

Steven's claim to fame was that he loved all women. Even at the age of seventy-nine it didn't matter what they looked like and it didn't matter how much they liked or disliked him, he just thought women were the best thing since chocolate éclairs. From the first time he realized that if he smiled at his nanny in just the right way she'd give him an extra dessert, he knew he was special, and it would be his lifelong job to share himself with as many women as possible. During his military stint and then working all those years for the Texas State Refinery Board, he'd traveled extensively, meeting many women in many countries. He had never failed to appreciate their talents and beauty and they never forgot him—at least that's the way he saw it. *God's gift to women,* if he did say so himself.

As he looked at Natalie he was reminded of his first wife. She was short and trim too, and bossy just like Natalie. She hadn't understood his need to know many women nor had his second wife. After the last ugly divorce those many years ago, he'd decided marriage was not where he was at his best. Even now that he was retired and moved back home to Haven Port and then simplified his life by moving to this retirement center, he'd slowed down some, but his world was going along as usual... *so many women, so little time.*

"Thank you." Natalie primly sat down in the chair across from him. "It has come to my attention that we need to have a meeting to help Emily. Would you like to be on this committee?"

Steven thought, *Sure, why not. Beats sitting here alone.* "What do I have to do?"

"Could you come to a meeting in the library after lunch at one o'clock?"

"Okay, I'll be there." Emily reminded him of his daughter-in-law but with sad eyes, and he would be happy to help her in any way he could.

Natalie smiled at him and stood up. "I'll see you at the meeting then."

More people were coming into the dining room now and Natalie moved towards her own table so she could put her notebook down before getting into the food line, but she saw Mary was just coming in too and Natalie called to her, "Mary Adele." She was Natalie's choice for heading up the number three spot, the sub-committee for checking on Emily after a date. *She's always a dependable person.*

"Mary Adele. A moment please?"

Mary turned to see who was calling her... and using her middle name. When she saw Natalie she thought, *Who else?* Only the teachers and her family ever called her by her first and middle name, except of course those that had known her since grade school.

Mary Adele and Natalie Ann started the first grade together here on the Island and had continued right through high school. They'd also worked on committees and volunteered on so many of the same projects, Natalie knew she could count on Mary Adele to be agreeable, to follow instructions, and to do what was necessary. Keeping a good eye on Emily's progress was going to be a big job.

"What is it?" Mary asked.

"I'm forming a committee to help Emily. Can I count on you, Mary Adele?"

"Of course you can. Why a committee, and what for?"

Natalie smiled. "Could you come to a meeting in the library after lunch to discuss the details? One o'clock?"

It was just like Natalie to make this a need-to-know situation so Mary just said, "Yes I can," and smiled and then thought, *maybe this will be fun.*

Natalie went back to her table and Mary continued toward the food line. She could smell the barley soup and decided she was hungrier than she thought. As she walked she felt her hip give a little twinge. Not a pain but a reminder that medication was due. Arthritis was her constant companion but mostly she kept it calmed. The pills were in her pocket and she took them with food so it wouldn't be long now. *At eighty you have to expect some discomfort,* she thought.

She shifted her weight and moved ahead in line. *I'll have a lay-down this afternoon,* she decided. The line moved forward and she took a tray and slid it along, choosing a cup of tea, a bowl of soup and half of a grilled cheese sandwich. *Yes, after the meeting a lay-down is exactly what I need. I'll just give this hip a rest.*

Natalie sat down and added a few notes to the list. Next to number two she had already written SX for Steven Xavier, and next to number three she wrote MAM for Mary Adele Murray. At the bottom of the list she added: Item number 5—See Emily. It would only be fair for Emily to have some input and to be able to give some specifics about what kind of man she would prefer. This was exciting and surely Emily would be as excited and delighted with this plan too.

She was smiling at everyone as she joined the lunch line. It was good to be in charge of something again.

Natalie started the meeting as soon as Stephen and Mary were seated. "Thank you for coming. As I mentioned to Steven and you too Mary Adele, it has come to my attention that Emily is having a bout with depression and my plan is to help her be happy again by finding her a male companion."

Mary couldn't believe her ears. Natalie wanted to fix Emily up? But who with?

"Steven, I am asking you to be the Chairman of the Procurement Committee. I think you should choose a couple of other people to help you find viable young men for Emily to date. Do you think you can do this?"

He was smiling because he thought he could easily get dates for Emily by himself but with a couple of helpers, it was a done deal. "Yeah, I can."

Natalie turned her attention to Mary. "Mary Adele, we need to check on Emily after each date to see if it was a success. I would like you and your group to perform this job. Will you?"

Mary thought for only a moment and decided. "Yes, I'd like to help. I thought this meeting would be about getting her a birthday gift, but this much more fun."

"Would you prefer to get the additional people for each of your groups or should I?" They both responded, and almost at the same time. They would fill their own slots and after a short discussion it was decided that a three-person committee was large enough. "We can always add more people if necessary," Natalie said. Mary and Steve nodded in agreement.

Natalie also pronounced they should have a secretary to take minutes. "After all, our memories aren't what they used to be and it would help us just in case there are any disagreements about decisions." Both Mary and Steven said this was a very wise idea too, and Natalie of course, already had someone in mind.

The meeting was adjourned and as they left the library, Natalie saw her candidate Sarah Ann Sampson hurrying towards her. Exactly the person she wanted to see. "Sarah Ann! I need to speak to you."

Sarah didn't even slow down. "Sure, but I'm in a hurry. Don't make me late for pottery class."

Natalie took a few fast steps so she could be beside Sarah, and as they raced down the hall, she said, "Sarah Ann, please stop for one second, then you can say yes and be on your way."

Sarah wasn't much taller than Natalie but she had improbable red hair that suffered from home permanents and not exactly professional haircuts. Her legs were short so she took quick steps when she walked and always appeared to be in a hurry.

Natalie cringed when she looked at Sarah's outfit. It consisted of a polyester printed smock, much like what the nurses wore in children's hospitals. It had bright primary colors in geometric patterns. The smocks varied, but this, along with her red polyester pants with the crease sewn down the front and her white orthopedic shoes, was her daily uniform.

Sarah did stop but turned around glaring.

"What do you want?"

Natalie wasn't offended. She was used to Sarah's attitude and these two ladies had a history too. They'd had children in the same grades at school and in many of the same organizations and activities over the years. Natalie had heard that Sarah thought Natalie was a pushy broad, and there were times when Natalie considered Sarah as more or less common, but they had never had a major confrontation because they both respected the other's strengths, at least committee wise. Over the years it became accepted that Natalie would be the chair and Sarah the secretary. They made a good team.

"We are planning to have some meetings in the library and we need a reliable secretary. The meetings will be to help Emily. Will you take the minutes?"

"Does Emily know we're helping her? And what're we helping her do?"

"I will speak to Emily when she gets in today, and we're going to help her be happier in her life. Sarah, I really need a dependable person. I'll ask Sister Nora if you can use the typewriter in the office. Will you do it?"

"I like Emily so I will. But ask Sister if I can use the computer instead. I've taken classes and I'm not using a typewriter anymore. When's the meeting? It can't mess up my classes."

"The first meeting will be after breakfast tomorrow. That shouldn't interfere with any of your interests, do you think?"

"Okay I'll do it, now move, you're blocking the door. I got a pot to paint." Sarah disappeared into the craft room and Natalie patted her lips and brow with her handkerchief.

She'd forgotten how excitable Sarah was when

the project was new and unknown to her, but now that this task was finished she turned back down the hall towards her own apartment, mentally making changes to the original list. She opened her door and immediately sat down at her desk. On a new page in the notebook she rewrote and updated the list:

PROJECT: EMILY

NAG 1· CHAIRWOMAN
SX   2·Leader of PROCUREMENT COMMITTEE
MAM 3· Leader of SURVEILLENCE COMMITTEE
SAS 4· Secretary
        5· Chat with Emily

This list was not complete but certainly getting there. She still needed to add the other committee members' names, but for now she would have time to read her magazines, then at four o'clock, she would be off to see Emily.

CHAPTER 2

At the age of fifty-seven, Emily Bray Barnes *was* too young to be alone but here she was and she was feeling guilty because she felt relieved.

She'd been a caregiver her whole life. As the oldest child in a family of four, she pretty much raised her three siblings because her mother was of *fragile health,* and of course she cared for her twin boys and husband as a young mother and wife, along with the second grade children she taught. Then, when her boys were grown and moved away, she enjoyed her time of just teaching, but it ended too soon. Her husband Sam had been a heavy smoker, and after emphysema was diagnosed, he decided to become an invalid and only moved from the bed to his recliner and back to his bed, using oxygen to help him breathe. His main communication with Emily was to complain about his quality of life and yell at her. For eight months he grew more and more lethargic and depressed and angry, and when they found the cancer in his lungs he stopped getting out of bed entirely. Emily was the only caregiver he would tolerate, so her fulltime teaching stopped and she took care of Sam the short five months he lasted.

Then, only four months after Sam's funeral, her mother came down with numerous real and imagined illnesses and of course they required Emily's full attention again, since all of her sisters and brothers lived many miles away. She cooked and cleaned and generally baby-sat an irrational, quarrelsome woman until her Mother too was gone.

Now, being alone was a peaceful but lonesome time for her and she couldn't help feeling guilty because she felt so relieved.

Emily smiled when she saw Natalie in the doorway of her office. "Hello. Can I help you?"

Natalie came into the office and sat down in the chair at the end of Emily's desk. "I just thought if you weren't busy, we could chat for a few minutes." She smoothed her skirt and placed the notebook on her lap, then smiled as she looked directly at Emily. "Tell me what occupies your time during those hours you're not here."

Emily thought this was an odd question but she figured Natalie probably wasn't here to just find out about her life, and she could certainly spend a few minutes until Natalie got to the point of the visit.

As she sat down Emily said, "Well, I read a lot and..."

"Did you know about the book club at the library?"

Emily smiled. "Nellie, the librarian... do you know her? I think she's new."

"No, I don't".

"Well, Nellie did invite me to join their Bookery Club. I've always enjoyed reading and now that I have the time, the book club sounded fun. Nellie told me their books of choice were only biographies of women in politics and that they discussed the book and how the heroine's actions might have affected current events in the political world. I was very intrigued."

"Yes, I would be too." Natalie was leaning a little forward. This might be something she would like to do too.

"Unfortunately the discussions always turned into arguments about the local government and then escalated to include the White House, and comments and thoughts were expressed with loud words and very red faces. I decided this was not what I was looking for."

"I don't think I would enjoy that either, and thank you for telling me about it." Natalie leaned her back against the chair again. "And you've stopped teaching completely?"

"Yes I have. I tried substituting but it wasn't as satisfying as having my own classroom and the second grade teacher they have now will probably be here a long time so..." Emily was beginning to wonder what this conversation was all about. She thought Natalie probably already knew all these things about her because Natalie seemed to know everything that went on here at St. Francis and on the Island.

"A little birdie told me you live in a condo now. Do you like it?"

"Yes, I do. It's on Front Street, about six blocks from here. It's called the Marina Condos. Do you know where they are?"

Natalie nodded yes and said, "I often go up that way when I take my constitutionals. So many people in that neighborhood have lovely gardens, don't you think? I especially like the roses on the corner."

Emily had also seen and admired the rose garden too. "I love those too, but I don't think I know the family."

"Well, I just know their name is Owens but I think they're just summer people." Natalie pressed her hanky to her lips and cleared her throat, getting back to the business at hand. "Do you live alone?" She knew perfectly well Emily was a widow and did live alone but it was her way of getting around to the subject.

"Yes..." *What in the world was on Natalie's mind?*

"Don't you ever find it lonely?"

"Oh, sometimes, but now that I'm working here it's not so bad." *Darn*, Emily thought. *I didn't mean to admit that.*

"Well, some of us thought you *just might* be feeling a little alone and wondered if you were dating?"

Emily sat back in her chair and laughed. "No, not really. Dinner with friends is about all. Why do you ask?"

Aha, thought Natalie. Now the door was open. "A few of us have some friends we would like to introduce you to, but we wanted to find out first just what sort of man you prefer. Would you like to share that with me?"

CHAPTER 3

Emily was astounded. She took a deep breath and sat up straighter in the chair, trying to think just what this meant. "Natalie," she finally said, and then she paused again. "I, uh, thank you and whoever else is doing this with you, but I'm not sure it's necessary. I'm happy the way I am and any relationship..."

"Now Emily, we're not asking you to marry these new friends we find for you. We just want you to have someone to take you out to dinner or the theatre, someone who will make your life interesting again. Now is this meddling?" She smiled her most winning and appealing smile and then answered her own question. "We don't think so. We truly think of you as a friend to all of us, and as friends, we want to help you be happy. Won't you let us try?"

Emily just looked at Natalie in disbelief. "I really don't think I want you to do this."

Natalie's shoulder slumped and her eyes got

shiny with tears. She pressed her hanky to her lips, then said, "Oh, Emily. Please let us. We're so excited and... and what would it hurt?"

Emily closed her eyes, took another deep breath and thought, *Oh my. Well, what indeed would it hurt to have these lovely people who so obviously care, introduce me to their single friends? I can always say no to any dates I don't want.* She opened her eyes and said, "If I do let you go on with this, you must promise you won't have hurt feelings if I choose not to date everyone you present and..."

Natalie's shoulders immediately lost their slump and she was smiling again as she straightened up, and cut off Emily's sentence. "Of course. It's only fair to you. Now, tell me what sort of man do you enjoy knowing?"

Emily smiled and sighed inwardly. *Well, in for a penny.* "Well, I ah...."

Natalie got right down to business. "What sports do you like to play?"

"Not many since my boys grew up. We used to bowl and go ice skating in Seattle, and of course fishing."

Natalie was making notations on her list. "And do you like football and basketball?"

Emily answered the rapidly fired questions: Yes, she did enjoy an occasional football game on TV, and yes she had been to a few professional games, both basketball and football... "but I prefer to see the high school games. Those boys are usually someone I taught and it makes the game more interesting."

"Do you like to dance?"

Emily smiled as she remembered the dance lessons in the dining room she'd held for her teenage boys. "Yes, I used to like to dance but it's been many years."

She also admitted to enjoying an occasional cocktail or glass of wine, and no, she didn't care for skiing.

"I know you had lovely gardens when you lived on the Cliffs. Still enjoy puttering?"

"I only have a few containers on the deck now. Some are flowers and I planted tomatoes this year. Not really much of a garden." Emily smiled thinking about the flowers and her gardens at her home on the Cliffs. That area got an afternoon wind most days and her boys always teased that her garden leaned to the west. It didn't actually, only the scrub Elder trees leaned, but this was fun to remember.

The questions continued.

Yes, she had played golf during the early years of her marriage but *no* to tennis. When Natalie asked if she liked strolling in the moonlight, Emily laughed. She had her doubts about that happening.

Natalie finally stood up. She had a good basis for screening the potential gentlemen callers, and she couldn't wait to get her notebook up to date. PREFERENCES would be a new heading under Emily.

"Thank you, my dear. I'll be getting back to you. Now, are you going to be at the movie tonight?" Natalie straightened her sweater and patted her hair as she spoke.

"No, I don't think so. I've got some work to do here. If you're going you can tell me about it the next time we meet."

"All right. See you soon." Natalie picked up her notebook and left Emily's office feeling this part of the plan had gone very well and she now had some definite guidelines. As she walked down the hall she thought, *I love it when a plan comes together.*

Emily watched Natalie go out the door and down the hall and she felt unaccountably refreshed. She smiled thinking of what Natalie was doing. Maybe she did need to get out more and maybe this would be fun. Maybe.

Natalie wasn't the only one putting the plan into action.

After her nap, Mary found her committee members just where she expected them to be. Checking on Emily wouldn't be a hard job but she needed partners who would be discreet. She spotted the two men she had in mind at their table in the dining room waiting for dinner to start. The other occupants of this table hadn't come in yet so she sat down to talk. "Paul, I have a favor to ask of you and George."

"What is it, Mary? What favor?" Paul Engles pulled his glasses down from their usual resting place on the top of his balding head and leaned forward. He was the kind of person whose emotions showed on his face long before his mouth could make a sound, and his eyes were saying he would do anything this woman asked of him—anything.

"Natalie Greene has a plan to help Emily find someone to date. I'm on the committee to check on Emily after she has these dates to see if they went well... if she's happy or what. Do you and George want to help me?"

Paul was already smiling and nodding yes.

George looked confused.

"I want you fellows to be part of the Surveillance Committee because I know you won't feel the need to talk to others about what we're seeing or doing or why we're doing it."

"Count me in," Paul said. "What do you think, George?"

George Masters usually wore his false teeth in his shirt pocket, but now they were in their proper place and ready for food. His speech was easier to understand when his teeth were in, but he didn't care about that. When anyone did mention this teeth and speech problem, he would loudly proclaim, "When they make 'em comfortable, I'll wear 'em all the time."

"Can you hear me, George? Do you want to be on her committee? I think it would be a great deal of fun and very interesting."

"I don't think I caught all that. What're we going to do? Go commit a... what're we supposed to do?" George also had a little trouble hearing but he didn't think he needed to wear those *damn hearing aids* he owned either, so he kept them in their plastic container in his pants pocket. In case he did need them, they would be handy, like at the movie tonight, but what was there to miss hearing while you ate?

Paul looked directly at George and spoke very distinctly, "Watch my lips. We're going to help Emily. Do you want to join this group with us?"

"You bet I do. I like Emily. What do I have to do?"

Paul turned back to Mary. "What do you want us to do? Tell me and I'll explain it to George."

Mary laid out the details as she saw them. "Our responsibilities might change later but for now we'll do a dry run to check on Emily and then after each date we'll check again. My immediate plan is to do our first surveillance trip tonight around eight-thirty. Not necessarily to get information but just as a practice. I know you understand Paul, but can you tell George without telling everyone in the room?"

Paul assured her he could.

"I'll meet you both in the hall outside the dining room at eight-thirty, after the movie. Okay?"

Paul nodded. He smiled at he watched Mary cross the dining room going back to her table and as he turned back to the table George had a few questions, so Paul got busy explaining.

Secretly Mary thought this was exciting, and she wasn't alone. Paul was excited too. A break in the routine and helping Emily and being with Mary, how much better could it get?

Steve was also gathering his committee. Dolly McBride and Larry Williams were the ones he wanted on his team. He was certain they would know the kind of man that would be a good fit for Emily.

That afternoon Steve found one of them on the smoking porch. Larry had that craggy-man look, sort of like Clint Eastwood. His eyebrows were heavy, and he squinted when he looked directly at you, and it seemed he looked beyond your face and was able to read your mind. He always thought this was a useful tool for a lawyer. He still stood six feet two inches tall and he thought of himself as thin, but since he'd quit drinking he'd added some weight and now he was not only tall, but big.

Steve said, "Hey Larry, how you doin'?"

"Fine. Pull up a chair."

Steve sat down and said, "Have you noticed Emily lately... how sad she looks?"

"She always looks sad. Is there something new wrong with her?"

"I didn't mean there's anything wrong with her but she's feeling low so there's this committee Natalie Greene formed to help Emily by finding guys for her to date. Want to help?”

Larry took a drag on his cigarette and let the smoke out slowly. “Why can’t she find dates for herself?”

“Well, look at her. Where could she find a guy? I suppose she could go to Seattle and walk around Pioneer Square until someone talked to her or she could go to Mickey’s Bar...”

“Okay I get it. She’s a lady and ladies get fixed up. Sure I’ll help. I even know a guy that might be fun for her to know. Lives here on the island too. Yeah, count me in.”

“Thanks, now I gotta go see if I can find Dolly.”

Larry laughed. “You just keep trying boy, but I don’t think you’ll make any headway there.”

“It’s not what you think. I want her on this committee too, but now that you mention it...” Steve’s laugh was a low rumble. “Doesn’t hurt to cover all the bases, does it?” He opened the door and went back into the building. He thought maybe he’d knock on Dolly’s apartment door but as luck would have it, he ran into her in the hallway by the library.

“Hey, Dolly.”

“Why Steven, hello. Havin’ a nice afternoon?” Dolly McBride had a small frame and spindly legs that made her look fragile. This look suited her. She wore her hair long in an upswept do, with just a few wispy curls that escaped to surround her sweet face. At eighty-two she wasn’t as spry as she had been but she was just as feisty and quick witted.

The name given Dolly at her birth was Ima and she’d married Phillip Stump three years after her first husband’s demise. She would only admit to a few very close friends that the reason she’d divorced Phillip was only because she was tired of having people laugh when they heard her name was Ima Stump. Phillip didn't understand her discomfort and wouldn't hear of her using her maiden name while they were married, so she got un-married. Then, when she moved here to the retirement home she changed her name from Ima Irene Stump back to Dolly, her nickname since childhood, and went back to her maiden name of McBride. Those who knew her before her move made the adjustment with a knowing smile. And those same people knew her deep southern accent started after a trip to Atlanta when she was fifteen. She'd gone with neighbors as a baby-sitter and it took just one week of listening to these soft southern conversations to convince her that this was perfect for her. Her Mother had to agree, it suited her small, blond, blue eyed daughter but Dolly's brother never tired of telling people she was from southern Oregon, that's why she had such an accent.

"Hello Dolly." He smiled his most winning smile and said, "I have a question to ask you."

"Well, Stev'n you can ask but prob'ly the answer will be..." Her southern inflections were strong.

"Wait a minute. This is something different." He smiled again. "There's a committee being formed to find dates for Emily so she can get happy. I'm asking you to be on my team and find someone to introduce to her to. Will you, or rather do you think you know someone who would be right for her?"

Dolly smiled. This certainly wasn't what she thought Steven was going to ask her but she was delighted to help with this plan. "Well, yes I do know someone. My ex-stepson, but, how will we ever get them together?"

"There's going to be a meeting about this. I'll let you know when. Now, do you want me to walk you to your room and maybe visit for awhile?"

Dolly smiled. "No thank you, Steven. I'll just say goodbye here and do tell me when the meeting is. I'd like to help Emily meet someone nice and my ex-stepson is nice." Saying this she turned and tottered away.

Steven smiled as she left. He was happy she hadn't taken him up on his offer. Dinner was being served soon and then he had plans for quick a nap before the movie.

That evening, before dinner started, with the good smell of pot roast wafting around them, Mary Adele and Steven both told Natalie the names of their fellow committee members. She immediately switched to chairwoman mode, saying there would be a very short meeting held in the library immediately after dinner. "Do you think everyone can attend?" They did. "And tomorrow morning after breakfast we'll have a more detailed meeting to discuss the particulars." They agreed again and went off to inform their fellow committee members. She would tell Sarah.

Natalie sat down at her table in the dining room, and opened the notebook. She wanted to make notes and enter the initials of these committee members in their proper space. She wouldn't admit it to anyone else but really she was afraid she'd forget them if she didn't do it now. Under Surveillance she listed MAM, for Mary Adele Murray; PE for Paul Engles; and GM for George Masters. Under Procurement she put DM for Dolly McBride and LW for Larry Williams. All the names were properly entered but, to her, the list felt incomplete. *If this is to be concise, I really need those middle initials.* Perhaps a peek at the St. Francis's resident list was in order, so she headed for the office. She had just enough time before dinner to make the additions. As she walked down the hall she realized this was a fault she'd lived with her whole life. Details considered meaningless to some had always been critical to her. *And why change at this stage of my life*, she thought. *At this age I can do as I please as long as it hurts no one else... and if it makes me happy.*

Emily must have stepped out but Natalie saw the resident roster posted just inside the office door on the bulletin board, and made the necessary additions to her list:

PROJECT EMILY

1· CHAIRWOMAN:
    NAG -- Natalie Ann Greene
2· SURVEILLANCE COMMITTEE:
    MAM – Mary Adele Murray
    PEE – Paul Edwards Engles
    GUM – George Underwood Masters
3· PROCUREMENT COMMITTEE:
    SEX – Steven Edgar Xavier
    DIM – Dolly Irene McBride
    LAW – Lawrence Anthony Williams
4· MEETING MINUTES:
    SAS – Sarah Ann Sampson

The inventory of likes and dislikes she'd gotten from Emily was on a page of its own and a copy had been made for the Procurement Committee head. She smiled to herself. As usual, she was ready for the next meeting.

The Tuesday after dinner meeting was about to begin.

"Attention, please. Let's get right down to business. Everyone here?" Natalie was at the lectern in the small meeting room. She'd pulled it from the corner where it stood ready for any speakers or meetings, and this was a meeting and she was speaking. She found it necessary to stand on a stool to see over the top, but this was not new to her either.

"We're all here. Let's start," Paul said. He was impatient to get back to his own apartment and bathroom.

Natalie looked at Sarah and said, "Are you ready to take minutes?"

"I'm ready." She gave her a disgusted look that said she was always ready, wasn't she?

Natalie gave her a look back that said *yes you are,* then smiled as she addressed the group. "Are you all aware of what your duties will be?"

Steven said, "My people are Dolly and Larry. We know we're supposed to find fellows for Emily to date. Right guys?"

Both Dolly and Larry nodded.

Mary said, "George and Paul and I are ready. We're going to check on Emily to see how happy she is after these dates. We'll do a practice run tonight... before she leaves for the evening."

Natalie beamed at her group. "Very good. Steven, how long do you think it will take your committee to find prospective friends for Emily?"

"I think we could have some names by tomorrow. What do you guys think?"

Larry again nodded and Dolly said in her best southern drawl, "Why certainly."

"I have a guy in mind," Larry added.

Natalie smiled at him, then turning to the group she said, "I discussed specifications with Emily and I've given the particulars to the Procurement Committee head. Stephen, I presume you will share them with your committee."

Steve nodded yes.

"Now, do you think you could get these gentlemen to come to a meeting on Sunday? Don't you think we should meet them before they're introduced to Emily?" Natalie looked around waiting for a response and was met with nods and some added murmurs of *sure* and *yes*.

"Let's make it two o'clock," Paul said. "Then for sure we can be done with the interviews before Emily comes to work at four."

"She doesn't work on Sunday," George said, hearing aids in place for once.

"That's true but remember she fills in for Anita sometimes."

Again heads were nodding agreement.

"Alright then." Natalie took a breath and smiled at *her people*. "We'll have a meeting here tomorrow after breakfast so the committee heads can make their reports and any discussion can follow. Thank you all for coming." With this said she took off her glasses and let them hang on the golden chain around her neck. She stepped down from the stool and started to wrestle the lectern back to the corner. To her relief, Larry and Steven took over the job. She made a slight bow to them and said, "Thank you kind sirs," and they smiled back.

As they left the room, Steve moved in close to Dolly and almost whispered as he put his arm around her shoulders, "If you need help, let me know. I'm free for the rest of the evening and I could come to your apartment at any time. Should we say around eight?"

"Oh, Steven you are such a caution. No, I don't need any help. Don't bother coming by, but I thank you for the offer." Dolly's deep southern accent made the response sound like "Ohhh, Steev'n, Yar such a caaaaution. No, Ah don' neeed any hep. Don' bother cum'ng bah, but Ah thank you for your awefer."

Hearing Dolly talk like Scarlet O'Hara, with all those soft breathy pauses, sent a wave of desire through Steven, and since he was sure this was only a temporary rejection, he just gave her a friendly pat on the shoulder and with a gentlemanly bow and a nod of his head, went to his apartment. Once there he picked up his jacket and Stetson and went out again. It was poker night at Jake's Place so he really didn't want to see her later, but he thought, *Never let an opportunity pass you by.*

Dolly was smiling too as she opened the door to her apartment. A *lady might not always say yes, but it is always nice to be asked.*

She was just shutting the door when the phone started to ring. She answered with a soft, "Hello?"

It was her daughter Maybelle. "Mama, I'm just calling to remind you about the birthday lunch on Saturday. Donny will pick you up at eleven o'clock. Do you want him to come to your room?"

Dolly sat down by the phone. "Oh, Maybelle," she crooned. "Ah haven't forgotten and tell Donny Ah'll be by the front door."

"Okay Mama. See you soon. 'Bye."

"Bye-bye dear."

It was so kind of her daughter to remind her of the birthday party for her grandson, but she had it on her calendar and wouldn't have forgotten. And since she was already by the telephone she looked up the number for her ex-stepson Ronald in her personal telephone directory and dialed.

"Hello," she heard.

"Hello, may I please speak to Ronald?"

It was her ex-husband who answered. "Hello Ima."

"Hello Phillip. How are you? Is the feeling coming back into your foot yet?"

"I'm better every day and I'm in physical therapy now and the foot's acting better. Just started going to exercises by myself. I call that progress. They say this stroke was just minor and I'll be able to drive again soon so then I can go back to my own house."

"Are you not being treated okay there at Ronald's? Aren't you happy?"

"Sure, its okay here, but not like being at home. How you doin'? Do you still like living at that nursing home? Because you know if you want to, you can always come back home to me."

Dolly spoke slowly, each word soft but firm. "First of all, I'm living in an apartment at St. Francis Retirement Center, not a nursing home. People are available if I need them, but otherwise I'm taking care of myself. It's the ideal life. They clean my rooms and feed me too much, and I have all these friends and things to do. You should consider comin' here to live. You just might like it."

"I'll think about it. Could we live together again? That would make me come for sure."

"No, I don't think so. I'm all settled in now, but you could be close by and we could just see each other all the time. Now, may I speak to Ronny?" Her southern accent was working overtime.

There was a hesitation on Phillip's end of the line. "You didn't just call to check on me?" He sounded disappointed but hopeful.

"Not this time. I called to talk to Ronny. Is he there?"

"Sure." She could hear him sigh, then take a ragged breath and yell, "RONNY, IMA'S ON THE PHONE." Then into the phone again he said, "What do you want him for?"

"I have someone I want him to meet," Dolly said.

"Oh. Well, here he is."

After a slight pause she heard, "Hi, Ima."

"Hello Ronny. Remember you said you would like to meet someone nice for a change? Well, a group of us met together today to find someone suitable for one of our friends. Would you be interested in participatin'?"

"Well, Ima, if you think I'm suitable, I think I would be interested. When and where?"

"On Sunday. Please come in the afternoon to meet the committee? Could you come by 'round two?"

"Sure, Ima. Two o'clock. Does she know about my funny eye? And... will there be an interrogation?" He sounded a little worried.

"Oh Ronald, it's not going to be an interrogation and don't worry about your eyes. It's hardly noticeable, usually. This is just for meetin' the committee. You'll enjoy yourself, I promise. I'll meet you by the front door and we'll be together all the time."

"Well okay, you can count on me. See you Sunday, Ima."

"One more thing. Don't forget everyone here knows me by the name of Dolly. No one calls me Ima anymore. Can you remember, dear?"

"Okay, I'll remember." Then after a slight pause

he said, "'Bye Dolly."

"'Bye-bye."

She hung up the phone and made a notation on her calendar—two o'clock, Sunday. Then she picked up her paperback and settled into the recliner. This was fun. She loved match making.

She was still smiling as she turned to the marked place in the James Patterson book she was reading. It was at a very exciting part and she couldn't wait to start reading again.

CHAPTER 4

Breakfast at St. Francis of Assisi Retirement Center was a very busy time. Dishes clanked and the conversations were loud to accommodate those ears that didn't hear well. Natalie was busy this Wednesday morning too. She stationed herself at the end of the food line so she could rally her troops.

"Meeting in the library right after breakfast," she said to George.

Today George's sparse white hair was standing up in tufts on his head. After his morning shower he'd wiped his head dry but had forgotten to comb his hair. Natalie noticed but didn't say anything.

George just nodded at her. Her voice was one he could hear even without the hearing aids. *How can you be so cheerful and talkative this early in the morning,* he thought. His wife had been the same way... full of life and happy when she first got up. He thought about Beth and the happy idiotic morning chirpings she made and all the sweet hugs and kisses as she tried to get him out of his regular glum morning mood. *God, how I miss that woman.*

"Meeting in the library right after breakfast, Mary Adele, do you have your report ready?"

She preferred to be called just Mary but Natalie always ignored her wishes. *Nothing ever changes with her,* she thought. "Yes, the Surveillance Committee did a run last night and we do have a report." It was the first report of this fun adventure, even if there was little to tell. "I'll tell Paul and George about the meeting."

"No, it's my job. I'll do it," stated Natalie in no uncertain terms. After all, she was in charge of this whole Project. This plan was hers and she knew you had to keep the chain of command firm.

Mary nodded and carried her breakfast tray to her table. "Yoo-hoo, George," she said. He didn't look up from his oatmeal so she knew he hadn't heard. She set her tray down and went across the room to get his attention. "Don't forget the meeting in the library after breakfast," she said.

"I already know," George answered. "Natalie told me."

"Oh," Mary said and went back to her table muttering, "Of course she did."

Back at her position at the head of the line, Natalie continued the reminding. "Meeting in the library right after breakfast," she said to Sarah.

"I know. I know. You told us yesterday. I'll be there."

Dolly was next in line and Natalie put her handkerchief to her lips. "Oh, Dolly. You forgot to wear a sweater. Do you want to go get it or change your blouse?" When she recovered somewhat she added, "And, don't forget there's a meeting in the library after breakfast."

"I didn't forget my sweater," drawled Dolly emphasizing her accent. "This is the new organza blouse my daughter gave me and I felt underclothing was unnecessary today since it's going to be so warm. Don't you think the tucking and the ruffles on the front are sweet? And this color is just perfect. Pink has always been my best color." She smiled sweetly at Natalie. "I won't forget the meeting this morning'. I'll be there right straight from this breakfast meal."

Natalie cringed. Maybe she should talk to someone about the dress code again, or really, the lack of one. She hoped Sister Nora would notice Dolly and say something.

Steven was next in line and he said, "My, don't you look just luscious today Dolly. I really like your blouse. You should wear it more often." Then, turning to Natalie he said, "And, good morning to you. Yes, I know about the meeting and I'll be there, especially since Dolly is attending." He smiled briefly at Natalie then his smile turned into a lecherous grin as he followed Dolly into the dining room.

Natalie shook her head in disapproval, but what could she do. *I wish this management would let me instruct these people about their attire.* She had noticed repeatedly that several of her fellow residents did not know about proper dress and decorum, and she could only imagine what was going through Steven's mind now with this display of Dolly. *Well, Dolly will just have to handle him.* She herself had to handle and deal with Steven right after he moved here. She was sure he thought because she took time to apply makeup and wear appropriate dress for the time of day, she would be an easy mark. First he tried to hold her hand during a movie, and then for goodness sake, he tried to kiss her when they met accidentally in a dimly lit hall one night. Well, she was not that kind of woman and she surely didn't appreciate having to watch these goings-on either. She made up her mind. *As soon as my committee duties were over and we've found someone for Emily, I'll have a talk with Sister Nora, and if need be, I'll go to the Board.* They needed to realize what really went on here at St. Francis.

Everyday at the close of breakfast, Sister Nora read the announcements:

"Today is Wednesday. Remember the book club meets today in the library after lunch, at one o'clock.

Remember also that this evening there is a movie scheduled at six-thirty in the meeting room. We're showing *The Sundance Kid*. When we voted, it was the one that got the most votes as a see-again movie. For those who care to have popcorn, come to the dining room just before the movie and pick it up.

And one last announcement... it's about shoes: Remember you must wear hard soled slippers or shoes any time you leave your apartment. These floors can be dangerously slippery for those soft, cloth bottomed slippers."

Announcements by Sister marked the end of breakfast. Everyone stood up almost in unison when they heard her finish with the usual reminder, "Have a safe and blessed day."

Most of the residents headed to their rooms for an after breakfast wash-up, but the committee members went dutifully to the library for their meeting. When everyone was settled, Natalie turned to Sarah but before she could say anything Sarah growled, "You don't have to give me directions every time."

"All right, Sarah." Natalie patted her lips with her hanky, took a deep breath and said, "Everyone is here so may we please have the report from the Surveillance Group?"

Last night at eight-thirty, Mary, Paul and George, the Surveillance Group, met in the hall outside of the dining room door. They were ready to do a practice check on Emily. George was not wearing his teeth but he did have his hearing aids in place. He thought if they were going to do surveillance, it certainly would include hearing, so he was ready.

Mary led the two men down the hall past the office door in a nonchalant stroll. At the end of the hall Mary said in a low voice, "Do you think she looks happy?"

Paul said he thought so, but George couldn't tell.

"Let's go back by and then we'll talk about it at the other end of the hall."

The group started back, hoping it would look like they were on another stroll but at the office door George leaned in and said, "Hello Emily. Are you happy tonight?"

Emily turned from the filing cabinet and looked at him. "Yes I am, George. How about you?" He nodded his head and returned to the group. He was smiling broadly and didn't understand what Mary was upset about.

Back in the main hallway George said, "Well, mission accomplished. I'm gone." And he turned down the hall towards his apartment.

Paul patted Mary on the shoulder and said, "Maybe we could go about this in a different way if we need to do this again."

Mary nodded. *Yes, and just maybe I'll be doing the surveillance alone after this.*

Mary stood up slowly to give her report. Her hip was a little bothersome this morning again, and the pain pill she took at breakfast hadn't quite kicked in yet. "We, my group of Paul and George and me, checked on Emily last night. She was here at work and she was happy." She didn't mention how George found out.

"Thank you for your succinct report," Natalie said. "Now, could we hear from the Procurement Committee?"

Steven stood up. "My Group is Larry, Dolly and me, and I have a list of three potential lays for Emily."

Natalie looked at him with wide eyes and her head was vigorously shaking no. "Steven, could we please use language that is not so offensive? Prospective suitor is a much nicer term. Sarah, put *suitors* in the minutes instead of those other words."

"I did it before you told me. I'm not stupid."

"Steven, please continue with your report." Natalie said. Her smile was thin but it was the best she could offer, and she hoped it was encouraging.

"By the way, the name is Steve. Only my mother and the nuns called me Steven. My group has three *pro-spec-tive suit-ors*," he mimicked. "Did I say that right? I guess we'll just call them now and set something up."

"All in good time, Steven... um, Steve. Could you please read us the names?"

"Your nephew Patrick Kelso, Dolly's ex-stepson Ronald Stump, and Carl Randall, recommended by me. Larry says he has someone in mind but wants to talk to him first."

"Did you say Donald Trump? Do you think he

would come here to date Emily? It'd be a damn good deal if you think you could pull it off," George said. He'd forgotten he would want to hear at this meeting and his hearing aids were in his pocket again. "Who knows him anyway, and isn't he already married to some foreigner or is he divorced again?"

Paul said. "The name is Ronald Stump. RRRRR. You didn't hear right. But Donald Trump just might be single again so maybe we could write him a letter."

Paul and George both laughed and so did some of the others, but not Natalie.

"No, we will not write to Mr. Trump unless we completely run out of prospects here. And of course, rich men are as easy to love as the poor ones." Natalie had heard this somewhere and she thought she was making a joke. She laughed, but no one else seemed to catch on, at least they didn't laugh. She pressed her hanky to her lips again and cleared her throat. "Sarah, please read back the report from the Procurement Group."

"They have three names they call referrals. Steve wants to call them for a meeting." Sarah wrote in her own style of shorthand and she read it back just as she put it down.

"Thank you Sarah. Steven... Steve... first we will have to study their characters. How else will we know if they are suitable for Emily?"

Dolly stood up. "About these referrals, do you-all think we would refer someone not suitable? My family is all just like me. Good upstanding citizens and generally speakin', very nice people." She was crooning in her best wounded southern voice. "Why, my own brother's daughter thought Ronald would make a perfect husband. It didn't work out, but there's a reference, don't ya-all think?" She sat down still looking offended.

Natalie nodded. "I guess I should rephrase what I said. I now think we, as the committees, need to meet these young men first. Do you agree?"

Everyone nodded.

"Should we meet them all together or one at a time?"

Steve said, "I thought we said we would invite them for Sunday. I vote we interview them one at a time. It's the way Emily will meet them, isn't it?"

Paul said, "Let's hurry this up. I have to go."

"Where're you going," asked George.

"You know, GO!" Paul said with emphasis. "In fact, I'm leaving." Then to Mary, "Tell me what you decide." Mary nodded as Paul quickly stood up and left the room.

"Let's vote. All in favor of a meeting with all these young men one at a time raise your hand," Natalie said.

No one moved. "What are we supposed to do?" George was confused and so was everyone else.

"Oh, for cryin' out'loud, let's just vote," Steve said. "This is getting to be a hassle."

"Please, everyone. All those in favor of a meeting with the applicants one-on-one or in a group on Sunday, please say yes," Natalie said.

Again, no one spoke.

She realized the question was not quite clear so she rephrased again. "All those in favor of meeting these men one at a time on Sunday, please say yes or no."

Sarah was tired of this. "What she means is vote yes if you want to meet these guys in a group on Sunday."

Every one said yes and Natalie blotted her lips.

"Now we just need to know when," Steve said.

"Steven… Steve, will you make arrangements with your group to notify these young men to come on Sunday? Tell them we will have a little coffee hour, and I think perhaps Sunday afternoon would be good, say three o'clock? Most of us are available then and they most probably will be free on the weekend."

"Natalie, we already decided yesterday it would be at two o'clock on Sunday so we'll be finished in case Emily comes to work. Will you call your sister's boy to see if he can come to this little shindig?" Steve's voice was showing his impatience.

"Yes, I will," Natalie said and blotted her lips again.

"Dolly can you contact your ex-husband's kid Ronald, and ask him to visit here on Sunday at two o'clock?" Steve asked.

"Steven, I would be happy to do that," Dolly said. "In fact, I already called him and he is coming."

"Good. And I'll call Carl and we'll get this show on the road. Anything else, Natalie?" She shook her head no and he turned his attention to Dolly and smiled his special smile that lets a woman know she is of interest. "Do you need my help?"

Dolly smiled sweetly back at him and said, "Oh Steve, no thank you. I've already told you Ronald knows about the meeting and it's confirmed he'll be here."

"Thank you everyone." Natalie said. "You will all be informed when the next meeting is necessary, and this meeting is adjourned."

Dolly walked back to her room on her pencil thin legs, still thinking she looked so special in her pink see-through blouse.

Sarah went to check on her pot. It might need more glaze.

Mary and Larry each headed to their apartments, and George headed for the patio to have a smoke. He found Paul already there, enjoying a cigar.

"Get your job done?" George asked as he pulled a pipe and tobacco from his pocket and folded his still tall frame onto a canvas chair. "Wish I'd thought of a reason to leave." These meetings were certainly not his style. He'd always tended to be a work-alone type of guy with little conversation needed or wanted, and he'd been considered a loner by all his crews. Before his retirement he owned a company that specialized in stone, wood, and brickwork for homes and the interiors of those fancy office buildings in Seattle and a few other places. He was a master craftsman in his trade. His once thick brown hair had thinned and lightened to a sparse white fringe and there were small patches that still grew on the top. His shoulders stooped a little but he still loved to play golf and he was often mistaken for a man in his sixties, instead of the eighty years he was.

"Yep, took care of that and could have come back to the meeting, but I decided to come here instead. Did I miss anything?"

"No. They're calling the fellows they have lined up so they can come on Sunday and we can look 'em over. That's all."

"Good."

"All this meeting stuff is BS. Can't hear what's being said half the time with all those people talking at once. Might as well just leave these contraptions in my pocket. And just who made Natalie in charge anyway?"

"I guess it's because she came up with the idea and we all want to help. I like Emily and I want her to be happy, don't you?"

"Of course I do. It's just... you know, the meetings. I didn't like 'em when I was working and I sure don't like 'em any better now."

Paul laughed. "I think the best way to stop the meetings is to find a guy for Emily." George just grunted. He sure hoped it would be soon.

The patio door opened and Steve came out to join them. A special room had been set aside for smoking, but you got to it by coming out across this patio first. In nice weather you could find the smoking crowd out here. "You okay now, Paul?"

"Yep. Just the juice and coffee caught up with me. We're discussing the fact that we don't much care for all these meetings, and I've been thinking... has anyone asked Emily if she even wants to do this?

"Natalie gave me a list of specifics I think she got directly from Emily herself." Steve sat down and chuckled, almost to himself. "I figure anyone would be happier if they got screwed sometimes, don't you?"

"Well Steve, not putting it quite that crudely, I would say anyone would be happier if they were loved," Paul said. "And, I'm sure Natalie did get the list from Emily and has that part under control." He stood up and crossed to the door, heading again for his apartment. "Now, I have to go. See you later."

CHAPTER 5

Hello, Patrick? This is Aunt Natalie."

"Hi. How are you?"

"I'm fine. Thank you for asking. Remember I told you about the friend I wanted you to meet? The one that works here where I live?"

"Sure I remember our conversation last night. Is this the one you got a committee working on? You know, I was thinking, this lady really must be a hard sell or a real loser if she needs a committee to fix her up." Patrick sounded whiny.

"Oh Patrick, I hope I didn't give you the wrong impression," Natalie said. "Emily is a lovely young woman and she's about your age. She's retired from teaching, and she's not a loser. Really, she's not. I like her."

"What's she look like?" Less whine, but still not a very positive response.

"She has long dark hair that she wears pulled back and secured at her neck. She's slim, and she sometimes wears glasses. What else do you want to know?"

"Does she drink? Is she interested in traveling? Does she know anything about business or the stock market? All those things."

"Well, dear, I think this is something for you to talk with her about when you meet, don't you? But first, before you do meet her, my committee would like to meet you. Are you available on Sunday?"

He said yes and they chatted about the time, what ferry he would catch from Seattle, and where exactly he should come for the meeting.

"How should I dress? Suit or regular clothes," he asked.

"What do you consider regular clothes? It's not those ugly suits you sweat in, is it?"

Patrick laughed. "No, Aunt Natalie. I don't do sweating except when I go to Mexico. I'll just wear slacks and a jacket."

"That would be exactly right. See you Sunday." After she hung up she couldn't help but feel smug. *Patrick is perfect for Emily,* she thought. *He's a little shy, just like she is and he has all that money he makes from his parking lot business.*

Natalie sat down at her desk. Today's meetings had been productive but she had something else on her mind too. She had been wondering how she could get Emily to update herself? She did have that lovely long hair but she wore it so plain, and those black rimmed glasses, and the clothing that seemed to be too big for her, and the lack of make-up... it all made her look the part of an old schoolmarm. *Just how could I convince her to dress her age and not look quite so frumpy? Hmmm... maybe another committee was needed.* Natalie smiled as the idea started to brew in her head.

Lawrence Anthony Williams was making calls too. He was Larry to everyone at St. Francis but still LAW to his old friends and right now, he was calling an old friend. His plan was to get Brian Junior to come meet Emily. Brian was a good boy, at least he had been while living next door to Larry... well, when he finally grew past the rock throwing age, he was good. Brian Senior had been his friend for many years, but not very friendly lately. Larry knew he didn't need to get Senior's permission to talk to Junior since Junior was now fifty-nine years old, but the problem was that Larry couldn't find the slip of paper with Junior's phone number on it. It was supposed to be in his wallet, but somehow it was gone, so he was making this call to Senior.

"Hello?" Brian Senior answered.

"Hi, this is Larry,... ah... Law. How you doin'?" LAW had been Larry's nickname since grade school days because of his initials... and being an attorney made it stick even harder over the adult years.

There was a hesitation on the line then, "I'm fine. What do you want?"

Larry chuckled at the expected response and said, "Brian, I want to be friends again. I'm calling to apologize for the last fight we had over the dog. I'm sorry. I'm not drinking at all now so there shouldn't be that sort of problem ever again. Did you get all those flowers replaced?"

Brian was silent.

"Aw, come on. We've been friends for to long to let just an argument ruin..."

"Law, there wasn't just one argument. It was forty-seven years of arguments every day over something. I'll tell you the truth, I was glad when you had to move to the retirement home and I hope you *have* stopped drinking for good. Is that all you called about?"

"No, not really, but it was the most important thing. We okay again?"

Brian hesitated again, and then said, "Oh, hell. Why not? What else did you call for, Law?"

"I don't go by my initials any more. When I moved I wanted a new start so I go by Larry now. And, I thought I'd like to call Brian Junior and apologize too. Could you give me his number?"

"Good idea. You were pretty rough on him the last few years he was home." Brian told him the number then added, "He lives up on the Cliffs now, did you know? Got his self a nice little condo and a nice little girlfriend named Annie to share it."

"He still working for the same airline?" asked Larry.

"Yep, and now he's head of a department and isn't flying as much. Doin' real good."

"Well, nice talking to you. Guess I'll call Junior now. Let's get together for lunch sometime, okay?"

"Okay Law. Give me a call. As long as you stay sober, I'd like to be friends again." And Brian Senior hung up.

Larry sat there wondering if he should find someone else to meet Emily since it sounded like Junior was hooked up. But he wanted to make amends there too, so he dialed Junior's number.

A sweet voice answered.

"May I speak to Brian?"

"He's not home yet. May I take a message?"

"When do you expect him?" Larry was thinking this probably wouldn't work out for Emily.

"Well, he was supposed to be home on the

twelve-thirty ferry after playing golf in Seattle, but he hasn't called and I'm not sure if he'll be home before he goes to work. If you want to talk to him you should try him at his office. Do you have the number?" He said he didn't so she gave it to him.

"Okay, I guess I'll catch him there. Thanks," Larry said, and he hung up rethinking his hesitation. That relationship didn't sound very strong at the moment. Maybe Brian Junior *would* be available. Larry wrote the number on the back of an envelope and put it under the phone then looked at his watch and decided to go to the dining room for a cup of decafe and make this call later. Maybe he'd run into someone to talk to, but if not, he'd just get his coffee and wait. He was glad to be living here. He ate the right foods and sure didn't get to drink anymore which, thank God, he'd finally realized was a good thing. When he drank his judgment turned to crap, and he wanted to fight with anyone that looked at him. Now he was happy to just drink coffee and talk. *Too bad I didn't learn that trick years ago*. Booze had lost him two wives, most of his family, and not many of his old friends still talked to him. AA said to take it one day at a time and that sure was a help. He was now up to Step Nine and making a list of those he had harmed and had already started on the reparation of those wrongs. One day at a time.

CHAPTER 6

Natalie seemed to call for a meeting immediately after every meal but she said this Wednesday evening it would be very short. When they arrived she was standing at the front table holding a gavel in her hand. It had been a gift from the Haven Port School District, given for her many years of service. She looked at it fondly. During her last year of volunteering, besides her other committees, she'd taken on the job of running the silent auction fundraiser to upgrade the swimming pool at the high school. It was a huge success but very tiring, so when her granddaughter Charlene graduated from high school that spring, Natalie decided to retire. There'd been a big dinner and many speakers saying how well she'd done her job over the years, and how much she would be missed. This gavel with its silver dedication placard that read TO NATALIE A. GREENE, WITH MANY THANKS FROM HAVEN PORT ISLAND, was the parting gift, and holding it in her hand tonight brought back the old feeling of *being needed*. She pulled herself upright, pressed her hanky to her lips and smiled, realizing that once again she was *in charge of something important and necessary.*

Tap, tap. "Everyone—this will be a short meeting." She had decided the lectern was too much trouble for these short meetings so she was standing by a table. She tap, tap, tapped on the table again. "Steven, please could we have the report from the Procurement Committee?"

He gave her his best *serious and understand-this* look and said, "My name is Steve." He continued to look at her until she smiled, then he said, "My committee has invited four prospective dates to a meeting at two o'clock on Sunday. Do you want the names again?"

"Well, it would be nice for us to hear," Natalie said. "Yes. Tell us the names and anything you can about them. This way we can get a head start on any questions we may want to ask of these gentlemen. Steven..., ah, Steve, do you have this information or should we hear from your group members?"

"I'll let them speak about their own guys," Steve said. "Dolly, do you want to go first?"

"Ah would be pleased to be first. I'm presenting my ex-stepson Ronald Stump..."

"I thought we weren't going to write to Donald Trump. We were going to wait and use him only if all the others fell through," George said.

Mary looked directly at him and said, "You didn't hear again. We're talking about Ronald Stump. Don't you have your hearing aids with you?"

George's cheeks got red as he fumbled in his pants pocket.

"I'll continue," Dolly said, bestowing a sweet

smile on George. "Ronald will be here at two o'clock. Do y'all I think we should have cookies and tea too?"

"I've arranged to have cookies, tea and coffee," Natalie said. "I talked to Sister Nora and she said Edith it would set it up for us. She's the one on kitchen duty Sunday."

"I should have known you would think of that," Dolly drawled and she gave a knowing look at Mary.

"Can you give us some details about the young man?" Natalie said.

"Why certainly. He's my ex-husband's boy. Fifty-seven years old and quite handsome, except for his one eye that seems to look at the ceiling or somewhere else when you're talking to him. Sometimes one eye looks at you and the other one wanders around a bit. He was born with it and it still does have a mind of its own. He's been working for the government since he graduated from the University and now he's a consultant. He does a lot of traveling, he likes the ballet and opera, and I guess I should tell every one that he has a shy side. I think he'd just be perfect for Emily and she's so kind, I just know she wouldn't mind his funny eye, do y'all think?"

Some of the committee smiled, some nodded yes they thought Emily was kind, and George just looked confused. He didn't quite get all that Dolly had said. He was thinking maybe it was necessary to hear everything for these meetings after all, and he was still fumbling with his hearing aid box.

"How about you, Larry?"

"I haven't talked to Brian yet. Might still get him tonight. I'll tell you about him later if he says yes to Sunday.

"All right. And now you, Steve? Natalie smiled because she had remembered not call him Steven.

My guy's Carl Randall, an old golfing buddy. He owns a car dealership in Seattle and one in Tacoma, and he's doing pretty well. He's sixty but acts younger. Dresses pretty good and his mother liked dancing and taught him, so he's pretty good at it, at least my second wife thought so. What else do you want to know?"

"I think that is enough for now, Steve." Natalie was proud of herself for remembering to say Steve again. "Thank you everyone for you report. Now for Sunday... the young men will be coming at two o'clock, is that right Sarah?

Sarah nodded yes.

"...so we should all be gathered in the meeting room by one-forty-five. Everyone agree?" They all did and the Wednesday evening meeting was over.

The group filtered out of the library but Paul and Larry left immediately, Paul to take care of his urgency problem and Larry to call Brian Junior at his work.

Back at his apartment, Larry looked at the envelope and dialed. It was a little after six-thirty but Steve knew Brian's office was open until seven on weeknights.

"Mr. Daniels office."

"Hello, this is Larry Williams. May I speak to Mr. Daniels please?"

"One moment please." Elevator music played when he was put on hold.

"Hey, Law. Dad said you'd be calling."

"How's everything? Work going okay?"

"I'm staying in the office more now and not flying as much. Being a pilot's fun but being gone all the time gets to you. How are you?"

"I stopped drinking and I'm okay. Just called to apologize for all the times when I *was* drinking and making everyone's lives a mess. Hope we can be friends again."

"Hell, Larry. I really liked you when you were sober, and I still like that part of you. If you're not drinking it's a good thing and yeah, we're still friends."

"Thanks, Brian. Now... how's your love life?"

"Well, that's not going very well. Why?"

"If you're not attached, I have someone I think you would like to meet." And he told Brian about Emily and the reception on Sunday. "Can you make it or are you even interested?"

"I think I remember her from school, she's a few years younger, right? Are you sure she likes my type?"

"Well, are you willing to find out? I think you'll be surprised at how she looks now. And she's a teacher you know."

"Didn't know that but why not? Sunday at two?"

"Yes, I'll meet you in the lobby, okay?"

"Okay. See you Sunday."

Larry was happy he would be seeing Brian again, and just maybe Emily would like him too. He smiled to himself. Maybe a good woman *was* all Brian needed to be happy.

CHAPTER 7

It was Thursday afternoon and Steve had been tracking Dolly all day. After breakfast she went back to her apartment but didn't answer the door when he knocked. Then after lunch, she'd hurried back to her room again, but at three o'clock he spotted her going to the library and he followed. Bella was playing the piano today and Dolly just loved classical music. Even the occasional wrong notes didn't interrupt her memories of the wonderful honeymoon she'd taken to Europe with her first husband. They'd made a point of going to all the musicals and operas they could find. It had been a wonderful time.

He sat down in the chair beside her.

"Oh, Steven, Ah didn't know you liked this kind of music."

"I usually don't, but I wanted to talk to you," Steve said. Funny, he didn't mind Dolly calling him Steven. "I just wanted to ask you if you knew anyone other than your ex-stepson who could come to meet the committee on Sunday. I think we need more than three guys, don't you?"

Dolly placed her left index finger on her cheek, just under her eye. This was her *I'm thinking* pose. "Why yes, I do believe I could find someone else too, and I agree, three is certainly not enough to choose from."

Steve reached over and gave Dolly's hand a squeeze. He was surprised how soft and warm it was. "Okay, see what you can do for Sunday. Talk to you later," and he hurried out of the library before Bella struck the first note.

Finding Larry was easier. He was in the dining room talking to Dr. Pete. "Hi," Steve said. "Is this a private meeting or can anyone join?"

"Not private at all. Sit down," Dr. Pete said. "How's everything today, Steve?"

"Going good. What's new here in dining room land?"

"Dr. Pete and I are talking about starting up some AA meetings here. I thought I was the only one who needed to attend those Friends of Bill coffee klatches, but it seems there are twelve of us fellow drunks living around this island who could attend."

"We'll discuss this further and I'll check into what has to be done to get started," Dr. Pete said. "Steve, would you like to join the group?"

Steve laughed. "I probably should participate even though drinking doesn't seem to be a problem to me much anymore. I have other interests now."

Dr. Pete chuckled and said, "I've heard about some of those interests." He stood up and said, "Well, if you two will excuse me I have some things to attend to" and he headed towards his office.

They watched Dr. Pete disappear around the

corner and Steve said, "Larry, I've been thinking about Emily."

"She's a little young for you, isn't she?"

Steve laughed. "Not really but that wasn't what I meant. What I want is for us to find more than just three guys for Emily to choose from. What do you think? Could you find another guy too? Dolly and I think we can."

"I might be able to come up with someone else, if anyone else is still talking to me. But, yes, sign me up for two at least. I think I can help... at least I really want to and I'll try."

"Good, that's what we need. Desire to help," Steve said. "Ready for another cup of coffee? I'm getting myself one."

"I'll go with you. I might get juice instead. After all it's cocktail time somewhere." Larry was laughing. But the laugh was more self-deprecating than happy. "Maybe a be-sure-its-shaken-and-not-stirred apple juice on-the-rocks. What do you think?"

They were still laughing on their way back to a table when Sister Nora came in. "What's so funny? Anything I can laugh at too?"

Steve smiled at her. Sister Nora Uma Nickels was a tall Nordic beauty, a little over five-foot-ten inches tall, broad shouldered and had very light brown, almost blond, curly hair, cut short. Her beautiful blue eyes always seemed to be happy and Steve thought, *What a waste. I sure would have liked to know her before she signed up for this job.*

Larry smiled at her. "Just mentioned it was almost cocktail hour but here I was having juice and not even an olive to put in it."

"Well, if all you need is the olive, I could arrange it."

"Thanks anyway, Sister. I'll just go with the juice, but I'll remember the offer. Maybe another time."

"Just let me know," Sister Nora said, and as she went by him she patted his shoulder.   "She's such a nice gal," Larry said.

"Yep," Steve said and turned as Mary and Paul came into the dining room.

"Hi, you two," Mary said. "Paul do you want coffee or juice?"

"Just coffee and are there any cookies out?"

"I'll look." Mary went to get their coffees while Paul sat down at one of the tables and he looked a little disappointed as Larry and Steve joined him. He had hoped to have Mary to himself for a few minutes. *Oh, well, another time*, he thought.

Mary came with two cups of coffee, a plate with several kinds of cookies and some napkins on a tray. "Thought maybe you two might enjoy a cookie too."

"Thanks," Steve said. "I like these peanut butter ones."

"I'm glad we ran into you. I have something on my mind and I'd like to discuss it with all of you." Mary had a look of concern on her face.

"What is it?" asked Larry.

"It's a little delicate and I think we should keep it confidential until we come up with a plan. Do you all agree?"

"Agree with what? Easy to keep a secret if you don't know what it is." Larry was always a little impatient with so called polite conversation. Get to the point was his motto.

"Well, I think we should do something about getting Emily a makeover and maybe update her wardrobe and modernize her hairdo. Maybe even get some makeup information for her. What do you think?"

Paul smiled at Mary. *It is so like My Mary to be thinking of someone else's welfare.* He always thought of her as *My Mary,* even though he was pretty sure she didn't know how he felt. "I like the idea of making her feel better about herself, so if it would help, I vote yes, but why the secrecy?"

"Yeah," Larry said. "Why not ask her if she wants improving?"

"I think it would be very tactless to have Emily hear we think she doesn't look good, don't you? I wouldn't want to hurt her feelings but I do think she could use a little advice. We would have to ask her somehow, and then if she doesn't want our help and says no, we can just forget it." Mary looked at the men as she spoke. She hoped they understood what she was talking about.

"I think you should be the one to talk to her. You have a wonderful tactful way of putting things," Paul said.

"I agree," Steve said looking at Larry.

"Yes," Larry replied. "I think she could use some help in those areas, and yes I think Mary should have a chat with her."

Mary was pleased they did understand. "Okay, I'll do it. Do you think I need to involve Natalie or any of the others?"

All three men said an emphatic NO.

Mary smiled to herself. "I'll see her today when she gets to work, but now I'll leave you gentlemen to your coffee." She stood up slowly, thinking it was almost time for another pain pill.

The men were already back to chatting as she went out the door and back to her apartment. She picked up the mail that was on the table where she'd left it earlier, and she decided to sit down to look at it. The first one said she had qualified for a new credit card. Next she read about a limited offer to just buy two magazines and she could pick a third one for free. Finally she saw that a mortgage company could help her obtain a new loan. Next was a catalogue for "candy and fruits delivered right to your door monthly" and lastly a catalogue of shoes.

She opened the shoe catalogue and when she was finished she looked at the clock and saw it was four-thirty. Emily would be at work now, so, after she dropped her mail in the trash can, catalogues and all, off she went.

Mary Adele Murray had occasional flare-ups of soreness and stiffness from the arthritis in her hip and shoulder, but other than these annoyances, she felt pretty good for her eighty years. Although it was definitely gray, her hair was still thick and she wore it braided and pinned on top of her head in a coronet. During her younger years she'd worn it falling down her back, framing her face much like Veronica Lake, but as her children came along, wearing her hair braided was much more convenient and she never got around to changing the style. Being tall hadn't always pleased her but now, even with the little bit of roundness in her shoulders, she still stood a stately five-foot-eight, very tall while she was in school, but just the right height now. She somehow didn't need to watch her weight either... not like Natalie. She seldom missed her daily walks and still did her stretching and yoga exercises, sometimes more than once a day.

For the shape I'm in, I'm in pretty good shape, she thought. Her husband always said that. Everyone thought Milt was so funny, but sometimes a little aloof and always the quick wit, even if it was sarcastic and aimed mostly at her.

Emily smiled when she turned around and saw Mary at the door. "Hello."

"Hello. Do you have a minute? I need some advice."

"Sure. Come in and sit down. Want some tea? I turned on the electric tea pot when I came in. I only have chamomile…"

"That would be lovely." Mary sat down on the straight chair by Emily's desk. These wooden chairs were easiest on her hip. Getting out of those overstuffed settees in the library could be a struggle sometimes.

Emily busied herself with the mugs, pouring the boiling water over the tea bags and then she brought the two steamy cups back to her desk. "Here we go. Sugar?"

"No, this is fine." Mary took a tiny sip of tea and realized it was still too hot, then she took a deep breath and plunged right into the subject on her mind. "Have you ever thought of cutting your hair?"

The question was a surprise. "Well, I don't give my hair much thought. Why do you ask?"

"My hair's long like yours, and I was thinking it would be so much easier to take care of if I got it cut. Do you ever think about doing that?"

When she was younger, Emily's mother made all her girls wear their hair long, so as the oldest child, Emily learned to braid early on but now she mostly wore it straight and hanging down her back. It was true it took her over an hour to dry it after shampooing, but what else did she have to do with her time? She smiled back at Mary. "Until now I hadn't really considered it. Are you thinking of cutting yours soon?"

"Yes I am, and I could use some moral support. Would you have time to go to Harriett's Beauty Shop with me tomorrow morning? I have a little bit of natural curl and I don't think I'll need to get a permanent but... would you have time?"

Emily smiled. "What time's your appointment? I'm filling in for Anita tomorrow evening so I'll need to be here by four. Should I drive us there or do you feel up to walking?"

"Unless it rains I'd rather walk. I haven't actually made the appointment yet. Should I make an appointment for you too? Change is good for the soul they say." Mary was almost holding her breath waiting for Emily's answer.

There was a short silence while Emily obviously thought about it and with only a slight hesitation in her voice she said, "Why not. If I don't like it I can always grow it back, right? Make two appointments and, if we get it done early enough, we could go to the food court at the mall for lunch."

Mary stood up and said, "I'll get us in as early as can be. What time's too early for you? Harriett opens at nine so maybe we can be their first customers. Did I mention she has a new man working for her so I just might have him do mine. He's from Chicago and maybe he'll update me in a fancy way." Mary was excited and showed it. To her surprise, so was Emily.

"Do you want to call from here?"

She did. They found the number in the phone book and Mary dialed. Sebastian, the new man, answered. "Harriett's Beauty Salon. How may I help you?" He had a lovely Italian accent and it surprisingly made her think of romance.

She made the two appointments for ten o'clock... one for Emily with Harriett and one for herself with Sebastian. She hung up and said, "We're all set. Let's leave here at nine-thirty." Emily agreed and then as Mary was leaving the office she turned and said, "I'm not going to tell anyone I'm doing this, it'll be a surprise. Thanks for going with me. As my granddaughter used to say, "It be fun."

Emily laughed. "Yes, it be fun."

Marry left with a lighter step, and funny her hip wasn't hurting at all as she headed back to her apartment.

Emily sat down at her desk and smiled to herself. Yes, this would be fun. She hadn't done an *us-girls* thing for so long. *Hair cut and lunch, and maybe be fixed up with someone nice by Natalie's group...* if nothing else life was starting to have some flavor. Plain vanilla is good sometimes but variety is the spice of life. She smiled at the trite old saying and promised herself she would enjoy tomorrow's outing to the fullest.

CHAPTER 8

At nine-thirty Friday morning, Mary was standing outside on the east side of St. Francis. The grounds, and especially the flowers, were being attended to by a young man from the landscaping service. Rockrose hedges surrounded the building on three sides and the young man, in a sleeveless T-shirt and jean shorts, was snipping them into shape. Mary loved to garden. The vegetables and flowers at her big house on the Cliffs just east of town had been her joy and Dahlias had been her specialty. When the decision was made for them to retire and downsize to a condo, she had taken up golf and turned to putting potted plants on the deck. After Milt's death almost two years ago, and with her children's encouragement, she'd decided to move to St. Francis. It had been a good decision. No housework to speak of and no maintenance worries. Her children said it gave her a new attitude and lease on life and she agreed, but she still missed her big gardens on the Cliffs.

Emily came down the sidewalk towards her. "Aren't those rose bushes beautiful? I love the way they trim it to form a hedge, but all rounded on the top."

"So do I. And I don't mind watching the gardener either." Mary laughed but it was more of a giggle.

Emily laughed with her. "Just one of the many perks at St. Francis."

They headed down the street to Harriett's still smiling about the perks, and waved at Delores, the office manager in the real estate office as they walked past. Then they crossed the street and looked in the window of the book store, all the while talking. When they opened the door to Harriett's, Sebastian came forward to greet them. His voice was low and smooth and sexy. "Ah, ladies." He smiled at each of them. "Please to come in. We are so happy to see you."

Harriett finished saying good-bye to her nine o'clock appointment and turned to Mary. "Do I understand you're getting your hair cut? What brought that on?"

"I just decided a change was in order and my friend Emily decided to join me and also make a change. And I was wondering, do you know about donating hair to the Cancer Society for wigs or something like that?"

"I certainly do and won't they be pleased to have two donations of such lovely hair. Shall we get started? Emily, let me take your jacket and come with me. Sit here and let's discuss what you have in mind."

Sebastian turned to Mary. "Would you like me to take your coat?" He hung it in the closet, turned back towards her and gave her the most beautiful seductive smile. "Please come with me."

Mary almost sighed.

He led the way to his station and Mary settled into the chair. He put a rose colored drape around her and said, "Your hair is so beautiful. Let me take it down and we'll have a look at what is needed?" He took out the pins and the long braids fell down her back. He unbraided each one in turn then ran his fingers though the waves, smoothing as he went. "You want it cut but do you know how short? Do you know what style we can give to you?"

Mary could have listened to his soft accented voice all day. It brought to mind so many romantic memories of her husband, back when they were young and he still seemed to care if she was happy. "I'm not sure about the style but I need updating, and I would like it to be easy-care. Is this too much to hope for?"

"Oh Mrs. Murray, I think I know exactly what you would like. Let me get you a picture I just saw in *Today's Hair Magazine*." He went to the waiting area and sorted through the stack of magazines until he found the one he wanted. "Ah, here it is." He opened the magazine and turned a few pages then said, "Look at this. Do you like it?"

Mary looked at the page he was pointing to. The woman had her hair cut just below her ears and tapered a little longer around the back. The soft curls and waves looked exactly as she had pictured herself. "I think I have a little natural wave in my hair. Will it be enough? I really don't want to have a permanent if it can be helped."

"Let's get you shampooed and then we can tell better, but I do think you have enough body for this cut and we'll look at the curl." He led her to the washing station. She sat down and he put a short waterproof drape around her shoulders and pulled the lever that elevated her legs. She put her head back on the head rest and relaxed. A change for her would be good at this point in her life. It would help sweep away the heaviness of spirit she fought every day.

Sebastian tested the water and asked, "Is this too warm?" When she said it wasn't, he sprayed her head with a warm stream of water and applied a floral smelling shampoo then went to work with his magic fingers, even massaging her neck muscles. She found the whole procedure very pleasant.

Meanwhile, Emily and Henrietta were also discussing styles. "I don't want to look like a kid again but I would like something easier to maintain."

"Have you ever worn it short?" Harriett was combing through Emily's hair.

"No. My mother thought all women should have long hair, wear no makeup, and should be quiet unless spoken to. This rule applied to us girls but not to her." She was thinking about her mother's loud, brash, domineering ways.

"You know, I think I remember your mother from church. She liked to sing, didn't she?"

"Yes, that would probably be my mother." Although she couldn't carry a tune, it didn't stop her from singing, and singing loudly.

Emily was led to the washing station too, without a break in their conversation she was draped.

"I was behind you in school, but I do remember you from church and in that Junior class play. What was it... that Shakespeare thing? You were the one that said something about a dagger still in you hand."

"Yes that was me. I was so scared I never was in another play. Mother pushed me into that drama class so I could *get over my shyness*. It didn't help much."

"Well, I still remember you in it so you must

have been pretty good. I also remember that jerk Claude that was supposed to be the dead guy. He was on the floor writhing and moaning for ten minutes. I thought the audience was going to have to kill him again." Both of them were laughing as Henrietta helped Emily lean back in the chair. As Emily felt the warm water on her head she sighed. This was so nice.

Once the shampooing was finished and Emily was back in the other chair, the conversation continued.

"Have you lived here all your life?" Emily asked.

Henrietta smiled but didn't miss a beat. She had gathered comb and scissors and was securing a dry cape at Emily's neck and over her shoulders.

"Except for when Les was in the Army and we lived in Texas, I've been here forever. I was born on the ferry when my mother was coming home from Seattle, and mostly never left except for a few vacations. Have you traveled much?"

"It was almost the same with me. Except for living in Seattle when I went to the University and a few vacation trips, I've been here forever too."

"I read about your husband and then your mother both dying. I'm sorry you lost them. What are you doing now?"

"I'm starting to enjoy life. I moved to a condo on Front Street, and I work part time at St. Francis, and now I'm getting my hair cut. Adventurous, aren't I?"

They both laughed.

"And, new adventures can lead to wonderful things. I'm glad you decided to do this and I think you'll like the cut I have in mind for you." She parted Emily's hair and picked up the scissors. "Let the adventure continue."

A little over an hour later, both Emily and Mary were finished and couldn't help admiring their new hair-dos in the store windows in the mall as they strolled by.

"This really feels good, doesn't it? And, you... you look wonderful. A whole new person." Mary was smiling and admiring Emily's haircut. "Now, I need to do some upgrading of my wardrobe. Want to come with me... maybe next week?"

"Thank you for your help and suggestions, Mary." Emily was smiling broadly. "I would be delighted to come shopping again next week. This is certainly fun." Emily was thinking maybe she might do some shopping too. "All of a sudden I'm hungry. Let's go eat. What shall we have? There are so many different foods up there in the food court to choose from."

On the way up the escalator, they did a little more window shopping and Emily decided she wanted to come back again and try on the flowered dress with the little flounce on the hem. She and Mary giggled again like teenagers when they discussed the neckline of the dress.

"I think they call it a halter top," Mary said. "Remember Marilyn Monroe used to wear those. I think you could too, but you might need special underthings."

Emily nodded. Yes... new undergarments certainly would have to go on her shopping list if she bought that dress. She smiled to herself. *Why have I waited so long?*

By the time they finished lunch it was almost one.

"I think I better go. I have a couple of things to do before I go to work. I'll walk with you back as far as

St. Francis…"

"Nonsense, you just go on ahead. I come here often and I'll just take my time going home. I'll see you after dinner and we can compare notes on the reactions to our new look."

"Okay," Emily said as she got up to leave. "Thank you again. I don't know what took me so long to decide to live again, but this surely has been a fun day of pulling me up and out of my hole," and she leaned down and kissed Mary's cheek. "See you later."

Mary felt like she was watching a flower begin to open, and she not only shared Emily's physical transformation but she could feel the lifting of her spirits too. She was smiling as she walked toward the escalator. *Now*, Mary thought, *all that's left on this updating Emily plan is new clothes and maybe, new glasses. But for today, the new hairdo is enough.*

Once on the first floor she walked out the back door of the mall and then cut across the parking lot to Adams Street. From there it was only a block back to St. Francis. As she neared the building she noted the young gardener had finished his work and the sprinklers were on. She thought again how happy she was to be living here. Most of the residents had been her friends or at least acquaintances for most of her life. It was like moving to a smaller town where you knew everyone. Milt's job at the bank in Seattle had dominated most of his free time, but Mary had loved being part of her children's activities at school and around Haven Port Island during all those years they were growing up. She'd joined every school and recreational committee she could so she would be totally involved. And Milton was totally happy with her interests, as long as he didn't have to participate. It meant he could travel and have interests of his own.

He thought Mary didn't know about these other interests, but she did. And, what he didn't know was that after a few years, it didn't matter to her. She loved her children more than any other humans and the fact that his schedule didn't allow him to be involved or that he was sarcastic to her when he was there, was okay. She had the children and didn't need him.

Mary planned to go directly to her apartment but as she started down the hall, she could smell the coffee from the dining room. She detoured to get a cup and as she was pouring Sister Nora came in.

"Well, look at you. My goodness."

Mary smiled.

"What a lovely thing you've done to your hair. It absolutely suits you."

"Thank you. You're the first person to see me. I was wondering if anyone would notice, and Sister, wait until you see Emily. She went with me."

"Our Emily? She got her hair cut? I certainly can't wait to see those results. How did this happen?"

Mary started by telling Sister Nora about the committees and ended with, "...and I thought Emily needed a little updating so I invited her to go with me and she decided to get a hair cut too. She looks so beautiful. I can't wait for everyone to see her."

"Who else is on this committee if you don't mind my asking?"

"Natalie's the Chairwoman, of course. Steve is head of the Procurement Committee, and I'm head of the Surveillance Committee. Steve's committee is inviting young men to come to our screening party on Sunday. Do you know about it?" Sister nodded her head yes about the Sunday get together. "And then if the committee finds any of them suitable, we'll have a reception and invite Emily."

"Does Emily know about this?"

"Yes, and she's agreed to meet them as long as we don't have hard feelings if she decides not to date the men we present." Mary stopped to catch her breath. "Don't you think it's nice to help her meet someone to make her life happier?"

Sister Nora was almost speechless. She knew there had been meetings after breakfast and sometimes after lunch but often groups would meet to plan outings, so she hadn't really paid special attention. "If Emily is willing, I guess I have no problem with it. Is this why you wanted cookies and coffee on Sunday? I thought it was just guests being entertained."

"I'm sorry if Natalie didn't tell you everything. You know how she likes being in charge, and sometimes she gets in a mode where it's everything's on a need-to-know basis. Is this going to be a problem?"

"I don't see any problem. I just hope Natalie remembers the part about *won't have hard feelings.* Is she bringing a young man?"

"Yes. I think it's her nephew from Seattle. Larry is bringing an old neighbor, Dolly has invited her ex-husband's son, and Steve has invited someone he knew in business or maybe from the golf course, I'm not sure. Do you know anyone suitable?"

Sister Nora smiled. "I'll have to think about it. Thank you for filling me in and I really like your haircut. Now I think I'll go share this information with Dr. Pete. Do you mind?"

"Of course not. I don't think it's a secret. Sunday at two o'clock is our first meeting of the prospective dates. For the sake of getting along,

Natalie should be the one you tell if you do think of someone, even though Steve is head of the Procurement group. You know how Natalie is."

And indeed, Sister Nora did know how Natalie could be when she wasn't kept in the loop with any information pertaining to her plans.

Mary picked up her coffee and as she went around the corner into the hall she ran into Natalie—literally. There was no spilling, but Natalie's reaction was loud and accusatory.

"Mary Adele! What happened to your hair?" Her face was flushed as she said, "What have you done? Where did you go today?"

Gathering her courage, Mary said, "Well, I got my hair cut then we went to the mal for lunch. What did you do today?"

While Natalie hesitated and tried to regain her composure, Mary walked past her and into her apartment.

CHAPTER 9

Mary's Friday night dinner was interrupted several times. People were stopping by to say how much they liked her new haircut, and how flattering it was, and many said, "It positively takes ten years off your age." It wasn't really a surprise when Natalie ignored her, and secretly Mary hoped to be there when she saw Emily.

And, when Natalie finally did see Emily, her reaction was more shock than surprise. She was aghast and more than a little angry. She was sure this never would have been done without some prompting.

"Emily, have you a moment?"

Emily smiled as she looked up and saw Natalie. "I always have time for you. How was your day?"

"Well..." she was a little hesitant in her reply. She just now realized Mary had said *"we"* earlier... that must have meant her and Emily. "My day was very simple. I took a walk, wrote some letters, read some magazines, and then watched Dr. Phil and a news program. Tell me about your day." Then she blurted out, "Who made you do this?"

Emily was surprised at Natalie's questions, and her reaction. First, why should it make any difference to her about the hair, and secondly, what was this *who made you do this* accusation? "Mary asked my advice about getting her hair cut and I decided to join her and get mine done too. Does it make a difference?"

Natalie took another very deep breath. So it *was* Mary Adele. *Well!* She decided it would be best not to involve Emily in this matter so she tried her best to smile and said, "I must say the results are lovely. It certainly is a very good permanent they gave you. To make it look so soft and natural. I know I need to perm every six weeks to keep my hair tidy and you too will need to get a schedule, don't you think?"

"I probably will get on some kind of a cutting schedule but I didn't need a permanent. Aren't I lucky? Both Mary and I got cuts to let the natural curl in our hair take over. We had so much fun today both at the beauty shop and at lunch. We're going again next week to shop. Want to join us?"

Natalie could feel her face getting red. *It was my idea to update Emily and Mary Adele just stepped in and took over.* To Emily she said, "Let me know when you plan to go and I'll see if my schedule will allow it, and thank you for asking me." She somehow forgot why she had come to see Emily in the first place... to tell her about the dating prospects... and Natalie left saying, "You look very pretty."

Now she had to find Mary Adele and get some things straightened out. She would inform her of what *was*, and *was not* her duties, and to tell her to stop overstepping her boundaries. Natalie didn't have to look far. She found Mary just outside the library talking to Sister Nora and Dr. Pete.

As she approached she heard Sister Nora say,

"Well, I approve of both of you updating your hair-dos. Change is fun."

Dr. Pete said, "And I think I see a new spring in your step, Mary. I also approve of that."

Natalie joined them and smiled her stiff I'm-not-happy-but-I'm-trying-to-be-pleasant smile.

"What do you think, Natalie? A new Mary, and have you seen Emily? Two new ladies with just a snip of the shears." Dr. Pete noticed Natalie's stiff smile but thought maybe he could jolly her out of whatever mood she was in. "Hair cuts never did that much for me." When it didn't seem to be working he said, "Excuse me ladies, I was on my way out to the hospital when I saw Emily and she told me about Mary's haircut too, so I just had to see it for myself. Now I'm really running late. I'll see you all tomorrow." And tomorrow he'd check with Sister Nora to see what Natalie was so bent out of shape about.

As he walked away he heard Natalie say, "Excuse me too, please. I'm on my way home." The sharpness in her voice had both Sister Nora and Mary watching her walk away wondering what this was all about.

"I'm so pleased to see you getting out and taking Emily with you." Sister Nora said.

"Well, I'm not sure who took who on this trip. I thought Emily could use a little push to fix herself up and the next thing I knew we were getting our haircut together and even stopping for lunch, and next week we're going shopping."

Sister Nora chuckled. "Whatever happened and no matter who took the lead, it was a good thing for the both of you. It's so nice to see you happy... I mean walking around smiling is a nice change, and Dr. Pete's right... there's definitely a new spring in your step."

Paul came around the corner and smiled broadly when he saw Mary. "Excuse me, but Mary, if you're going to play cards tonight would you be my Bridge partner?" Paul was blushing slightly. He was hoping he would be spending the evening with Mary.

"Yes, I'd like to, but now I need go to my place." Then smiling at Sister Nora she said, "See you both later."

Sister Nora watched them both walk away and thought, *What a nice friendship they have.*

The couple parted at the hallway and Mary found Natalie waiting in front of her door. "Mary Adele, I need to talk to you about some things." Her voice was almost a croak and she was barely holding her temper in check.

"Okay, but what's the problem?" Mary felt herself slipping back into the *yes-ma'am* person she always was when Natalie spoke to her.

"Well, the first thing is that you are not following the rules. You went behind my back and took matters into your own hands without consulting me."

"What did I do?"

"I'm speaking about your hair. You cut your hair and made Emily cut hers."

Mary was speechless. "Yes we cut our hair but what does it have to do with you?"

Natalie found it incredulous that Mary didn't understand. Now she was no longer holding her temper and she was almost sputtering. "It was my idea. MINE!" And her voice was rising in volume. "I had the idea first to have Emily upgrade her image and you... you just took it out of my hands!"

"How was I supposed to know?" Now Mary was

starting to get impatient. "Did you tell me you were working on a plan? How could I have known?"

"Mary Adele. When I put a plan into action you know I cover all the details. You couldn't possibly believe I would forget Emily needed some fixes to her appearance, and that I would take care of the details when the time was right. You couldn't possibly think that I..."

Mary suddenly realized what the problem was. Natalie had this on her list and when she had accidentally stepped in before this part of *the plan* could be implemented, it was just too much for Natalie to handle. Mary felt her *yes-ma'am* feelings slipping away and her newfound self-assuredness was building. "Natalie, please calm down. The haircut had nothing to do with the plan. I wanted to get my hair cut and I talked to Emily about it. She decided to go with me and she got hers cut too. That's it. I had no knowledge of your plan and it was just a series of spur of the moment decisions. Please don't think you aren't still in *full* charge of the dating project. You are, and I'm still in charge of Surveillances. Would you like me to get you a cup of tea or would you like to come in for a minute while you collect yourself?"

Natalie just looked at Mary. "Well, this time I will overlook it but please don't overstep your responsibilities again," and she was off in a huff. She wasn't much calmer but she knew that she, Natalie Ann Greene, was still in charge and she had certainly straightened Mary Adele Murray out on this point.

This was the first time Mary had ever stood up to any of Natalie's angry reprimands. *Maybe I'm getting a backbone*, she thought, and then she smiled. *But what will I ever do with a backbone?*

The Bridge game that night was what they called a Couples Switch. Four tables were set up with four players per table. They started the first round with their partner but kept individual score cards. A round meant playing four hands then you totaled up the score and changed partners so you played with someone else at your table. After playing with all of the other three at the first table, the two players with the top scores moved to the next table and the games continued. This way everyone played with someone different for each set. By the end of the evening, the individual with the highest score was the winner. To add interest, each player put a dollar into a bowl, and at the end of the evening, the first place score got ten dollars, the second place got five dollars. The poor person who ended up with the lowest score received the last dollar as compensation. Tonight Dolly won the single dollar.

"Oh my," Dolly declared. "I simply could not concentrate." She accepted the dollar and put it into her little sequined coin purse, while laughing her tinkley laugh.

Everyone standing near her laughed as well.

Steve said, "What're you going to do with all the money, Dolly. Go night-clubbing?" He thought this was so funny he said it after every Friday night's Bridge game.

"Oh Steven...you are so funny," she crooned.

"Funnier than a broken leg," Larry said as he turned toward Dolly, "Want to get some coffee? They have decaf."

"Why, I'd like to Lawrence. Thank you," and as they walked away she took his arm.

"Struck out again?" Paul was smiling.

"Heck no." Steve smiled too as he watched

them. "When the time's right, she'll cave in, just watch." He walked over to the refreshment table. No coffee this late, it would keep him awake, but a cup of mint tea and a cookie, along with some conversation was what he really wanted. He liked playing Bridge but also looked forward to the Tuesday night poker games at Jake's Place, one of his favorite haunts when he was still drinking. Now he went for poker and companionship. They made sure to have lots of iced tea, coffee and snacks for the guys, and in deference to Steve, not many of them drank beer or wine. He was happy to be among his friends without the pressure to drink. He'd learned it at AA, but he was also realizing on his own that it was possible to have a good time without getting sauced.

Mary was more tired than she realized. It was all the excitement of the day she knew. She turned to Paul. "I'm going to skip the refreshments tonight. I'm ready to go home. Congratulations on winning second place." She squeezed his arm. "I'll see you tomorrow at breakfast."

"Okay. Want me to walk you home?" He was smiling and hoping.

"No thank you. Goodnight."

Paul smiled again but not as wide. "Goodnight and have a peaceful sleep."

Mary walked back to her room thinking it was certainly a nice way for Paul to say good-night. She really liked Paul and she knew he had special feelings for her. Lately, it was something she thought about often, and it gave her such pleasure to be held in that special place in someone's thoughts again. As she unlocked her door she was humming the Irving Berlin song, *It's a Lovely Day Today.*

CHAPTER 10

Not all of the residents of St. Francis were early risers, but for those that were, coffee, juice, and toast was always available at six o'clock, and on this early Saturday morning Paul was headed for the coffee pot. Because of all those get-up-in-the-middle-of-the-night trips he was a restless sleeper, so as soon as his clock showed five-thirty, he felt he could finally get up for the day. He was shaved and showered and at six-fifteen he filled his cup and decided to sit on the patio. He was thinking he would be the only one there, but he was surprised to find Steve sitting by the table with half a pot of coffee next to him.

"Mornin'."

"Hi. Nice day today."

"Yep, gonna be warm," Paul said as he moved a chair. He always sat as close to the door as possible because of his condition. He never could stay anywhere very long but today the coffee was good and before they knew it, it was seven o'clock and the pot was empty. Paul was standing up ready to leave, when the door opened and Natalie stepped out onto the patio. "I'm looking for Lawrence. I see he isn't here."

"He hardly ever is," Steve answered. "And I think he likes to be called Larry."

"Do you know where he is?"

"Probably in bed. Go look there." Steve didn't like his mornings upset and Natalie was an up-setter if ever there was one.

"He didn't answer his door."

"What do you want him for?"

"I think we should accommodate more gentlemen for this Sunday's interview and I was wondering if he'd gotten confirmation yet for his intended person. I think you've already reported on your young man but..."

"I might know someone who would be interested in Emily," Paul interrupted. "And she might find him interesting too. I'll call him when it gets to be a decent hour."

Natalie looked at him in surprise. "That would be wonderful, Paul. Please do that. I think we'll have a meeting right after lunch. Will that give you ample time?"

He nodded as he started through the door, headed to his apartment.

"Wait," Natalie said. "Tell me about him."

"No time now. I gotta go," and the door to the patio closed behind him.

Steve felt trapped but he needn't have worried. Natalie was anxious to get on with her day and followed Paul back through the door without another word to Steve.

At seven o'clock sharp, three days a week, Natalie started her constitutional at a brisk pace. She liked walking before breakfast and weather dictated her route. Today the sun was shinning and the air was warm so she headed out the front door and up Elm to Front Street. This direction took her by several homes, past those beautiful rose gardens near Emily's condo, and back down Maple and past the garden center.

Home again she walked around the side of the Retirement Center and back through the front door. She always did her best planning while she walked and she'd been turning this Sunday meeting over in her mind. *Sunday's our first meeting and I know of five gentlemen who are invited, but is this enough? I've checked with almost everyone but I still need to see Lawrence, err, Larry. Now why doesn't he like his given name?* She entered her apartment and as she prepared to shower she thought, *I wonder if Patrick might know someone he would like to bring with him.* She made a mental note to call her nephew, really to remind him about Sunday but to also ask him about bringing a friend. *And, I must not forget to call everyone to a meeting right after lunch.*

Breakfast was almost finished and Sister Nora was ready to make the morning announcements but she stopped by Natalie's table first. "I was just thinking about Sunday and the cookies. How many do you think you'll need? How many people will be there at your party?"

Natalie thought a moment, ticking off the numbers on her fingers. *Five gentlemen, six committee members, herself and Sarah Ann...* "I think there will be thirteen people."

"Are they male or female? I think men eat many more cookies than women."

Another pause and Natalie said, "Nine will be males."

"Okay, peanut butter and chocolate chips then. They seem to be favorites." Sister Nora had hoped to hear the reason for Sunday's meeting from Natalie, but at least she found out there were nine males attending. She wondered how many would be there for Emily, or were they mostly committee members?

Sister took her usual place in the front of the room and started the announcements. "Good morning everyone. Today is Saturday, and this is movie night. The show starts at seven in the meeting room. Tonight we have a Greta Garbo comedy for you. As usual, popcorn is available here in the dining room beforehand.

A reminder... if you take coffee or food to your apartment, remember to bring the dishes back to the dining room. Better yet, drink your coffee and eat your snacks here and, who knows, you might find a little conversation to go with it.

And lastly, don't forget to look at the roses on the south side of the building. They're in full bloom and extra beautiful this year.

Have a lovely and blessed day and I'll see you at lunch."

The announcements over, Natalie motioned to Mary Adele. "There will be a meeting in the Library after lunch today. We'll need to know the names of the gentlemen coming on Sunday. Will you tell your committee?"

Mary said she would, and then Natalie blocked Steve's exit from the dining room to give him the same message. Next, she waved at Sarah Ann as she was walking down the hall and she said she'd be there as she hurried past Natalie and went down the hall. All her tasks done, Natalie continued on to her apartment without a backward look. She had many things on her mind and when she unlocked her door, she went directly to the phone. First on her list was to call her nephew.

"Patrick? Aunt Natalie." She listened a minute then said, "I'm just fine and I too am looking forward to tomorrow. I do, however, have a favor to ask. Would you like to invite a friend to come along with you just in case you…" She listened again for a moment. "Well, I do understand." More listening, "Patrick, dear, please don't get so excited. Of course you can come alone and meet her." Pause. "Yes, of course I think you're right for her." She listened again. "Patrick I apologize. You are very welcome to come meet the committee alone." Another pause. "All right. See you on Sunday, dear. Two o'clock?" She hung up the phone and sat down, pressing her handkerchief to her forehead and then her lips. *Now just what got him so excited?*

CHAPTER 11

After breakfast, Paul headed for his apartment too. As usual, he took care of the urgency problem then sat down at his desk. He took the Haven Port phone book out of his desk drawer and dialed the number for Oscar Hanson. "Hello, is this Harry?"

Oscar Hanson worked at the University of Washington's Satellite Marine Center in Haven Port. Paul had worked there and had been head of the Ichthyology Department before his retirement, and Harry was his assistant and right hand, so he was the natural replacement as department director. Since Harry's father was also a well-known ichthyologist, Oscar Harrison Hanson Jr. went by Harry, taken from his middle name.

"Glad to find you home." They talked for a few minutes about what's-happening-in the-department-these-days, then Paul asked how Harry's dating life was going. He listened then said, "...because I know someone I think you'd like to date. She's pretty, a retired school teacher, around fifty-five or so, same as you—and she's really nice."

Harry said he was always interested in meeting a friend of Paul's, especially pretty ones, and they made arrangements for him to come over on Sunday at two.

"One last thing, this meeting on Sunday is for... Well, a few of Emily's friends are having a little reception and inviting guys they want her to meet, so do you mind coming for a little examination first?"

"She must be pretty special for you to go to all this trouble. Sure, I'll be looked over by a committee." He laughed, then said, "...but what if I don't cut the mustard with these people? Will I get to meet her anyway?"

Paul assured him he would and the date was made. Harry was a nice guy and Emily might just enjoy dating a smart man.

When Dolly got back to her apartment she found the message light blinking on her answering machine. "Hi Ima, err, Dolly, I almost forgot. Just touching base. Are we still on for tomorrow at two? I'll assume we are if I don't' hear from you. 'Bye."

It was Ronald. She immediately dialed his number and heard, "Stump residence."

"May I please speak to Ronald?"

"Can I say who's calling?"

Dolly wondered why there was a woman answering the phone. "Yes you can. This is Dolly."

"I'll get Phillip for you."

Before Dolly could make it clear she wanted Ronald, her ex-husband was saying hello.

"Phillip... I called for Ronald. Could I please

speak to him?"

"Ima, he's not home but he said if you called, to tell you he'd see you tomorrow."

"Oh, good. Thank you, that's all I wanted."

"Ima. Wait," Phillip said, catching Dolly just as she was hanging up. "Let's talk for a few minutes. I miss talking to you."

"Well, not very much evidently. Your lady friend answered the phone when I called."

"For crying-out-loud, it's Jenny from next door." Dolly heard him take a deep breath and she could almost see him trying to calm himself down. "She comes over to clean for Ronny and she was just here to tell me she couldn't come on Tuesday. Don't you remember Jenny?"

Dolly certainly did remember her. Thirty years old with two children and plunging necklines. She had sometimes helped Dolly with dinner parties. "I'm so glad she can be there for you. Tell her I said hello, and now good-bye Phillip. I'm hanging up," and she did before he could say another word. She sat for a minute thinking about Phillip and the old neighborhood. She was a little surprised she cared that this young woman was with her husband but after a few minutes she decided these thoughts were not productive. She reminded herself he was her ex-husband and then she got up to get her book. She wasn't jealous but did sort of wish for her old life sometimes, but only if her name wouldn't be Ima Stump.

As Larry opened the door to his apartment he could hear the phone ringing. He picked up to find Brian was laughing on the other end.

"Hi Law. Just calling to see if I'm still coming to the party? You didn't change your mind, did you?"

"No I didn't, did you?"

"Nope. Looking forward to it. The girlfriend is moving out so now I guess I'm on the prowl."

"Well, don't' forget Emily's a lady."

"They all start out that way. I'll see you tomorrow at two. That still the plan? Where do I go when I get there?"

"I'll meet you by the front door."

"Okay, see ya."

"'Bye," Larry said and put the phone down hoping he hadn't made a mistake.

Steve wasn't as lucky as the others. Carl was not at home nor at his dealership. He left a message both places. *Well, guess that's the best I can do,* he thought. He switched on the TV, and then turned it off. He was restless. He left his apartment and headed back towards the cafeteria. It was empty. He looked out on the smoking patio and it too was vacant. What he needed was someone to talk to. Since no one seemed to be around, he decided it might as well go for a walk. He left by the patio door, strolled down Lincoln Street and turned left on Willow. Jake's Place was just two blocks away and Steve decided to go there for coffee and conversation. In his drinking days he'd spent many hours at Jake's, a bar and restaurant just down from the golf course, and although now he usually only showed up for Tuesday Poker Night, today he felt he needed people and Murph would probably be behind the bar.

Jake's Place was the neighborhood establishment owned by Michael Murphy, Murph to his friends. He was a retired police officer from Seattle but was born and raised in Haven Port and it seemed he would now spend his retirement years here too. He was a fixture of the neighborhood but couldn't be a candidate for Emily because he was already keeping company with Lisa Stanton, and besides she would kill him if he looked at another woman.

Steve was right. Murph was behind the bar.

"Hey, Steve."

He sat down on his favorite bar stool, feeling like he had come home. "Cup of coffee, please."

Murph had already picked up the pot and a cup. "Glad you're here. I got something to run past you. Are you planning to play next Tuesday?"

Steve nodded and took a sip.

"Do you know a guy named Tom Taylor? He wants to join us. He's a fireman but he's only lived here a couple of months."

"No, never heard of him. How did you meet him?"

"He comes in pretty regular. He lived on the peninsula but move here to go to work for the fire department. I like him. Seems like an okay guy."

"Well sure, it's okay with me. I'll take anyone's money." They were both laughing when Ed Casey came in. "Hi Ed. What's up?"

"Got a tee time in half and hour so decided to have a cup of coffee first." He looked at Steve. "How you doing? Don't see you very often outside of poker night."

Ed Casey had been a fisherman in Alaska and still owned part of the operation, but now his nephew ran the business and Ed retired back to his home town of Haven Port. He spent his time playing golf or skiing depending on the season, and taking care of his house and the house of his lady friend Flo Janson. When he asked Steve how he was doing, what he really meant was: How's retirement home living?

"Well, so far I really have no complaints. Good food, stuff to do, usually people to talk to, and they seem to keep me busy."

"Good... glad it's working out. If I didn't have Flo I'd be thinking along those lines." He gave Steve's shoulder a little squeeze.

They were all smiling.

"Ed, do you know a guy named Tom Taylor?" Murph asked.

"Yeah. He's a fireman. Got an apartment over on Maple, doesn't he?"

"That's the guy. Wants to join our poker game. Is it okay by you?"

"Sure. Why ask? I thought anyone could play."

"It's always been that way but this is the first guy that's inquired who I don't really know. Just asking around. I'll tell him to come on Tuesday."

They chatted about Ed's golf game, Murph's business here at Jake's, and about Steve's new life at the retirement home, then Ed looked at his watch and said, "Better go. Flo's meeting me and I don't want to be late." He got off the stool, left a dollar on the bar for his coffee, and went out the door.

"What's on your agenda today Steve?" asked Murph.

"Busy day planned. Lunch at eleven-thirty, then a nap. Dinner at five and then tonight is movie night. Big day ahead for me."

"Don't you really like it?"

"I make fun of it but I do. I still think I need a woman in my life and I'm doing my best to incorporate all the ones at St. Francis into my fold, but it's slow going when you take a nap every day and don't really care if you catch one or not."

"I can't believe this is you talking."

"It's true, but if you tell anyone, I'll deny it. Turning eighty slowed me down in the woman department and each additional month seems to slow me some more... but I don't want them to know yet." He laughed as he stood up and put two dollars on the bar. "See you later. Going to walk a little then head for the barn."

"See ya Tuesday."

"Yep, you surely will. Bye," and hands in his pockets, Steve went out the door.

CHAPTER 12

The after lunch meeting was very short. No one even sat down.

Mary spoke first. "Dolly has gone to her daughter's, but she wanted me to tell you her ex-husband's son is coming. His name's Ronald Stump, retired but still a consultant for the IRS. And, oh yes, she says she is just sure Emily won't find his funny eye an intrusion."

Natalie looked at Mary Adele but her smile was tight. She was still a little miffed at her but trying hard not to show it.

"Carl Randall is coming at my invite," Steve said. "He owns car dealerships and right now, he's between lady friends."

Natalie looked around. "Is there anyone else?"

"Yes," Larry said. "Brian Daniels is my old neighbor. I watched him grow up and he's coming."

"I invited a kid who used to work for me at the U," Paul said. "He's head of the department now and he's teaching too. Name's Harry Hanson."

Natalie was excited. "That's nice, Paul. Thank you for your participation. Four young men for the committee to meet, and I've also invited my nephew, Patrick Kelso. He's interested in the business world. That makes five interviewees." Her eyes were shinning. "All right everyone. See you tomorrow at two o'clock."

CHAPTER 13

olly wasn't at the meeting because she was at a birthday party.

Saturday at eleven o'clock she was waiting by the front door when her grandson parked and came in. *My,* she thought, *he is so handsome.*

"Hi Gram. You ready? Can I carry anything?" He towered over Dolly's five foot petite frame. He was eighteen today and he was already six feet tall. His father was six-four so it wasn't a surprise. She handed him a shopping bag that held two boxes wrapped in very bright blue and gold paper. "Hey, these're wrapped in my high school colors." She thought he would appreciate her knowing this little detail of his life and he did.

"Is this goin' to be a big party?" Dolly was hoping some of his friends would be there too. She so enjoyed meeting these young people. It gave her hope for the future and renewed her energy just being around them.

"No, not really big. Billy from next door and his girl friend Jo, Grandpa Stump and Ronny of course, Janine my girlfriend, and some guy Dad knows from work that's alone so we invited him, and a lady from Mom's work, and you and me. Just enough. And after I take you home today, Billy and I and the girls are going to Seattle to a Broadway Show. I forget which one. It's at the Fifth Avenue Theatre. Mom and Dad gave me the tickets for my birthday. Neat, huh?"

"Why yes, I think that is *very* neat." Dolly loved this conversation with Donny. He was such a good boy and she was so very proud of him, in all ways.

They arrived at the house and while Dolly waited for Donny to come around to open her door, she admired the view of what had once been her home. On this east side of the island at the corner of Monroe and Cliff Side Road, she had raised her child, buried one husband and had divorced another. Four years ago, when her daughter's husband found he could teach here at the University's Satellite Campus, they moved back to the island. Dolly was divorced by this time and to make her life simpler, she decided to move to St. Francis, and her daughter and family took over the old home.

The landscaping is so nice, she thought. Maybelle and her husband John loved to garden and it showed. The rockery held ferns and lovely primroses and lilies. Dolly felt a moment of nostalgia for her old familiar home but quickly put a smile on her face. *For heavens sake, you still have the best of both worlds. You live in a perfectly wonderful place and can visit here any time and stay here as long as you like. Your room is always ready.*

"Grandma, want to take my arm on these steps?" Dolly happily moved closer to him. They walked up the seven stairs and onto the wide porch that wrapped around the house.

"Donny, I'd like to see the other side of the house before we go in. Would it be all right?"

"Sure." He kept her hand on his arm as they walked towards the side of the house that faced the water.

Of course Maybelle saw them on the porch and came out. "Mama, you're here." They were hugging when Grandpa Phillip Stump came out to join them.

"Ima. I'm so happy to see you." His voice was shaky and he might have started to cry if his son Ronald hadn't come up behind him to whisper, "Call her Dolly." There was a little more hugging and then they all moved into the house.

Dolly was just getting settled into a lovely comfortable wing backed chair with Phillip next to her when the front doorbell rang. Maybelle went to answer. It was her husband's friend from work and right behind him, coming up the stairs, was a woman with noteworthy red hair.

"Well, both of you together. Hello Sally," and turning she said, "I'm sorry I've forgotten your name."

"My name's Brad and hello Sally. I've been looking forward to meeting you. John said you were beautiful and he was right."

Sally's smile was wide. She liked the looks of Brad too.

"You both come in now and meet everyone else." Introductions were made and while John offered drinks, Maybelle excused herself to see to lunch. Sally and Brad sat down on the loveseat, chatting and getting to know each other, Billy and Donny set the chairs up to the table, and Janine and Jo opened a card table to set the presents on. Grandpa Phillip was happy he had Dolly pretty much to himself and Ronald helped John serve drinks. Everyone was happy.

The conversation was lively and noisy. When everyone had been served with a drink, John said, "Thank you everyone for coming." Conversation stopped. "This is a special day for us."

Donny said, "Dad, can I make my announcement now?"

"Sure, but let me get your mother first."

When they were all gathered in the living room John said, "Okay son, fire away."

"Some of you already know this, but earlier this week I got notified that I've been accepted at Annapolis. I'll be starting there later in the summer."

Now everyone was talking at once.

Dolly said, "I'm so proud of you. You're just like your Grandpa McBride."

Grandpa Phillip said, "Why not West Point?" Donny just smiled at him. He knew his Grandpa had wanted him to be a Navy man and that this was just his way of joking.

Brad said, "It's a good way of life. You'll like it."

Sally said, "You'll be so handsome in that uniform."

John and Maybelle stood by beaming at their son, while the teenagers were laughing and hugging Donny.

"What are you going to do until you leave?" Ronny asked.

"When school's out I'll just go full time at the golf course. It'll only be for a couple of months then I'm going on a short vacation. After that I report in. I'm pretty excited."

There were comments like "We know you are" and "We're all so happy for you" but when Maybelle said, "Let's eat. Would everyone please come to the table?" the whole room moved. Maybelle went to help Dolly up from the chair and walked with her to the table. "Grandpa, you over there, and Ronny beside you. Sally and Brad, you two sit here. Donny you and your friends sit on this side, and Mom you sit here. I'll be right next to you. John will be at the head of the table. Everyone, get settled and I'll be back with food."

The teenagers cheered at the mention of food but Dolly noted the sweet smile Janine gave Donny as he sat down next to her. She wondered how serious the relationship was.

Maybelle set a large plate of sliced ham on the table and behind her was John with a large tray of relish, mayonnaise, mustard, pickles and olives. Maybelle went back to the kitchen and returned with a basket holding Kaiser Rolls fresh from the oven, and two baskets full of chips. John made his return trip carrying a large bowl of macaroni salad and a plate with several cheeses. He sat down and Maybelle made her last trip from the kitchen carrying a platter of sliced onions, tomatoes and lettuce. She set it on the table and said, "Well, Donny, did I forget anything?" Then to everyone she said, "He wanted his favorite lunch today so here it is. He'll want a cola to drink, how about everyone else?"

John always planned ahead and now he pulled a full cooler up next to the table and handed out colas, orange drinks, and beers to Ronny and Grandpa Phillip, and Dolly had her water glass refilled as the platters were passed. Again the conversation became noisy, punctuated with laughter. All four teens decided they would eat onions so they could gross out everyone at the theatre.

The food was delicious and several commented

on how good the ham sandwiches tasted. When it was time for cake, Sally got up to help Maybelle clear the table and John helped too. It took no time before the smaller plates were brought in along with the four-layered cake.

"Now that's a cake," Brad said. It was German Chocolate with coconut frosting dripping down the sides.

"Donny, before we cut the cake, how about opening the presents? Stand by the side of the table so we all can see, please."

His father didn't need to tell him more than once. Maybelle was ready with paper and pencil to make notes for those thank-you cards Donny would be writing tomorrow and Donny picked up the first box. It was small and wrapped in bright red foil. "It's from Janine," he said, and opened the box to find a silver medallion and chain. The medallion said, *Friends Forever* and showed two hands clasped. Donny looked at her and slipped it over his head. He smiled at her and said, "You bet. Thank you."

Janine was blushing and smiled back.

The next present was in a flat white box about ten inches long and about six inches wide, with a green ribbon tied around it. "I could only find Christmas ribbon when I was wrapping this," Grandpa Phillip said. "It's from Ronny and me both."

Donny slipped the ribbon off to find a very nice split leather wallet. "Thank you. I can really use this."

"Look inside," Ronny said.

"Wow! Look Dad. A hundred dollar bill!"

"Hey. That'll come in handy too, I bet." His dad was laughing as he said this and everyone else laughed with him.

Donny continued to open presents. He got a

hand knitted scarf in his high school colors and a check from Dolly, mud flaps from his friends Billy and Jo that said *America's Finest*, and a small hand-held electronic device that held several solitaire and other games from Sally. The last package was from Brad. In it was a small flat camera that could be carried in a shirt pocket. "Gosh, this is great," Donny said. "I don't see the instructions, though. Did I drop them?"

"It didn't come with instructions but I'll teach you how to use it. Actually I have to make a confession. I bought a camera last month and it wouldn't work so I took it back. They fixed it and it still didn't work, so when I went back this time, I was a little testy. To appease me they gave me a new one plus this little guy. I thought it would be just right for a young man your age."

"I'm sorry you had so much trouble with your camera, but it sure was worth it to me."

More laughing.

"Okay, cake everyone?" Maybelle lit the candles and after they sang, she cut the first piece for Donny, then a slice for everyone else.

Coffee was served with the cake and as Brad was asking for a second cup, his cell phone rang. "Excuse me, please," he said, moving away from the table and then out to the porch. He was back in a very short time and said, "I'm sorry but I must run. Sally I have your phone number, I'll call you. John and Maybelle, thanks for the invitation to this fun party, and I'm happy to have met all of you, and Donny... good luck. Hope I see you all again soon." He smiled and went out the front door.

"What a nice young man," crooned Dolly. She was thinking of Emily. "John, have you worked with him very long?"

"He's been here a few months. He's doing something with the seismic department at the U. Don't exactly know why he's here at Haven Port and not at the main campus, but I think it has to do with space available. He's only in his office a few hours a week, and he's joined us at Jake's on poker night. It's about all I know, but I like him."

Everyone agreed when Dolly said she thought he was nice, especially Sally. Dolly made a mental note to ask John for Brad's phone number. He was certainly someone she would like to see Emily meet.

After seconds on cake and the final clearing of the table, Dolly said, "Donny, would you mind taking me home now?"

"Sure Grandma. Janine, want to ride along?" Of course she did and the three of them walked out to the porch and down the stairs. Donny helped Dolly into the back seat and then Janine into the front. As he went around the car he was whistling. It had been a good birthday party.

CHAPTER 14

Finally, Sunday had arrived. The big day. The first group meeting for prospective dates for Emily. Everyone's excitement was evident.

It was almost two o'clock and Dolly, Steve and Paul were by the front door waiting for their young men. Natalie and Larry had already shown their guests into the meeting room and they were sipping coffee, eating cookies, and chatting.

Earlier Natalie had posted a sign on the door. It read PRIVATE PARTY and now, as the last of the guests entered the room, Sarah closed the doors and started passing out nametags. Dolly and Ronny moved to the refreshment table and he helped himself to iced tea and several cookies. Paul and Steve poured coffee for their guests and they all headed towards the chairs.

Natalie waited until she saw they were settling and then started the meeting by saying, "Attention everyone," tap, tap. Natalie was using her gavel today, after all this was an important meeting. "We all know why we're here. Does everyone have a refreshment?" She looked around then said, "If so, would you please take a seat next to your sponsor?"

Card tables had been arranged in at semi-circle with Natalie and her gavel presiding at a card table in the front. Sarah handed out a list of the nominees to the committee members. "Use this as a reference and to make notes on. You did bring something to write with, didn't you?"

The list read:

NATALIE-Patrick Robert Kelso (Business)
DOLLY-Ivan Ronald Stump (Accountant)
PAUL-Oscar Harris Hanson (Scientist)
STEVE-Carl Astairee Randall (Car dealership)
LARRY-Brian Allen Daniels (Pilot)

"How come their middle name's are on it?" Steve not only thought the list was unnecessary but even a little silly. He was starting to have doubts about this group meeting. "I agreed to this stuff at first but why don't we just introduce Emily to these guys and let them have at it?"

Dolly was sitting beside him and answered quietly, "Because, we need to find out if any of these boys are not suitable. Do you remember now?"

Steve smiled at her. "Well, okay. I'll try to be patient, but don't you think this would be more fun if we'd served booze?"

Dolly just smiled, turned away from him and over at Ronny.

Tap-tap-tap. Natalie called for attention again.

"Everyone settled? Good. I think the best way to

handle the introductions is for each sponsor to stand and introduce their young man, and then have *them* tell us something about themselves. Do you all agree?"

Everyone nodded in approval.

"First on our list is my name. I'm Natalie Ann Greene. May I present my nephew, Patrick Kelso. Patrick, will you tell us about yourself?"

Patrick stood up but his eyes stared off into space and as he spoke his Adams Apple bobbed up and down and his tall frame was thin to the point of being gaunt. "I'm not used to talking to a crowd but I'll tell you about my business. I own parking lots for people who want to park somewhere safe while they go on their airplane trips. I started with my first lot when I was in high school. Doin' tune ups and oil changes on the cars while they were there. We did so good with the first one that my dad helped me buy two more lots. We did good with them too. Now I have almost thirty parking lots across the northwest and some in the southwest." He sat down abruptly, still not looking at anyone.

Patrick had obviously thought about his appearance. His pocket protector was new and clean behind his two pens and an automatic pencil in the pocket of his sport jacket pocket. His haircut appeared fresh and his glasses were clean and his shoes were shined. When Natalie met him at the front door she had also noted his tan knit shirt was tucked into tan pants that were pressed, and his green twill jacket fit him in the sleeves, something he'd always had trouble with since his arms were just a tad longer than normal. She was pleased at the good impression he was undoubtedly making on the group.

While he talked he nervously pulled on his coat sleeves, then put his hand in his pants pocket, then took them out only to pull on his sleeves again, then hands back in his pockets. Everyone could see he was ill at ease but he did smile when he was talking about his parking lots, and his face took on more confidence. It made him almost look handsome but the smile was gone after he sat down.

"Thank you Patrick. Dolly, will you present your young man?"

She stood up. "My name is Dolly McBride and this is my ex-stepson Ronald Stump. Ronny, will you tell every one about yourself?"

"Excuse me Ronald, before you start," Natalie interrupted, "please tell us your full name."

Dolly spoke for him. "His full name is Ivan Ronald Stump. Ronny was named after his great-uncle so he goes by the name of Ronald so there won't be confusion."

Ronny stood. He could best be described as a look-alike for the Pillsbury Dough Boy in rumpled and well-worn clothes. Clothes had never been all that important to Ronny. If you were warm enough and everything important was covered it was okay. He had two suits that almost served as uniforms. In the winter he wore brown slacks and a polyester jacket made to look like brown herringbone wool. During the warmer months he wore brown slacks with a lighter weight polyester tan jacket. He wore the tan shirt and brown tie with both outfits. Today he had on the tan jacket and his shoes were brown suede Oxfords that could use a good brushing to do away with the shiny spots.

"I'm an accountant," he said. Then there was a pause. He looked at Dolly and said, "What else should I say. It's all I do."

Dolly smiled and said, "Tell them about the IRS."

"Oh, yes. I'm retired from the IRS. Now I'm a consultant and handle claims." And he sat down again.

"Thank you Ronald, or do you prefer to be called Ronny?" Natalie was smiling.

"Only my family calls me Ronny. Everyone else calls me Ron." He didn't stand up and spoke looking directly at Natalie.

"All right, thank you Ron. Now, next is Paul. Are you ready?"

Paul stood up and thought he had just enough time to introduce Harry before he had to make a trip to the necessary room. "My name is Paul Engles and this is my friend Harry Hanson."

Natalie interrupted again and said, "Oscar Harrison Hanson".

"Yes," Paul said. "But we all called him Harry because his father is in the same business and pretty well known, so Harry opted to have a name of his own, and I'll be right back."

Harry was accustomed to Paul's hurried departures and he was also accustomed to public speaking and giving lectures, so he smiled as he stood up. He stood, walked to the front of the room and as he turned to face his audience he buttoned his coat jacket and began: "Good afternoon everyone. My name is Oscar Harris Hanson. Unless you are interested in the field of marine biology you probably haven't heard of my father but he is well published and well respected in the field of ichthyology. I, on the other hand, work for the University of Washington as a teacher and researcher. My office is here on Haven Port Island at the extension building and if any of you are interested, I'd be happy to show you around over there, but there's not much to see. We have a few specimens in tanks and a few dried samples, but mostly we bring back data and pictures from our research trips and then write about our activities." He smiled while looking around, unbuttoned his coat and walked back to his chair.

"My, that does sound interesting. Thank you, Harry." Natalie looked at her list and said, "Next is Steven Xavier." She turned to Steve and smiled. "Steven, please?"

"My friends call me Steve," he said looking directly at her. Then to the others he said, "I'm happy to introduce you to my golfing friend Carl Randall. You can read his middle name on the list if you want to. Carl?"

Carl was handsome with a winner's smile. He'd worked on this smile in front of the mirror for several years before it became *natural*. He was six-foot-one, tanned and well muscled from the hours he spent sailing and working on his boat. He also wore clothes to their best advantage. His well-pressed black slacks, white golf shirt and pale blue cardigan sweater made his blue eyes especially noticeable. He wore his dark hair short in a military cut, and his shoes were highly polished loafers with tassels. He stood up, smiled at the group and seemed to make eye contact with each and every one of them. First rule of a good salesman.

"My name is Carl Astaire Randall. The middle name's from the great dancing star Fred Astaire. My mother met him once and thought he was wonderful, so here I am with his name." And, yes she taught me to dance." He stopped and looked around as the group politely laughed with him. "I sell cars for a living. I own one dealership just north of Seattle and another is in Bellevue and one in Tacoma, so if you need a good deal on a car, be sure to see me." He sat down to a sprinkling of applause. It had been a performance for sure.

Natalie smiled at Carl then said, "Larry, you're next on the list."

"My name is Larry and I brought Brian Daniels, my old neighbor."

Brian stood up and faced the group. "My name is Brian Allen Daniels. I fly airplanes. I was in the Air Force for twenty-one years and now I fly planes for United. My schedule's pretty well set. I'm out sixteen days of each month and home the rest. I like living on the island and since I grew up here I know lots of people, but I don't think I've ever met Emily."

Standing at five-foot-ten, he wasn't as tall as the last two guys but he was very confident. His eyes had a permanent squint to them so you couldn't really see their color, but his lips held a hint of a smile as he talked. He pretty much just stated the facts, but he looked pleasant doing it. He wore tan Dockers, a red golf shirt with a black windbreaker and his shoes were black canvas slip-ons with no socks. He hadn't really dressed up for this meeting but he looked very much like all the other men on the island when they were going casual.

As he sat down, Natalie stood.

"Gentlemen, that was a very nice way for us to get to know you, now does anyone have any questions of our young men?"

Ronny raised his hand. "Brian, do you do a lot of European flights?"

Natalie thought the committee would be asking the questions, but this was all right. Information was what they wanted after all, and it didn't matter who asked what questions.

Brian stood again. "I fly twice a month to England, twice a month to Italy and twice a month to

Russia. The rest of the time I'm stuck in an office in Seattle. Does that answer your question?"

"Thank you. Yes it does."

Then from Patrick, "Do you still like to fly or does it get boring after a while?"

"No I don't get bored. I still like to fly, but being gone from home all the time is hard on a social life, so I'm cutting back and I'll be more and more in the office and home."

Natalie thought this was going very well indeed. Look how much information was coming out.

Harry raised his hand and when no one objected he said, "I'd like to ask Ron a question. Does the IRS find a lot of fraud in the institutes of higher learning? Like the universities or even in the educational system in general?"

Ron was in his element now and showed no signs of his shyness. He stood up and speaking directly to Ron he said, "In every element of society there is fraud because there are people. The institutions you mentioned are run by people so draw your own conclusions. Do you think there is more fraud in these places than others?"

Harry said, "No, not really but since I have to account so closely for every cent I spend at the U and my reports have to be so detailed, I wouldn't think there could be, or would be, much fraud or any other underhanded spending that wouldn't be detected by the bean counters. What do you think Paul?"

Paul had returned but was fidgeting and fighting the urge to leave again. In preparation for this meeting he hadn't had anything to drink, not even his morning coffee, but still, here it was, that nagging feeling of urgency. "I agree with what you said, but I need to be excused for a few minutes. Sorry." Then

Paul stood and left at a hurried pace.

Dolly raised her voice up a notch and said, "I'm so happy to see all of you gentlemen here today. I hope you have had a good time."

There was general *yeses* and *thanks-for-inviting-mes* and then Mary stood up. Natalie looked at her wondering what in the world she would say.

"I'd like to ask each of you to respond to my question: Where do you see yourself in five years?"

Natalie relaxed. *Good question.*

Patrick answered first: "I think, or at least hope, to have another ten lots." He smiled at Natalie.

Ronny was blushing again but stood up when Dolly looked at him sternly. "I will be retired and then I would like to travel to Europe. It would be nice to have someone to go with me but even if I don't, I'm going to do a lot of traveling." He pulled at his sleeves, put his hands in his pockets and sat down again.

Harry stood up next. "I think I'll still be at the U studying fish, but maybe I'll be teaching more than I do now. I'd like that."

Carl didn't need any encouragement. "In five years I'll have two more dealerships. But, I don't intend to still be actively running the show. At least I hope not. I'd like to travel too but I'm thinking South America or Costa Rica, or maybe even Australia on my sailboat. I've been to Europe several times but now I'd like to go the other way and do some exploring. Maybe rent a car and drive around those countries for several months."

All eyes turned to Brian as he stood. "You already know I'm going to stop traveling as much and I'm hoping to get a place with some land so I can raise a couple of horses and maybe some chickens. For sure I'm going to want a partner to do this with."

Mary was happy with the responses. These were telling answers from these prospective dates.

Tap-tap-tap.

"Well, wasn't this nice," Natalie said. "Thank you all for sharing and for coming. Your sponsor will be getting back to you with further information. Please feel free to stay and chat... have another cup of coffee and eat some more of those delicious cookies. No need to hurry off." That said she picked up her chair and replaced it at the side of the room. Her movement signaled everyone else to do the same and Steve picked up Dolly's chair and Larry picked up Mary's.

The party started to break up then and Patrick gave Natalie a kiss on the cheek and made his way to the door. Ronny got a couple of cookies for his pocket and gave Dolly a hug. The others were shaking hands and before long, the meeting room was empty of guests, with just the committee left.

"Shall we have a meeting after dinner tonight to discuss our possibilities?" asked Natalie.

They all agreed and moved towards their individual apartments, except for Steve and Larry. They headed for the smoking patio.

"When they were seated and Steve had his cigarette glowing, Larry said, "Well, what do you think?"

"I think I'll smoke this cigarette then go have a nap before dinner."

"I'm for that," Larry said, and that's what they did.

George hadn't been to the meeting of the prospective guys because he was having trouble with his hearing aids and decided he wouldn't be able to hear anyway, so why bother. He was slowly coming to the realization that he did have a serious hearing problem, but these gosh darn hearing aids didn't help. Maybe he would see if he could get tested again. His daughter had stopped by after church this morning to say hello and mentioned it would be so nice to be able to carry on a conversation with him again and that he was missing out on the kids. He seemed so grouchy they didn't want to visit. She said she knew it was because he couldn't hear and she needed him to realize it. Well, he did know he'd been out of sorts, and now wondered why he was so resistant to this hearing aid thing. He didn't really know, but he could do something positive about it. Monday he would ask Dr. Pete to help him get an appointment. He still didn't think he was missing much but if it would please his daughter, he'd do it.

He told Paul about his plan at dinner.

"That's a good plan, George. I agree with your daughter. You're missing out on lots of things by being so stubborn."

George just nodded in agreement. For sure he would talk to Dr. Pete as soon as he saw him.

"Want to hear about the meeting today?"

George nodded and Paul noticed his hearing aids were ready too.

"A couple of real nice kids, and a couple of really interesting ones came."

"Any good enough for our Emily?"

"I think they're all good hearted but I'm not sure if all of them are for our Emily."

He told George about his friend who studied fish; Steve's friend, the almost-too-smooth car salesman; Larry's ex-neighbor the pilot who might be okay; and Dolly's ex-stepson, the shy IRS guy. He also told him about Natalie's nephew, the parking lot owner. "As I said, the whole bunch was very interesting. I think Emily might even enjoy knowing all of them, but I wonder if any of them knows to talk about anything other than their work?"

They spent the rest of their dinner time talking about Emily and how happy they would be if one of these guys turned out to be a keeper.

This business of having a coffee hour with prospective dates for Emily was more tiring than any of them expected. Dolly and Mary both told Natalie they were too tired to have a meeting after dinner and when Natalie told Steve and Larry, the said they were pretty beat too. Well, with more than half of the members unable to attend, she decided to postpone the meeting until tomorrow after breakfast. And, when she went back to her apartment after dinner, she realized she too was a feeling tired. Well, not so tired as weary. It was a big job being head of these committees. She put on her night clothes and crawled into bed, intending to read, but her eyes kept closing, and at eight, she gave it up.

CHAPTER 15

On this Monday morning, Natalie was up early. Six-thirty found her ready for her walk and certainly ready to meet the day. Yesterday had been very exciting and a little tiring, but exercise was the key to Natalie's energy and she needed to recharge. It was threatening rain so she put on her flannel lined, bright yellow rain coat with the matching hat, pulled on her yellow rubberized shoes, and took the red umbrella from the closet. *If it rains, I'm ready. A little rain can't stop me.*

Today she went out the patio door, intending to walk down Lincoln Street to the golf course, but when she pushed open the door there sat Steve and James Pritchard Reinhold III. Both had a cup of coffee and Steve was smoking. She was surprised to see James here and could only manage a weak smile and an equally weak "Hello."

"Well, hello back," he smiled as he stood up. "Haven't seen you in a very long time." James had been a golfing friend of Natalie's husband, Howard. She'd entertained him several times in her home and in turn had been invited to the Estate on the Cliffs. "I was just inviting Steve to a little impromptu get-together up at the house. Cocktails and dinner on Thursday around five-thirty. Could you come too?"

Natalie had recovered sufficiently to say, "I think I can, James. Of course I'll need to consult my calendar. May I call you later today to confirm?"

"Sure, call and just leave a message if I'm not there."

"Is there an occasion?"

"There certainly is. My nephew's visiting and I want people to hear him play the piano. Am I remembering right? You do like music?"

"Of course I do and I'm glad he feels well enough to play. I heard he'd been in a terrible car accident."

He smiled at her. "Yes, but he's on the way to being fully recovered although he still has bandages on his face. I decided he needed company so I'm inviting some in. Hope you and Steve can make it."

Steve finished his cigarette and drained his coffee cup. "I'm going for more coffee. Sure you don't want some? And how about you Natalie, can I bring you a cup?"

"No thank you. I'm off for my morning walk. James, I'll see you soon, and Steven, I'll see you after breakfast, won't I?"

Steve nodded as he went into the building, not waiting to see if James had changed his mind.

James was still standing. He tipped his bowler hat and made a slight bow to Natalie. "Well fair lady, I certainly hope to see you on Thursday, but now, are you walking in my direction? I'm going down towards the golf course?"

She couldn't help but be pleased that he would want her to walk with him. "Yes, that's the direction I'm taking and I'd enjoy having your company."

They walked side by side chatting, and with an occasional laugh coming from one or the other, or from both of them.

He said, "...and the doctor has suggested I get more exercise and eat less red meat and give up smoking." He made a face. "I did stop smoking, almost. And I eat less steak. As for the exercise, this is turning out to be very pleasant, especially when I can walk with a beautiful woman." He smiled at her while he talked. "What days do you walk?

Natalie was delighted to tell him. "I like to walk before breakfast and I try to walk on Monday, Wednesday and Friday, and sometimes I get a little extra in on Sundays. I walk rain or shine, but just shorter ones when the weather's bad." She smiled back as she looked up at him. "You're certainly welcome to join me anytime." She'd always thought he had the nicest eyes and she was pleased he felt she would be good company.

James beamed. He'd always liked Natalie but also had felt sorry for her, for the way Howard had treated her. Not exactly bad, but he ignored her mostly, and James thought this was why Natalie busied herself with all those volunteer things.

"Do you miss working on the Annual Art Auction or the Garden Tours?" He'd always enjoyed working with her and he thought she was still as cute as the first time they'd met, forty years ago. Also, he was truly happy when she called him by his given name of James and not JP, like everyone else in town. It made him feel special.

They were at the golf course by this time and James said, "Let's stop for a cup of coffee."

She accepted and suddenly felt a little shy, a very new feeling for her.

They walked down along the putting green to the Club House Café and went inside. The rain held off and the sun was trying to get out from behind the low clouds as the couple drank coffee and chatted like the old friends they were.

Breakfast at St. Francis went as usual and Sister Nora's announcements were short.

"Today is Monday and the Health Clinic is open all morning. The craft classes start at ten o'clock and there will be one of Dr. Chu's interesting travelogues at one o'clock in the library. I think today is about the Pacific Northwest, is that right Dr. Chu?"

Dr. Chu had a mouth full of coffee but nodded yes as he swallowed. Then he said, "I have some new slides for this presentation I think everyone will like."

"Oh, that will be nice. Thank you Dr. Chu. Well, that's it for today everyone. Have a safe and blessed day."

Natalie returned from her walk with just barely enough time to change clothes for breakfast and hadn't reminded the others of the after breakfast meeting but no one forgot. Even George was there. For some reason she'd forgotten her gavel but she called the meeting to order by saying, "Shall we all be seated? Is everyone here?"

Sarah stood up and said, "All present and accounted for, sir." She was being funny and the group smiled—everyone except Natalie.

She cleared her throat, patted her lips with the handkerchief and said with a forced smile, "It was an interesting meeting yesterday, don't you agree?" The response was nods and a couple of them said yes. "I think we should now vote on which ones will be invited to meet Emily. Sarah do you have paper for everyone?"

Sarah was ready. She passed out a pencil and a slip of paper with the numbers one, two, three down the left side.

"Thank you Sara. Now let's everyone vote for two people you think would make a nice gentleman caller for Emily." She took her own piece of paper and was starting to write when Dolly raised her hand. "Yes, do you have a question?"

"Yes, Ah do. I have three spaces on my piece of paper and you said to write down two choices."

Sarah spoke up. "I thought she would ask for three names but she only said two. Ignore the other space."

Dolly smiled sweetly. "Thank you for the explanation."

Paul said, "How are we supposed to remember the names of everyone. I think I remember the first names of a couple, but..."

Sarah to the rescue. She opened her notebook and pulled out papers with the names of yesterday's candidates. The same list she passed out at the meeting.

Steve said, "Wouldn't it be simpler if we just took a hand vote?"

Natalie had already finished writing her choices and she turned to look at Steve. "A hand vote? Then how would we have a record of the happening?"

Sarah looked at Natalie and said, "I could record it in the minutes."

"We could try that I guess. I'm hoping no one's

feeling will be hurt by the vote."

"Steve has a good idea," Larry said, "but I think there *will* be bad feelings if we vote that way, so I want to vote by writing it down," He could certainly see where this kind of open voting could be the cause for not only hurt feelings but rifts among the residents, and he also knew if you offended someone over a relative, you were dead meat practically forever. He'd had experience there and was still doing reparation.

"I do agree when you put it that way. I change my vote to using paper." Natalie pressed her hanky to her lips.

Everyone smiled and bent their heads to write.

It wasn't often Natalie changed her mind.

George spoke up. "I wasn't there yesterday so I don't think I'll vote."

Natalie smiled at him. "I think that would be best."

Sarah was as usual, vigilant. As each person finished writing and lifted their head, she collected the papers. When she had all six she started to tally. It only took a few second before she said, "I have the list ready but someone didn't vote."

Mary smiled. "I just couldn't make up my mind." What she really meant was that none of the candidates were right and she just couldn't saddle Emily with any one of them.

Natalie looked at the list Sarah presented and would have read it but Sara had written it in her own brand of shorthand. She handed it back and said, "Sarah, would you please tell us the results you do have?"

"I have two votes for Natalie's Patrick."

Natalie preened. *Of course he was perfect,* she thought.

"There are two votes for Dolly's Ron, and two votes for Paul's Harry, and two votes for Steve's Carl, and two votes for Larry's guy Brian. Everyone got two votes."

Natalie was speechless, but not for long. "Well. It appears we have all voted for our own person and for one other. What we need is a tie breaker. Sarah, you met everyone, tell us who you think would be a good date for Emily."

Sarah stared daggers at Natalie. "Oh no, I'm not getting into this. You're the ones doin' this interviewing. I just take the minutes."

Everyone started to speak at once. Finally Natalie said, "Attention everyone. Please. Quiet down. We need to discuss this so one person speak at a time please."

Steve said, "Sarah, please won't you help? It'll be anonymous and we could all promise not to vote for our own guy again so it will make it even more anonymous."

Paul said, "I think it's a fair way to do it. Agreed?"

They all did and Natalie felt the meeting slowly slipping out of her hands.

Sarah knew Natalie well enough to see what was happening so when she passed out the slips again she said, "Only vote for one person, right Natalie?"

Natalie was happy she could step in and take the reins again. "I think it would be nicer to vote for two."

This was starting to be a pain. Especially for George who was anxious to go to the clinic and talk to Dr. Pete, and for Paul who needed to just go, and Larry and Steve who were just plain getting tired of the whole thing.

Sarah collected the slips again and this time Mary voted. She decided maybe the pilot and the scientist could be fun. This time the tally was:

Patrick the parking lot owner – two
Ronald the accountant – one
Harry the scientist – four
Carl the car salesman – three
Brian the pilot – two

"Well, now this gives us a place to start," said Natalie. "Paul, I'll check with Emily and see when she's available and then you can tell Harry to contact her. In the meantime, we should vote again to break the tie between Patrick, Carl and Brian. Does everyone agree?" But she was losing her audience for sure this time. Paul was already walking out the door and George was standing.

"Let's can this meeting until after Emily sees Harry. Then we might be done." Steve was talking as he made his way to the door too.

Natalie said pretty much to herself, "Meeting adjourned." She wasn't exactly unhappy with the choice but she'd so wished Patrick would be chosen. *Oh well,* she thought, *there's nothing in the rules to say he can't ask her out anyway.* She gathered up her notebook and started for her apartment when she saw George coming towards her.

"Say, I've been thinking. I know a guy I think Emily would like. When're we having the next screening party?"

She hadn't considered that possibility yet but she said, "Well, how soon do you think we should have it, next Sunday?"

"Yeah, I think that would work. I'll call him."

He started to walk away but Natalie said, "Would you give me his name please? And perhaps a little about him?"

"His names Simon Smith and he's a retired librarian. Known him since we moved here. Used to come here just in the summer but now he's full time. Lives in a condo somewhere."

"Is he of a proper age and marital status?" Natalie was shifting back into her in-charge mode.

George turned and scowled at her. "Do you think I'd pick someone too old or someone who was married?" He walked away shaking his head. "Women," he said under his breath.

CHAPTER 16

Mary was excited. She could hardly wait for Emily to come to work today so they could talk about their shopping trip.

Emily worked Monday through Thursday, four to nine-thirty. These hours were perfect for her and sometimes she filled in on weekends. That was good too. Sometimes weekends got very long. She walked into the office this Monday afternoon to find Mary waiting. "Hello."

"Hello. I wanted to chat about the shopping we talked about."

"Good. I wanted to talk to you too. Would tomorrow be okay?" Emily seemed just as excited a Mary.

"Tomorrow is perfect. We could go over at ten and shop, have lunch and maybe shop some more. Make a day of it until you have to come to work. Will it be too much for you to do in one day?"

Emily smiled. "I can take it if you can." They

both laughed and it was settled. Tomorrow they would meet at the door by the patio and walk over together. If per chance it was raining Emily would bring her car and "...it might make sense anyway since we'll probably have so many packages to carry." That statement made the ladies laugh again. Two mature women but as delighted with themselves as teenagers and almost giggling.

Tuesday morning Mary was walking down the hall on her way to the patio door when Natalie stopped her. "When do you and Emily plan to go shopping? Emily invited me to go with you."

Mary stopped. *Oh no,* she thought. 'Hello Natalie. When did you talk to Emily?"

"It was one day last week. I don't exactly remember when. Oh yes, it was the day you did the thing to your hair. Do you remember that day?"

"Yes, of course I remember. Well, let's get together with Emily when she comes in today and figure out a shopping day."

Natalie smiled. "Yes, that'll work but I need to find something new to wear for Thursday so it probably will have to be tomorrow. I might even have to go alone if you can't make it. Would that hurt your feelings?"

Mary was surprised. It was not in Natalie's nature to ask about another's feelings. Now she felt guilty about today's shopping trip and not mentioning it. Should she say something?

Natalie smiled. "Where are you going now?"

Caught.

"I have plans for lunch with a friend."

"Well, have a nice day and would shopping tomorrow work for you? I'll take care of asking Emily."

"Yes, and morning is good," Mary said then turned to walk down the hall. She glanced back and Natalie was still standing there smiling. What was up with her today? She opened the door to the patio still in a quandary and saw Emily just driving up. She got into the car and said, "You'll never guess what just happened and I don't know what to do about it."

By the time Mary told Emily about the hallway conversation and they made the short drive to the mall, Emily had a plan. "Let's just go shopping again tomorrow, only we'll make it all her."

Mary thought this was brilliant and relaxed. Today for us, tomorrow for Natalie.

Emily's excitement heightened the minute they walked through the revolving door and saw all the shops spread out in front of them. "I haven't really been shopping for so many years. My clothes never seem to wear out." Her face was flushed and the added color made her look radiant.

As they walked down the corridor, immediately on their left was a candy store and they couldn't resist. Mary bought a quarter pound of orange jelly slices and Emily bought white chocolate fudge. The next store was full of toys then a jewelry store, and the next one was Women's Casual World, a shop full of tops, slacks, jackets, skirts and dresses. When they stepped through this door they knew the fun had really begun.

"I don't even know where to look first. These colors are not what I'm used to wearing." Emily stood in the door and tried to take it all in. "Aren't they all so pretty?"

Mary was secretly hoping Emily would pick something bright and cheerful and quickly agreed. "Why don't we look at some blouses? I would like to find something in a light blue to go with my navy pantsuit. What's your favorite color?"

It had been so long since Emily considered anything that wasn't mix and match with her wardrobe of black skirts, black pantsuits and tan or white tops that she wasn't sure what colors she liked. "I'm looking at this beautiful apricot one, and oh my, the pale green long sleeved blouse over there, and..."

Mary was excited because Emily was. They pulled out garments, discussed style and decided to try some of them on. Mary found a knit top she liked for her navy suit that had short sleeves, a slight scoop in the neckline and it was a perfect icy blue.

Emily found two tops in the apricot color she liked. One was a blouse with a collar and buttoned down the front. The bottom hem was slightly scooped so it could be tucked in or not. The other was more like a sleeveless sweater knit tank top but of a silky blend. And in the next isle she found a pair of white slacks with a plain front. Mary told her the pants were definitely in style and they asked the clerk what kind of shoes she had to go with them, sandals perhaps?

The clerk said, "Come with me."

They followed her to the back of the store and a whole wall of definitely fun shoes. Mary immediately picked out two pairs of sandals. One pair was white and had three-inch heels and the other pair was a nice apricot paisley sort of print and had a wedge heel and closed toes. Both were called slides, which meant no back and the white ones had just a wide strip of leather across the arch of the foot. Emily took them with her into the dressing room. Minutes later she emerged, looking not only ten years younger but also definitely in style. Mary could only stare at the woman that had been hiding behind the frumpy clothes and hairdo. "You look beautiful. How do you feel?"

Emily thought beautiful was going overboard but she did feel good, an unaccustomed sensation, and she was smiling. The apricot top fit just right but she said, "Are these pants too tight? There doesn't seem to be very much extra room in them."

"They don't look too tight, and remember they're made of a stretch material. Try sitting in them. It's always a good test."

Emily sat down on the chair by the dressing room door and said, "They feel fine. I'm just worried because they might show too much." She stood and turned in front of the mirror, looking at all sides of herself.

Mary thought she knew how Emily was feeling. She'd been hiding her body for so many years in those oversized clothes; it must have felt strange to be wearing these well-fitted slacks. "I saw a jacket that matched those pants. Let me get it for you."

Emily sat down to put on the white shoes. She stood up again and took a full look in the mirror. She smiled when she thought what her mother would have said. "Self indulgence will lead to trouble." But at the age of fifty-seven, Emily decided a little self indulgence wouldn't hurt. She then changed into the apricot paisley wedges and when Mary came back she slipped on the white jacket over the apricot knit top. She walked out to the three-way mirror in the store and was amazed. "I hardly recognize this person."

Mary agreed. She too could hardly recognize this woman with her stylish haircut, white pantsuit with a beautiful apricot color next to her face, and these fun shoes... and who could have known what a lovely body Emily had been hiding all these years.

While Emily paid for the pantsuit, both pairs of

shoes, and the three blouses—a bright blue, a green print, and the apricot one—Mary wandered over to the accessory department to look at the purses, gloves and funky jewelry. When Emily joined her, Mary had two necklaces in her left hand. They were different shades of blue and she was trying to decide if they could be worn with the top she held in her other hand. "Don't you just love this big, clunky jewelry? It's so popular now."

Emily didn't know. For so many years she had only worn her wedding ring and plain gold studs in her pierced ears. It's what her husband liked and it was all the jewelry she had. She walked around the display and looked at the earrings and necklaces. "Am I trying to look like a teenager if wear these sorts of things?" She had a white, pear shaped stone hanging from a very thin leather thong in her hand, and on the display was the miniature copies of the necklace made into earrings.

"No, I don't think so, and I do think it would look lovely with your new pantsuit. What do you think of these to go with the blouse I picked?" The two discussed the blue necklace and decided it was okay but not the exactly right and they needed to look further. Emily decided to buy the white necklace and earrings and Mary paid for her blouse and they were off again.

As they moved out of the store and back into the mall, both women were smiling.

They walked toward the next store and saw the headless torsos displaying bras and panties and what Mary remembered as Merry Widow waist cinchers. "Want to go in here?"

"Not really. I think I'd rather go where I usually go to get my underthings. Do you mind? But we could look if you want to."

Mary started to laugh. "No, I'm not really interested in wearing a thong panty or being pushed up." They both were laughing now.

Across the mall was a store featuring costume jewelry and Mary started towards it. "Might find a necklace in here, do you think? Anyway, let's look."

As they entered the store they were blasted with the rap music that was pouring from the speakers on the ceiling. Mary motioned to Emily and they walked back out. "I'm sorry but I can't really stand that much sound all at once. I can't bring myself to call it music even if the kids think it is. Guess it makes me an old fuddy-duddy."

"I think that makes you someone that cares if she goes deaf or not," Emily said and they walked to the next store that carried stationary and special papers goods. They went in and Mary bought some note cards and Emily found birthday cards to send to her twin sons. It made her happy to be thinking of them. Maybe she would take the cards to them next month instead of sending them by mail, just to see if they could recognize her now. It made her smile more to think of the changes going on.

Mary had been watching her. She had such a lovely, sweet smile. "I think I'm ready for lunch, how about you?"

Emily nodded. It *was* time to eat. She checked her watch; it was already twelve-thirty. "Where has the time gone? I can't believe we've been shopping for over two hours. Let's do go find some food."

Just like last week they took the escalator up to the food court. At one end were the food stalls. Chinese Kitchen, East Indian Cuisine, Mama's Italian, Cluckin' Chicken, and American Deli were just a few names Emily recognized. "What sounds good to you? Can you smell the pizza? Does that interest you?"

"I haven't had pizza for some time." Mary picked up the paper menu from the Mama's Italian counter and headed for a table to unload her bundles. They decided on a medium with double cheese, mushrooms, Italian sausage and roasted garlic. Emily went to place the order and when she got back Mary had paper plates, plastic forks and napkins laid out on the table.

"I ordered us iced teas to drink with it, okay?"

"Sounds good and I need to wash my hands," Mary said. "I'll be right back."

While she waited Emily thought about her new clothes. She really liked the trousers and the way they fit and she liked them paired with the jacket, but just where was she going to wear them? She really needed to get something to wear to work or church, or just to wear at home. When Mary returned, Emily said, "I need to get some thing not as dressy. Something more practical. The white suit is lovely and it makes me feel good but it's not exactly a work outfit."

"Don't forget you have some gentlemen who are going to be calling you for dates. Surely you'll have an occasion to dress up, don't you think?" Mary wanted to tell Emily about the results of the Sunday's coffee hour but decided it needed to be handled as the group planned.

"Well, maybe I will. You're right but I do need more than one outfit, don't you think?"

Mary agreed and they talked about maybe even looking at warm-up outfits. "My daughter is a little overweight but she looks so cute wearing those silky looking suits with the stripe down the leg. Let's look at some of those. You could wear them to ball games or walking or even playing golf if you want to. Do you play golf?”

"Yes I do, but not lately. And I saw a sundress when we were here the day we got our hair cuts. Do you remember? I don't have anywhere to wear that either but I'd love to try it on. Let's go there after we eat."

Mary was feeling so warm towards Emily. It was almost like watching a butterfly coming out of its cocoon. "And don't forget, shoes to go with them. Shoes make the outfit you know."

The pizza was delicious and they finished it, talking the whole time. Emily wanted to know about Mary's grandchildren, and Mary wanted to hear about Emily's boys. When they were finished Mary produced hand cleaners in a foil package and the ladies wiped their hands then put their plates and napkins into the refuse containers. Now they were ready to hit the shops again.

They started for the escalator and Mary said, "Before we go look at that dress, let's stop at this sports clothes shop. I want you to look at the running suits."

They didn't make it back to the shop that held the dress but at two-thirty Emily said she really needed to get home and she could see Mary was getting tired. They packed everything into the car and Emily drove them back to St. Francis. Mary got out of the car and as she said good-bye, she wondered if Emily would wear any of her new clothes tonight to work, then as she let herself into her apartment she realized she would be going to the mall again tomorrow with Natalie in tow. Maybe they wouldn't shop as long, at least she hoped not, but for now she would just stretch out on her bed for a little rest before dinner.

When Emily got home she put all the bags on the bed, and, one by one, unloaded the contents. This new jogging suit, as Mary called it, was pretty. It was a bright blue with a white stripe down the sleeve and down the pant leg and a white sleeveless cotton tee for underneath. She already had white walking shoes so this was all set. She hung it together on one hanger and put it in the closet.

Next she decided to just open all the bags, lay the contents on the bed, and she hung up the rest of the purchases. The dark green slacks and the lighter green cotton sweater set, then the navy skirt with the matching cardigan sweater, and the blue and red flowered blouse. She hung them all up then turned to the coral colored blouse and the red cotton cardigan sweater she'd bought for no reason except she liked it. They went on hangers and into the closet next to everything else.

Lastly, she opened the hanging bag that held the coat. Mary said she needed this for cooler evenings. It was of very lightweight wool with a button at the waist that made it wrap to the left and when she tried it on in the store Mary said it looked so elegant with her dark shiny hair. It made Emily feel elegant too. It was such a light beige color; it could almost be called off-white and it would go with everything.

By the time Emily finished hanging her clothes and disposing of the sacks and tags, it was time to head back to St. Francis to work. Half an hour later she entered her office and found Natalie sitting in the chair by her desk.

"We, the committee, have a surprise for you. We found a lovely young man for you to date." Natalie sat back and waited for Emily to be surprised.

But Emily didn't show surprise and that was agitating to Natalie.

"Is his name Harry? He called me just before I came to work today. He sounds nice and I already agreed to go out with him on Thursday night."

"Where are you going? Will it be a formal date or just for coffee?" Natalie forgot her snit and got excited. Her plan was really working, and fast.

"We're going to a dinner party up at the Estate. Mr. Reinhold invited some of the staff from the University and Harry invited me to go with him."

"Why didn't you call me after you talked to him? Never mind, it doesn't matter now. But, isn't it a coincidence. I happen to be going to that same party and I think Steven is invited also. At least you'll know the two of us in case of any problem." Natalie was feeling slightly maternal towards Emily. "And dear, maybe we could go shopping tomorrow and get something suitable for you to wear. I plan to get something for the party too, so let's start early."

CHAPTER 17

Wednesday morning Natalie hurried through her walk. It was a short circle down to the golf course and back and now she was showered and dressed and ready to have breakfast. She was thinking about the shopping and maybe getting something in chiffon or maybe a silk shift. She liked to shop but not alone, so she was happily looking forward to this day.

Mary was in the breakfast line behind Natalie and said, "Ready for our outing?"

Natalie had almost forgotten Mary was going with them but she recovered quickly. "Yes I am, are you?"

"Emily said she would pick us up in the car because it's raining. She'll be here at quarter to ten so we can be there when the mall opens."

Natalie stopped and looked at Mary. She was trying not to be angry. Why hadn't Emily called her to change the time? She was controlling herself very well she thought when she answered, "Well, it would have been nice of her to at least call me."

"I told her not to bother; that I'd see you at breakfast. You don't mind do you?" Mary knew perfectly well that Natalie minded but she was determined not to let this conversation turn into a disagreement.

Natalie had her tray filled and didn't answer. She walked to her table and sat down. As she spread cream cheese on her bagel she concentrated on calming down. She patted her lips and forehead with her handkerchief and stuffed it into her sleeve. She felt better now and what did it matter Emily had sent a message instead of calling directly?

Sister Nora made the after-breakfast announcements a little early. "...Because there seems to be so many early activities today.

"This is Wednesday and because of the broken projector on Monday, the travelogue by Dr. Chu had to be cancelled, so it will be held tonight. Remember, it's the presentation about the Pacific Northwest and Dr. Chu has new slides to present.

If you are going out today, mind the weather. Looks wet and cool so bundle up and have a blessed day." Sister smiled at everyone and they all smiled back.

Paul and George lingered over their coffee.

"He said he would get me an appointment in Seattle as soon as possible and he thinks I just need a different kind of hearing aid then I'll be able to hear. And he said it won't be uncomfortable like this one is. He said all I need to do is give my ears a chance to get used to them." It was a long speech for George but he was as excited as he had ever been. Dr. Pete had given him hope and that alone helped his depression. If you asked George what would make his life better, he would say immediately to be able to know what people were saying again. He didn't much care to talk but he sure missed knowing what was going on.

Paul was happy for George and would have stayed and talked some more but he had to go. "I'll be right back," he said and he hurried out of the dining room.

Steve and Larry were also sipping coffee at their table, happy not to have to go out in the storm they could see brewing outside the windows. Steve thought about going out to smoke, or rather to the smoking room across the open patio, but decided he could wait a little longer and even mentioned to Larry he might stop smoking just because of weather like this.

Larry laughed and said, "Knowing how much willpower you have, I wouldn't put it past you to do just that."

Steve looked at him and thought, *Yes, I do have willpower, don't I?* He'd almost forgotten that this was a by-product of not drinking. It made him smile.

Sarah had finished her breakfast and was already in the craft room, painting yet another pot for her daughter's garden.

The whole committee was happy and relaxed. The first round had happened and they had performed well, and with good results.

At nine-fifty-five Natalie and Mary were waiting by the front door. Emily drove up under the covered part of the entrance and the ladies got in. Natalie was surprised Emily drove a SUV but it hadn't surprised Mary at all. It was exactly the kind of car she expected this strong woman to have. Playing chauffeur to her twins and their friends, then hauling wheel chairs back and forth to the doctors made this the perfect vehicle for her. Emily drove them into the underground parking garage at the mall and the women took the escalator up to the main floor.

"Well, where shall we start?" Natalie felt she needed to be in charge. Obviously Emily didn't know anything about how to choose clothes, and she would never admit it, but she did feel it would be a reflection on her if Emily wore something inappropriate to the party tomorrow.

"The day I got my hair cut I saw some things in that store I'd like to see better. Let's go look." Emily didn't seem to notice the bossy directions of Natalie and turned towards the store leaving Mary and Natalie to follow.

They walked in the door and immediately to their right was the mannequin that had been in the window. There was the muted print of turquoise and orange on white and the all-over look was of flowers on a type of material that seemed to float. The halter-necked front was cut low and a still lower V in the back. The slim, straight skirt was short with a two-inch ruffle around the bottom. Emily touched the skirt and said, "I really didn't get a good look at this before, and now that I have, well I think all I really like is the material. I guess I'm not interested."

"There're other styles and materials on this side." A sales woman had come up to help. "Is it something for you?" she asked looking at Emily.

"Yes, for me and for this lady. Are you looking for a dress too?" Emily was looking at Mary.

Mary smiled and decided yes she would like a new party dress too. She looked at the smiles on Natalie's and Emily's face and decided shopping for dresses was making all three of them very happy indeed.

"Let's see. You must be a size four or six?" The sales woman was looking at Emily again. "Come over here and I'll get you started looking." When she returned she looked at Natalie. "I think your size is in this part of the store," and led the way towards the back."

While the other ladies were busy looking at their sizes, Mary was looking at the dressy pants suits on the rack by the front door. She immediately found a deep orchid silk with a short jacket and pants that were fully lined. The top closed down the front with pearl buttons and it had a jewel neckline. Her pearl earrings and bracelet would work for jewelry so she didn't have to look any further. She took it into the dressing room for a try on. If it fit, all she would need was new shoes.

Emily was having similar success. She found a dress in a burgundy wool and silk blend with a wide band at the waist and a flared skirt. It had a ballet neckline and the sleeves were three-quarter length and banded just like the waist. Emily headed for the dressing room but Natalie hadn't found anything yet. The sales woman was trying to help her. "Do you have a color in mind?"

Natalie didn't but turned down a dark green, a navy and a brown.

"Do you have a style in mind?"

Natalie didn't have that pinned down either, but she knew when she saw it she would know.

Emily came out of the dressing room and stood in front of the three-way mirror. Her eyes were shining and the deep color of the burgundy made her skin seem translucent. The tight, banded waist fit perfectly but she realized she would need to get a different bra and thought maybe a burgundy bra would be right, just in case a strap might show. Next she thought about shoes. She better ask Mary for help there.

Natalie saw her and smiled. "It's a perfect dress for you. Do you like it?"

Before she could answer, Mary came out of the dressing room and also smiled at Emily. "Oh that's wonderful. It won't even have to be altered. But you'll need to get shoes to go with it. Burgundy leather if we can find them."

Holding her tongue, Natalie forced a smile. *Just who put Mary in charge?*

The sales woman brought a dress for Natalie to see. It was an iridescent silvery-green silk with a slightly gathered skirt, long sleeves and a fitted bodice. It zipped up the back and the stand-up collar would be beautiful against her skin. She took it into the changing room while Mary and Emily talked about shoes.

"I have some black ones that will do if we can't find the right color," Emily said. "Maybe I could wear this tomorrow night."

Mary looked at her and smiled. "So you have a date?"

"Oh Mary, I'm sorry. I told Natalie and I guess I thought she'd tell you. Paul's friend from the U called and we're going to a cocktail dinner party at the Estate tomorrow night."

"Then I agree. This would be good for the dinner party. I'm so pleased."

Emily turned a few times in front of the mirror and said almost to herself, "I definitely need a new bra with this dress."

Mary heard her and agreed. "But that won't be a problem. We'll go to Macy's and get you fitted correctly." Emily didn't know what *being fitted* meant and Mary was explaining it when Natalie came out of the dressing room. They both stopped talking and stared. She looked beautiful. The icy green made her eyes even greener and the dress fit in all the right places.

"I think I can wear this with my diamonds, don't you?"

The sales woman was very complimentary to Natalie and after they all changed out of the new outfits she asked where they were going in their new clothes.

Natalie told her they were attending a function at the Estate on the Cliffs and was waiting for her to be properly impressed, but the saleswoman said, "My husband works at the U and we're going too. I think he's invited the whole town to hear his nephew play."

Mary suppressed a smile as she watched Natalie's face fall. She could almost hear her wondering, *Why are the commoners invited too?*

They left the store and Mary suggested they go to the foundation department at Macy's next.

"And we could look there for shoes too," said Natalie, struggling to be back in charge.

In short order Emily and Mary, and even Natalie had new garments to wear under their party clothes, all of them the appropriate color.

Natalie confided she had never worn anything but beige bras, "...but this gray silk one was, well, fun."

The shoes were harder to find. Macy's had some lovely leather pumps but not in a right color for Emily or Mary, and the heel was too high for Natalie. The shoe clerk suggested they also look at Harley's Shoes located on the upper floor so that's where they intended to go next, but Emily said, "Let's have a cup of tea first." She could see Mary was looking tired and they had time to sit for a few minutes. They went to the Starbuck counter and Emily ordered a cup of Chamomile Tea, Natalie a cup of Chai and Mary an Orange Zinger. They took their cups to a table and sat down.

"I didn't think finding a dress would be so easy," Emily said.

Mary thought Emily was glowing. "It was lucky, wasn't it?"

Natalie was still a little miffed about Mary being so pushy but they chatted while they sat and drank their tea and began to feel another burst of energy. Now, off to find shoes.

They found Harley's Shoe Store. The perfect pair of soft Italian kid leather, dyed the perfect burgundy color was displayed on a side table, just waiting for Emily to come in. They were pumps with a four-inch heel, handmade, and they were expensive. Emily and Mary were talking about the price but Natalie, always the practical one, asked Emily, "Can you walk in high heels?"

Emily didn't know. She'd worn high heels in school for various occasions and always when she went out with Sam, but it had been some time since she'd worn anything other than her standard two inch slip-ons. She had on hose today in preparation for this shoe trying, so she slipped them on and stood up. She took a couple of steps forward then did a turn. "I guess it's like riding a bike, you never really forget." She walked over to the door and back, looking like she wore them every day.

Finding shoes for Mary was not as easy. The

orchid color was difficult to match and finally she settled for a pair of pearlized white leather with a two-inch sling heel.

Natalie decided she already had the shoes for her dress and as they walked out of the store with their new shoes, Emily realized it was time to go home. It had been a successful shopping day and they'd found everything they needed. However, as they headed for the parking garage, they passed O'Brian's Jewelry and Emily said, "I don't think I have proper jewelry for this dress."

Mary decided to sit on the bench by the door with the packages while Natalie and Emily looked in the display cases. The salesman asked what they especially were looking for and they explained about the dress. He wanted to see the color and Emily pulled back the protective plastic from the hanging bag and held up the dress for his inspection. He was a grandfatherly type with white hair and a large bushy moustache. He heard Natalie call her Emily and said, "I think I know you. Did you teach here at the grade school?"

Emily smiled and said, "Yes I did, but it was a few years ago. Did you have a child in my class?"

"No, but my wife taught first grade and I think you were friends. Her name was Helen York. I lost her last year to cancer. Do you remember her?"

Emily reached over and laid her hand on his. "Yes of course I remember Helen and we were friends. I don't think we've met though, did we? I had to quit teaching to take care of my family and we lost contact. I'm so sorry."

"Thank you. I sort of thought you didn't know about her, and we did meet at the Cake Walk your class held one year, but it was a long time ago." He smiled remembering. "Now, let's find something to set off that dress." He pulled out a tray of very heavy gold chains and held them up. Emily thought they would look okay but Natalie had her own idea.

"Do you have something more delicate? Maybe a couple of fine chains of different weights and lengths? What do you think Emily?"

"Like these?" He was holding a set of five chains of graduated lengths and in the other hand... earrings to match.

"Let me show my friend."

Mary agreed they were right for the dress and so did Natalie so that part was finished. And the price was surprising. "Are you sure the total for this set is only twenty-five dollars?"

He was sure and leaned over the counter to speak softly. "They're costume jewelry but look every bit as good as eighteen carat gold if you take care of them." Then he winked at Natalie. Natalie blushed but she didn't know why except it had been a very long time since anyone had winked at her.

While Emily paid for the necklace Mary and Natalie picked up the packages and all three headed for the car.

Another fun shopping day, thought Emily.
Emily looks so happy, thought Mary.
Mission accomplished, thought Natalie.

CHAPTER 18

Emily hung her new dress on the back of her bedroom door where she could see and admire it. When they were buying the burgundy bra, Mary suggested they look for hose that would be good to wear with the outfit too.

She had never in her life worn any stockings that weren't the Suntan color her mother had approved of, so they consulted the clerk. She asked if this was for a fancy gathering and suggested the nearly nude pantyhose with the touch of gold. Emily hesitated but Mary pushed her. "Might as well make the outfit complete." Emily had reluctantly agreed but was so glad now. It certainly would make this dress look special.

Emily thought about her upcoming date. On Monday, Sister Nora warned her that the committee had a *look-see* at potential dates on Sunday, but she was still surprised when Harry called. He introduced himself as Paul Engles friend and asked if she had a minute to talk or would it be better if he called later. Emily thought this was considerate and said she could chat for a few minutes before she left for work. He told her about how he knew Paul and what he taught at the U. "You know Paul, of course."

"Yes, he lives at St. Francis, but you know that."

He then asked her if she liked piano music and told her about the dinner party on Thursday. "Would you like to go with me and do you mind if our first date includes Mary and Paul and lots of other people?"

She told him she wouldn't mind and that it sounded fun, then she gave him her address. The conversation lasted less than ten minutes but Emily felt it would be okay, especially with so many people around. So did Harry. He didn't date much so he thought this first date would be easier on everyone.

Back at St. Francis, Natalie also hung her dress on the back of the bedroom door and smiled. There had been a message on her recorder from James Reinhold saying he would *like to send a car for her if it was alright with her. It would be there at five-fifteen and perhaps Steve could ride up with her if she didn't mind.* She returned the call, leaving a message that said *it was very considerate to have a car sent and she would speak to Steven.*

Natalie found Steve in the dining room talking to Dr. Pete. As she walked up to them, they both turned and smiled. "Steven, may I have a word with you?"

Dr. Pete excused himself, saying he was on his way home and would see them both later. Steve could only imagine what Natalie had on her mind but it couldn't be good.

"James said he is sending a car for me and

wondered did you need a ride to the party on Thursday?"

Wow, he thought. *Sending a car for her and inviting me too? Maybe I misjudged her relationship with JP.* "Sure, I'd like to ride with you."

"All right, it's set. The car will be here at five-fifteen. Shall we meet at the front door?"

He said yes and as she walked away he reassessed her. She wasn't bad looking, but just so bossy. Maybe she would be pleasant during the ride. He was looking forward to Thursday's get-together. It would be his first cocktail party when he wasn't drinking but he wasn't worried he kept telling himself.

When Mary got to her apartment after the shopping trip, there was a note under her door to call Paul. *Oh dear*, she thought. *Is there a problem?*

There wasn't.

"I know this is late notice but tomorrow there's a cocktail and dinner party at the Reinhold Estate and I've been invited. I was wondering if you would like to go. I apologize for not asking you sooner but you know about my problem and it's hard for me to go to places where..."

Mary interrupted him and said, "Paul, if you feel comfortable going, I feel comfortable going with you. You know your limitations and I understand." She could hear his sigh, almost like he'd been holding his breath. "Would you like me to drive?"

"Well, the young man I brought to the party on Sunday, do you remember Harry? Well, he's taking Emily and asked if we wanted to go with them. Will that be okay?"

Of course it was okay and Mary was excited. She had a new outfit to wear and she hadn't been on a date since she'd been widowed, and she was very happy to be going with Paul. She left her apartment and went to see if Emily had come to work yet.

Emily was not wearing any of her new clothes and it surprised Mary but then she thought, *Why would she*? It had been a rainy afternoon and now a stormy evening.

"Emily, guess what? We're riding together."

They chatted about the party and the riding arrangement and Mary assured Emily about Harry. "He's a handsome young man and if he's a friend of Paul's he just has to be nice."

Then Mary brought up the subject of makeup. No one had mentioned makeup to Emily before and she didn't know how to respond.

Don't I look okay this way? "But I don't know how to put on the eye stuff and I'm not sure I even have a lipstick."

"Do you want me to help you? I can lend you a lipstick that would go with the dress and show you how to do your eyes. Just a little mascara and shadow would do wonderful things and set off your beautiful face."

"I'm so sorry to make you go to all this trouble, but yes I would like some help. Sister Nora got my replacement for tomorrow so I could come here. What do you think?"

Mary said she could show her right now if she had time and left to get the necessary equipment. A few minutes later she was back with a mirror, lip liner, lipstick, gray shadow and mascara. She demonstrated the lip liner on herself and then Emily practiced on her own lips. Mary then applied lipstick in a light coat and then Emily did it too. "It's better to put on two light coats then one heavy one. Let the first application dry a bit then apply the second coat. It'll stay on longer. Now let's do eyes."

They followed a similar procedure except first Mary applied gray eye shadow on one eyelid and Emily followed her instructions and did the same on the other eye. Then Mary applied soft strokes of mascara to the upper eye lashes then the lower ones and Emily followed these instructions on the other eye. Mary presented the mirror and Emily gasped. "Oh. I do look better. Less sickly."

Mary laughed. "You were always beautiful, this just plays it up. Wear it tonight and get a little used to not rubbing your eyes."

"How do I take it off when I go to bed, just wash it off?"

"If you have some cold cream you could use it, but just soap and water in the shower works well. It's just temporary, you know, and will wash off easily."

Emily picked up the mirror and looked at herself again. She was almost embarrassed that she looked so good. Once again she could hear her mother in the background saying something about *pride going before the fall,* but she decided not to listen. She was doing nothing wrong, and it made her so happy to look so, well, pretty.

As Mary left Emily she thought, *Just wait until they see her at the party tomorrow. And I just can't wait until Natalie sees her all made up.* She was humming a tune as she entered the dining room.

The after lunch Monday travelogue was postponed to Wednesday night. The projector was repaired and only the bulb needed replacing so tonight the talk was being held in the library. The chairs were comfortable and the crowd was, as usual, small. Tonight Dr. Chu had everything set up and the projector had been tested. The new slides he had were of sunsets around the San Juan Islands and behind the Olympics. They were spectacular and brought ooohs and aaahs from the group of nine who watched. When the show was finished, Dr. Chu stood up. He smiled at the audience and said, "Just a footnote to this lovely view of our beautiful Pacific Northwest, did you know that in 1792, Captain George Vancouver was sent to explore the western coastline of the new world? Part of Vancouver's duties were to name and identify islands and waterways and it was not unusual for him to honor favorite Saints and even some of his crew, by bestowing their names on points of interest. When he got to what we now call Washington State, Lieutenant Peter Puget had a waterway named for him, James Vashon got an island, and Saint John got the San Juan's, a whole chain of islands." The audience had heard the Professor tell this story several times but they all loved it and knew that this was the time for a laugh.

"However," continued CC, as he was fondly called, "the island that Vancouver must have loved the best was the one he found on a dark and stormy night. This island, located in the southern part of Puget Sound, hosted Vancouver's ships in a safe harbor during a particularly bad and stormy winter. The history books tell us that in his reports to his King, Vancouver often referred to this favored area, and legend has it that Haven Port is the name he bestowed on our island and the protective bay. The island has certainly changed since then, hasn't it?" More expected laughter from the audience, and knowing this was the end of the slide presentation, they all stood up to leave the library and this month's travelogue presentation.

Dr. Chu was retired from the University of San Diego's History Department, but spent the last ten years of his working life as a travel agent. The many slide shows and tapes of his travels were usually shown on the first Monday of each month and they were popular with a certain section of the residents. After all, what else was there to do on the first Monday of the month?

Dolly and Mary were part of today's audience. "I wish I could travel more," said Dolly. "My first husband and I loved to see new places."

Mary smiled. She was just happy to be here at St. Francis and there was enough excitement going on for her at the moment. However, traveling was a distant dream she felt she probably would never realize. "Maybe someday," she said, "but in the meantime I enjoy these travelogues of CC's."

All these comments added to Dr. Chu's pleasure of showing his photography and he decided to start collecting scenes from around Haven Port for a future presentation.

CHAPTER 19

It was not unusual for the Puget Sound and the island of Haven Port to endure a heavy storm that blew down from Alaska just for one day and then have the following morning's dawn be sunny with the air almost balmy. Thursday was one of these days that promised to be warm.

About ten o'clock, Steve strolled down to Jake's Restaurant and Bar for coffee and found a crowd. Murph was behind the bar and on the stools sat Larry and four other men he didn't know. Murph made the introductions.

"Hey Steve, come on in. Do you know these guys?"

"I guess I only know you and Larry."

"This young man is Andy Owens. He lives on Front Street in one of the houses. The one with all the roses."

Andy nodded his white head towards Steve and said, "Thanks for the young man title. I guess seventy isn't really so old, huh?"

Murph continued his introductions as he set a cup of coffee in front of Steve. "This is Tom Taylor. He's a fireman and he'll be joining our Poker group. This is Brad, he works at the University, and this is Sam Pitts, new resident of Haven Port. Well, he's not really new, been here for almost a year. He has the boat building place on the East Harbor. Guys, this is Steve and he's brave enough not to drink anymore."

Larry thought this was a kind way to say he was a drunk but he didn't mind. It was true and as he took a stool next to the young man named Andy, he said, "I wonder why we don't know each other. How long you lived here?"

"Well, I lived here sort of for twenty years. I've only been here now for about six months, but I owned that house for a long time. I just used it for business meetings and rented it out mostly. I haven't been back since the wife died, but I'm here now. Where do you live?"

"I'm living at St. Francis Retirement Center. Just moved there last year and its great. Good food, nice people and no yard work."

Everyone laughed.

The conversation continued. Brad and Tom were chatting about the wind action on the island and how tough it was to fight fires here, especially on the cliffs. Sam and Larry were discussing the weather and Murph and Steve and Andy started chatting about the Mariners.

Andy said, "I sure hope they get their act together again. They seem to fall apart in the middle of every season."

"Yeah, since Griffey left we seem to be short of consistent long hitters."

"Oh, I don't think I agree," Andy said. "What about Ichiro? He was certainly doing a fine job."

They were agreeing and disagreeing and discussing when Brad joined the conversation. "They certainly play good ball in Japan. Have you ever watched a Japanese baseball game?"

The conversation went on about baseball for awhile, then turned to the America's Cup Race. Brad seemed to know a great deal of inside stuff about the race and the others asked him questions. It was a spirited conversation until Brad's cell phone rang. He looked at the number, took a five-dollar bill out of his pocket, laid it on the bar and walked out without a word to anyone. He was concentrating on the phone call. The others watched him go, and then Larry and Steve decided it was time for them to leave too.

"See ya' Murph," Larry said.

"See you guys. Thanks for coming in."

They paid and then walked out into the sunshine and headed home. They could see Brad standing across the street still talking on the phone.

Steve looked at Larry and said, "What do you think about Brad, could he be someone our Emily would like?"

Larry just shrugged his shoulders and started walking. "I don't know. I'm getting a little tired of the whole business."

Lunch at St. Francis was as noisy as breakfast. However, unlike breakfast where some of the residents came in late or not at all, lunch time was in full-house attendance most of the time, except for today. Many of the ladies were gone to beauty appointments or were playing Bridge, and the dining room minus so many female voices was noticeably quieter.

Twice a month, on Thursdays, eight ladies met at each other's homes for lunch and Bridge. Today they were playing at Flo Janson's house. They usually started play at ten o'clock, had lunch around noon, then played again until four but today they decided to stop at two because some of the ladies needed time to rest a bit and then get ready for the event at the Estate.

This club started more than fifty years ago with one table of four ladies then grew to eight members sometime the next year. That was the year of the storms that were so bad they had to cancel Bridge. No ferries could come to the island, and the island was without electricity for twelve days. The ladies still played Bridge but my lantern light and that was when they all decided to use this as the beginning of the Thursday Ladies Bridge Club.

At two, Dolly rode home with Marilyn Chu, but Natalie and Mary decided to walk. Mary was surprised at how friendly Natalie was being. She talked about the concert and dinner scheduled for tonight, and how pleased she was that Emily would get to wear her new dress and, now that it was done, she did like the short hair on Emily. Mary decided that she would not contribute the fact that Emily would be wearing makeup tonight. This conversation was too pleasant to ruin.

At five-fifteen Anita from the office knocked at Natalie's door. "There's a man at the desk saying he has an appointment with you. He's dressed like a chauffer and he's also asking for Mr. Xavier. Do you know what this is about?"

Natalie did know and she was ready. It was the car James had sent. "Thank you Anita. Will you tell him I'll be right out? Did you tell Mr. Xavier?"

"I met him in the hall as he was coming to the office so I guess you're all they're waiting for."

"Thank you." Natalie picked up her shawl and purse and followed Anita to the front reception area. There stood Steven dressed in a navy blue blazer and gray slacks. He was with a handsome young man holding his chauffeurs cap in his hand. She said, "Hello, shall we go?" She liked this car-at-the-door convenience, and even though she was sharing the treat with Steven, she felt special.

A few minutes later, Paul was knocking at Mary's door. His friend Harry was here to pick them up and then they would go get Emily. When Mary opened the door Paul broke into a wide grin and made a small bow to her. "My lady. Your carriage awaits."

Mary smiled back and said, "Thank you, sire. I'm ready," and she stepped out into the hall, closed her door and took his arm. "Lead on Macbeth."

They were both laughing when they came out of the building. Paul helped her into the back seat of the car, then went around to the other side and got in.

"What a happy couple you two make," Harry said.

He got back into the driver's seat and off they went to get Emily.

Harry had spent the afternoon cleaning his car. He'd washed and polished and aired it out and moved all his fish books and sample jars into his garage. *Wouldn't be very impressive to have a date get into a car that smelled fishy.* Actually, he only used this car for going to conferences or to the mainland and usually took his Jeep to locations where he needed his diving gear, but he was just making sure the stray bits of his profession wouldn't be stabbing anyone.

It was a short drive to Emily's condo and on the way Mary said she and Paul would just wait in the car while Harry collected her.

Harry was a little nervous. Paul told him she had dark hair, was a retired teacher and a widow, liked a lot of the things he liked, and in his mind he saw her as an athletic, solidly built with wide shoulders and probably not too feminine. He was very anxious to see her in person. Was she a lady or a jock? He parked and walked over to the security intercom outside the covered vestibule. She buzzed him in and he took the elevator up to the third floor. When she opened the door to her condo he couldn't believe his eyes. Blind dates never looked this good. Her hair framed her face in very soft waves, her dress fit in all the right places and her eyes were sparkling.

"Hello Harry. Won't you come in?"

He stumbled as he stepped over the threshold and the first words out of his mouth were, "How lucky can a guy get?" Then he could have kicked himself. All day he'd practiced saying, "So nice to finally meet you, Emily," but instead had blurted out exactly what he was thinking.

Emily just smiled. He looked exactly as she imagined; tall with blondish hair going gray and with the broad shoulders and the narrow hips of a swimmer. He was neatly dressed in a dark blue suit with a lighter blue shirt and his tie was the same color as the suit. She held out her hand. "I'm happy to meet you in person, shall we go? Are Mary and Paul in the car?" She picked up her coat and continued, "I think I'll just carry this for now but I might need it later."

He said nothing, just turned around and opened the door and went out. She followed and locked the door. In the elevator he said, "Do you like to fish?”

She smiled and thought, *Oh my, didn't we already discuss this?* To him she said, “Yes I do. We discussed fishing and boating on the phone yesterday.”

“I thought you would look like a school teacher with long hair and horned rimmed glasses.” He'd blurted out what he was thinking again instead of saying *he remembered their conversation but was trying to expand on it.* And he thought, *Maybe it's a good thing we'll be with other people tonight.*

CHAPTER 20

The Estate, as the home of James Pritchard Reinhold III was called by the residents of Haven Port, stood high on a hill at the northeastern corner of the island. It afforded the owner a panoramic view of the shipping lanes in the Puget Sound, the Olympic Mountains to the west, and to the east presented the skyline of Seattle. The first sea captain named James Pritchard Reinhold built this home for his wife and nine children and it had been passed down through the family to James II and now the present James III. JP, as he was known in town, had never married but enjoyed entertaining. His sisters and their families visited often, and presently his nephew was living with him, recuperating from a near fatal automobile accident.

Edgar Bruce Simpson was his sister's son, and a concert pianist. For many years he'd studied at Julliard and in Europe under several master teachers, and at the age of twenty-nine, his career was taking him on tours all over the world. When he was in the United States and time permitted, he liked to drive to the cities where his concerts were to be.

It was during a drive from Seattle after a concert, to San Francisco, that his terrible accident happened. A drunk teenager crossed the middle line just outside of Portland, Oregon, and hit the car in front of Bruce. Although Bruce swerved, he was still involved in the crash and the ensuing fire. Both of the other drivers had been killed and Bruce had been severely burned. For several months he convalesced at Portland's Emanuel Hospital and then came to Haven Port and his Uncle James to continue his recovery. Tonight would be his first 'public' appearance and performance since the accident.

At the bottom of Estate Hill Road, a man asked for names and checked a clipboard list. The chauffeured car was waved through and continued up the hill, and as they got closer they could see several cars already in the parking lot in front of the iron gate. Natalie and Steve's limo pulled through the gate and stopped at the entrance. The driver came around to open their door and helped Natalie out then offered a hand to Steve.

"Thank you, I think I can just about make it by myself," Steve said.

They made their way up the nine, wide and deep marble steps to the front door. It was standing open and James could be seen just inside, greeting all his guests. He was dressed in an open throated, pale grey silk shirt and a dark grey, Italian silk suit. His nephew stood beside him dressed in black slacks and jacket, with his shirt open to accommodate the bandages that covered his entire face except for the spaces for his eyes, nose and mouth.

"Natalie and Steve. Welcome. So nice of you to come. Have you met my nephew Bruce?" Bruce presented his hand but didn't speak. "It's still a little uncomfortable for him to talk so please forgive him. His fingers will make up for his silence, I assure you."

Steve shook hands with James then Bruce. "Thanks for inviting me and I'm looking forward to hearing you play." Bruce took Steve's hand in both of his as a response.

Natalie put out her hand to James and he stepped toward her to enable an embrace and kiss on the cheek. She blushed. "I'm especially happy to see you," he said and she blushed more.

"Would you please help yourself to the drink of your choice, and we'll be with you soon."

As they started toward the tables set up in the dining room, James turned his attention to the next group coming up the stairs.

Just behind the limo was Harry and his carload. He maneuvered his car into a parking space and jumped out. He opened the back door for Paul then went around to Emily's door.

When she got out she left her coat on the seat. "I don't think I'll need this until later." She started towards the front door but stopped, looking at the view. "Isn't this beautiful, especially today with the sun shining across the Sound?"

"The original Reinhold sure spent a lot of bucks on this place," Harry said. Too late he wished he'd said, "Yes, it's almost as beautiful as you are."

Paul helped Mary out of the car then tucked her hand into his arm to help her up the stairs. He knew she really didn't need the help, but it was another opportunity to touch her.

James greeted Paul like the old friend he was

and Mary as a lovely woman he knew casually. He also greeted Harry with a handshake but when Emily was introduced, he was surprised. "Emily Barnes. I never would have recognized you. Look what a little retirement did for our school teacher. Whatever you're doing certainly agrees with you and you look beautiful tonight."

Emily smiled. She was thinking, *Do I look that different?* But she said, "Thank you. I'll take it as a compliment for all retired teachers."

James laughed and so did Paul and Mary. Harry smiled because he was certainly proud to be escorting this woman, and he agreed she sure didn't look like any retired teachers he knew.

"This is my nephew Bruce, and he isn't talking much yet but if you'll help yourself to drinks in the dining room, we'll be joining you soon." They shook hands with Bruce and moved off to see the wonders laid out on the hors d'oeuvre tables, and at the tended bar.

The foyer where they had been greeted was floored in an almost black marble. When they came through the door, the first thing people noticed was the large staircase with its beautifully carved handrails on the right side of the hall, just past the dining room doors. Then they saw the long hall that led to the back of the house and kitchen area. To the immediate the right was the dining room where table of appetizers and a bar were set up, and on the left side of the entry hall they could see chairs placed in the library facing the piano.

Several people were already sampling shrimp and sushi and all sorts of cheeses and meats. The bar was on the left side of this room and, not waiting for Emily, that's where Harry headed. She followed because that seemed to be the thing to do. He ordered a gin and tonic, never looking at her, and then stepped over to the food. It seemed he'd forgotten he had a date. Emily just smiled. *Oh well,* she thought, *there's plenty of other people here to talk to.* She asked for a white wine and then moved toward the food table too.

As Paul and Mary walked towards the bar Paul said, "Mary, would you mind ordering me a red wine and I'll be right back?" Mary smiled and said she would as Paul hurried off to find the men's room.

The room was abuzz with so many people talking and laughing. A few more people joined them and then so did James. Emily watched as he walked into the room, searched for Natalie and found her standing next to long time friends Flo Janson and Tom Casey.

He greeted the others and smiled but took Natalie's elbow and said, "Let's get us a little libation, shall we?" They moved to the bar and James ordered a Manhattan and to Emily's surprise, Natalie had a Martini. They waited for their drinks and talked like very good friends then moved towards another group standing by the window. Emily smiled. She was seeing Natalie out of her role as commander and in the role of woman, and she smiled as she watched James *work the room* with Natalie by his side.

Emily picked up one of the small china plates and added a shrimp, a couple pieces of cheese and crackers, some olives stuffed with garlic. Ordinarily she would have avoided the garlic but tonight she wasn't really planning to be close to anyone and she was certain there would be no kissing. She moved to the side of the room by the window, set her wine glass on a small table and took a bite of a piece of cheese on a cracker, then ate an olive while she watched the group. As she was biting into the second olive, a voice said, "I don't think I know you. Do you come here often?" She turned to see an athletic looking man with short brown hair and a sweet smile. He was holding a glass of what looked like soda water with a slice of lime.

"Well, actually this is my first visit." Emily felt a little shy. She'd never been approached like this by a stranger, and she'd never had the opportunity to make small talk with anyone so attractive, let alone someone who seemed to be flirting with her.

"My name is Brad. I overheard your name and that you're a school teacher?"

Emily smiled. This was familiar ground and she relaxed a little. "Well, I'm a retired school teacher. "

"What did you teach?"

"Second grade, here on Haven Port."

"You look so young to have retired. It wasn't for ill health was it?"

"Well, sort of," Emily said, and she told him about taking care of her husband during his last illness and then her mother. "I tried being a substitute teacher when everything calmed down again, but it wasn't the same for me so I retired." As she smiled she realized she was enjoying this chance meeting and the conversation.

Brad had listened carefully, with full attention. It made Emily feel as though he really cared. "I'm working at the University Extension Lab for a few months," he said. "Would you like to have coffee or a drink sometime?" Harry took this moment to remember he had a date and stepped up.

"Hi Brad. You met Emily yet?"

"Just did, thank you. See you both later," then Brad walked over to a group that was standing by the bar.

"He's a nice guy. I see him around the building sometimes. Want to go find a chair for the recital? I see some guys are already there so we better hurry so we can get a good seat." He didn't wait for her reply but headed off across the foyer. Emily followed and as they passed the group Brad had joined, he smiled at her. She smiled back.

Mary and Paul joined them with Paul sitting on the outside chair, just in case.

Soon everyone had moved from the dining room and the doors were closed.

James seated Natalie in the front row then walked over to the piano. The room got quiet and he said, "Bruce is going to play a selection of Broadway tunes then he'll take requests. Ladies and gentlemen, I give you E. B. Simpson at the piano."

Tonight was the first time Bruce was to play in front of an audience again and he was both excited and nervous. His fingers had not been impaired, and he hoped his memory could keep up. He started with *Gypsy*, then slipped into songs from *Chicago* and *The Producers*. The audience was tapping their toes and clapped enthusiastically after the first set. He continued with *Oklahoma*, and feeling better by the moment slipped in *Flight of the Bumble Bee*.

He played on and on and finally ended with *Jesus Christ Super Star*. Everyone applauded loudly and they gave him a standing ovation. He stood by the piano bench and bowed. Later Natalie would say she saw tears on his bandaged cheek.

The audience began their requests of classical and modern music and Bruce played until at last James stood up. He thanked Bruce for his wonderful performance and then announced dinner would be served in a few minutes in the dining room, but that there was time for the ladies and gentlemen to refresh themselves if they liked. He pointed out the salon just past the stairway and sent the gentlemen upstairs and on the right.

Mary and Emily excused themselves and headed for the salon, mostly to see what it looked like, and Paul headed upstairs and to the right. Natalie was already in the salon and all three exclaimed over the gold fixtures and dark red, flocked flowers on the gold wallpaper. It was circa 1900 and beautiful.

When they returned they found Paul and James waiting for them by the door but Harry was already seated at the dining table. When he saw Emily he just raised his hand and pointed to the chair next to him. She smiled resignedly and went to her seat. To her surprise and pleasure, Brad was seated on her other side.

The food was brought in by waiters who appeared to be boys from the college. They knew Paul and Harry and several other people. The wine glasses were filled with a very cold Chablis and the food serving began. First came a lovely tomato bisque and toast points. Then next the bowls were replaced with salad plates that held a bed of greens with four large shrimp and red grapefruit. This was drizzled with a honey mustard dressing.

Before the main dish was served, the wine glasses were replaced and a Merlot was poured. The main dish was thin slices of medium rare beef, roasted red potatoes and sliced green beans. Just behind the server came a waiter offering mushroom gravy.

Mary was seated across from Emily and several times they looked at each other as each new presentation was placed in front of them. Harry wasted no time digging in. He tucked his napkin into the neck of his shirt and ate with gusto. He didn't even notice that Emily and Brad were carrying on a conversation during the entire dinner. Finally the dishes were cleared away in preparation for the dessert.

"I just can't imagine having any room for dessert after all that lovely food," Mary said.

"I'm pretty full too and would you please excuse me for a moment?" Paul said.

Mary looked across the table at Emily. Harry was busy talking to Natalie on his right and Emily was talking to the handsome man on her left. *Now there was someone for Emily,* she thought. *Handsome, maybe a little younger but not too much. Emily certainly looks interested and happy... and so does he.*

Emily *was* happy. She was enjoying the conversation with Brad, enjoying the food, and just enjoying being out and with people. Even if Harry had turned out to be less than what she hoped for it was not a wasted evening.

"Would you be free for dinner tomorrow? What time do you get off work?" Brad was also very happy to have come tonight and so happy he'd met Emily.

Emily smiled. "Well I work until nine-thirty and I usually have Fridays off but since I traded days, I'm working tomorrow."

"How about lunch then? What time do you have to be at work?"

"Four o'clock. Yes, I'd like to have lunch with you. Shall I meet you somewhere?"

Brad realized he was really pushing this shy lady pretty fast so he agreed to meet tomorrow at Mickey's Restaurant on Front Street for a twelve-thirty lunch instead of picking her up.

  Emily was excited and couldn't wait to tell Mary about it. Harry was oblivious and heavily involved with the Cherries Jubilee.

CHAPTER 21

Mary was just walking into her apartment after Friday morning's breakfast when the phone rang. "Hello, have you recuperated yet?"

Mary laughed. It was Emily. "Well I didn't go for my walk yet and I slept in. How about you?"

"Well after Harry dropped you two off he drove me home and said we should have dinner again sometime. I said I was not available most evenings and he said okay. I walked myself to the door and he drove off. Guess he wasn't any more interested in me than I was in him.

"Well you tried, and you certainly were a good sport about it. I don't think he was being rude, do you?"

"No, not really. In our phone conversation, the one and only, he said he didn't date much because his work was so consuming, so I guess he was just being himself. But what I wanted to tell you is that I'm having lunch with the nice guy that sat next to me. His name is Brad and we're going to Mickey's. And I need your help. What should I wear?"

"It's not all that warm today so why don't you just wear slacks, a blouse and a sweater. What do you have that would fit that bill?" They discussed Emily's wardrobe and decided that black slacks, a bright sapphire blue blouse and a black cardigan would work. She had pearl earrings and of course black low-heeled shoes.

"The restaurant is only a block away from me but I didn't give Brad my address because I don't really know him. Was it rude not to?"

Mary assured her that her instincts were good and to keep following them. "I'll see you when you come to work to hear all the details, that is if you want to share."

Emily laughed. "I'm sure I'll want to. Thank you for the help. See you later."

Although she was still a little tired from the excitement of last night, Mary decided she would take a short walk. She tried to walk every day to keep her hip from getting worse. She changed into a navy fleece sweat suit and walking shoes and went out her door. Standing by the front outside door she found Dr. Pete.

"Hello Mary. How is everything today?"

"Oh... Dr. Pete. Hello. Everything's wonderful. I thought I'd see you last night at the Estate party. Where were you?"

"I meant to go but there was a small emergency down on the beach and it turned into a long drawn out session. By the time I was finished I was too tired and it was too late to go. Was it fun?"

"That boy can surely play. I enjoyed the music so much and the food was wonderful. Be sure to go if there's another opportunity. You'll really enjoy his music."

"How did Emily do on her first date?"

Mary smiled. She didn't know Dr. Pete was aware of the committee doings and also surprised he would ask about her. "Well, it was a learning experience and I don't think we'll see those two on another date, but it was so good for Emily to get out and she looked beautiful."

Dr. Pete nodded. "Emily is very beautiful where it counts, but I heard she looked extra special last night."

"Yes she did. New dress, new hairdo, and she wore make-up. You might not have recognized her."

Again Dr. Pete smiled. "Oh, I think I'd recognize her. I'm glad she had a good time and I do wish I'd been there to see her."

Paul joined them and said hello to Dr. Pete. "Mary, are you going for a walk?"

"Yes, just heading out. Want to come?"

Paul looked down at the floor and said, "No thank you. I'll wait for you here. See you at lunch," and walked away.

"What's wrong with Paul?" asked Dr. Pete.

"Well, he has this little problem," started Mary and then she decided to tell Dr. Pete all about it.

Yesterday had been beautiful and warm but true to the Pacific Northwest weather patterns, today was cloudy and the sun shone only intermittently. It wasn't cold, the thermometer read sixty-five degrees, but it wasn't warm either with the wind coming off the water. Emily left her condo at twelve-fifteen and walked the short distance to Mickey's Restaurant.

To reach the front door of the restaurant she had to walk down the pier by the Boat Repair Shop and when she arrived, Brad was standing just outside the door, talking on his cell phone. "Okay, I'll do it," he said and closed the phone. He put it back in his pocket and reached out towards Emily. "Hello. I just got here too."

They were offered a table on the deck but opted instead to sit by a window inside. Brad was wearing a rust colored suede jacket and tan slacks and loafers. His knit shirt was the same tan as his slacks and he looked so handsome. As they walked to their table several people looked at the couple—the beautiful woman and handsome man.

Emily wanted hot tea and Brad joined her. They talked about the various types of tea available. He liked Chamomile and also liked her favorite, Earl Grey, but confessed it didn't really matter the flavor, he pretty much liked them all. Emily agreed except for the ones that tasted of licorice. "I just can't like that flavor."

"Do you know the history of how tea was discovered?" Brad was smiling.

Emily shook her head.

"In 2700 BC, an Emperor named Shen Nung was sitting in his garden with a cup of very hot water. Some leaves from a nearby tree fell into his cup and, being a lazy sort, the Emperor did nothing about it and continued to drink the water. The story goes he enjoyed the taste of the leaf in his water so much that forever after he had a leaf added. He also felt it made his aches and pains better."

Emily laughed. "Are you sure that's a true story?"

"No, but I like to tell it. I read it somewhere and it sounded plausible so... okay so it's a simple story told by a simple man." He smiled at Emily. "Want to order?"

They both had clam chowder in a bread bowl and for dessert, Burnt Crème.

They talked about the weather and the changes from yesterday and about the Mariner's and Seahawks. They talked about Emily's teaching career and about her children. Then Emily asked him if he had a family.

"I have two boys I seldom see. One's a Marine and one's in the Army Special Forces. They're all over the place and not allowed to tell anyone what they're doing most of the time; however I know one of my kids is in the Middle East now."

Emily felt sorry for him. It was sad not to be able to talk to your children. "Do they contact their Mother?"

"She's dead," Brad said and then changed the subject. "Let's do this again soon. Do you work on the weekend?"

"No not usually, unless I trade with someone."

"I was thinking of us going to Seattle and just puttering around at Pike Street Market and the city for the day and then maybe coming home after seeing a Mariner's game or something like that. What do you think?"

"It does sound fun."

"How about tomorrow? We could catch the nine o'clock ferry and start the adventure."

She smiled. "Okay. Tomorrow at nine, but the Mariners are away this weekend. I think they're in LA."

Brad smiled. "Okay, we'll find something else to do after we get there. Wear walking shoes and—" The William Tell Overture started to play. It was his cell phone. He looked at the number and said, "Sorry, I have to take this." He stood up and walked to the entrance and out the door while opening his phone and starting to talk. In a few minutes he was back and looking sad. "I'm so sorry I have to renege on the tomorrow thing. Duty calls."

Emily was disappointed but said, "That's okay. We can plan it for another day."

Brad sat down and said, "Let's have another cup of tea. I don't have to be anywhere for another hour, do you?"

She said she didn't and they ordered another pot of Earl Grey and talked about all the things they could investigate on their Seattle trip.

CHAPTER 22

At ten o'clock Saturday morning Emily's phone rang. She answered and found Brad on the line. The connection was full of static but after the hello's Brad said, "I'll be back in Haven Port on Monday. How about lunch again?" She said yes and they made a plan to meet at Alice's Tea Room. Emily would make the reservation for twelve noon.

She was happy to hear from Brad and wondered briefly where he was calling from. She started away from the phone but it rang again. This time it was Carl Randall, Steve's friend. With little preamble he said, "Hey babe, how about dinner in the big city tonight? If you walk on the ferry I'll pick you up and we can go somewhere fun. Sound good?"

Emily hesitated. He sounded so... so forceful, but he was a friend of Steve's so he must be okay. "That sounds nice. How will I recognize you at the ferry terminal?"

He laughed. "Just come down the stairs and

you'll see me in a blue convertible with the top down, and I'll take off my sun glasses so you can see that my baby blues match the car."

She hesitated again but only for a second more, then agreed. They ended the conversation with the promise she would be on the five o'clock ferry to Seattle.

As soon as she hung up she called Mary. She told her about the date and then said, "I know I always ask you this, but what should I wear today? Is it warm enough for the white pants suit and would it be dressy enough? And what shoes?"

"I was just going for my walk. Want me to come by and help put something together?"

Emily was very appreciative. "Oh please, if it isn't too far for you. Do you know where it is? I'll take you home afterwards." Mary did remember. She'd been there only last Thursday and as soon as they hung up, Emily headed for her closet to start looking until Mary arrived.

When Mary hung up the phone, she picked up her keys and headed out. She left by the front door and went straight up Elm Street, speaking to other walkers as they passed, and was generally enjoying the warm air, and her general feeling of happiness. She thought about how Emily had been transformed from plain to striking, and she thought about how happy she was that Emily thought enough of her to ask for help. It was almost like having another daughter. She arrived at the condo and pressed the button on the security phone. Emily recognized Mary's voice and buzzed her in. She was waiting on the outside walkway when Mary got off the elevator.

They hugged and Emily said, "You're such a dear to come running every time I feel like I have a problem."

"Well you wouldn't be having these questions and needs if I hadn't been part of the problem." Both laughed at this and walked inside. Emily led her right to the bedroom.

"I laid out the blouses. I have the green one to wear with the white suit but I'm not sure about wearing those sandals? It might be cold when the sun goes down."

Mary looked at the blouses. "Did he say where you were going to dinner?"

"He only said *somewhere fun*. But I'm not sure where it might turn out to be. I guess I should have asked him to be more specific. I'm so dumb when it comes to this dating stuff and I'm so glad I have you." She gave Mary a hug.

Mary was glad to be there for Emily but she hadn't dated for more years than she could really remember so she doubted she could be of very much help. "This is what I think about your dating. You are a sensible woman with good morals, and you should not do anything that makes you uncomfortable. However, you should have a little adventure in your soul and be willing to try different things, like wearing open toed sandals even if it might not be warm when you come home."

Emily laughed. "Yes, I guess I do worry a lot. I'm a big girl and what terrible thing could happen just going to dinner, and what fashion police are going to stop me from wearing what I feel is right?"

"That's the spirit. We've agreed the white suit would be appropriate, right?" Emily nodded her head yes. "...and this green silk sleeveless is nice but would you feel comfortable taking off the jacket if it gets warm at dinner?"

"No not really, it has low-cut armholes and my bra shows. What about the flowered blouse?"

"I like it but it shows through the back of the jacket. How about trying it on and we can see."

Emily took off her sweatshirt and put on the blouse then the jacket. She turned with her back to Mary and said, "Does it show?"

"It doesn't show but let's try on some other blouses, than we can make the choice. Are you settled on the white sandals?"

"Not exactly." Emily went to the closet and took down the box with the paisley print slides with the wedge heel. "Maybe these would be better for walking on and off the ferry. I really like them too."

"Well that settles the blouse part then. The apricot silky knit tank is our choice. Then you can wear the necklace and earrings you bought. What do you think?"

"I'm so nervous," Emily confided. "What if he sees me and is disappointed, then we have the whole evening to suffer through."

"Emily, remember you're only a phone call away from coming home. No matter where you are, you can call a taxi to take you to the ferry and then come home. If it would make you feel any better, how about calling me after you see him. I've met him and I can tell you he's good looking, tall, and has a beautiful smile. His mother loved dancing so much she taught him how and even gave him the middle name of Astaire, after Fred. He has three car dealerships so he is a working man and he likes to travel."

"What kind of feeling did you get about him?"

"I didn't get bad vibes, if that's what you mean."

"Okay, I guess it's just me being so silly."

Mary patted Emily's hand and said, "After you

meet him, why don't you just call me on your cell phone? When you get to where you're going, just excuse yourself and go to the ladies room. You'll feel better and so will I. And don't forget, if you find any situation is uncomfortable, you can just leave from wherever you are and get yourself home. How's that for a plan?"

They laughed and hugged. Emily felt better but still nervous.

"If things seem out of my control or bad, I will call you."

"Good, now I must start home." Mary said no to the ride and went out the door with one last bit of advice. "Have a lovely time and I'll look forward to hearing all about this tomorrow, or even maybe tonight, okay?"

Emily hugged Mary again. She was trying hard to look confident for Mary's sake but it wasn't really what she was feeling.

CHAPTER 23

By four-thirty Emily was showered and shampooed. She'd put on makeup just as Mary had shown her, and she was dressed in the new suit with the silky apricot tank. She'd put on her new jewelry, then sprayed White Linen perfume up into the air and walked into the perfume spray. Mary taught her how to do this too. The last thing she did was to put on her new paisley print shoes and then she went to look in the full length mirror. Never had she felt she looked so up-to-date, almost pretty. She could hear her mother's voice warning her, but with her newly found self confidence she decided she was okay without parental approval tonight.

Although the ferry landing was only a few blocks from her condo, Emily decided to drive because she would be coming home late and the weather could possibly change. She parked in the ferry parking lot, locked her car and took a deep breath. The ferry was almost finished unloading the cars, and in just a few minutes it would be leaving for Seattle to take her on adventure number two. With a determined step she walked into the passenger waiting room and onto the ferry, admonishing herself for her doubts. She *would* have fun tonight she told herself, and what was there to worry about anyway? After all, this was a friend of Steve's.

Bedroom communities are very familiar to people who work in big cities. That's the place where the kids function during the day waiting for mama or daddy or both to come home from their job in the city. In the Seattle area, the bedroom communities also extend across the Puget Sound and involve the Kitsap Peninsula and a couple of islands. Commuters board the Washington State Ferries from very early morning until the last ferry run which was well after midnight. These ferries present a clean, safe way to travel for both cars and people during their commute, and on the weekends the ferries are filled with tourists and their families.

The trip tonight, from Haven Port to Seattle, would take approximately thirty minutes. Emily took a seat in the bow of the boat and watched sailboats tacking back and forth, people in fishing boats that didn't seem to be catching and she watched as the passengers interacted. A small boy about three years old wanted to go out on deck then back in, then back out. The father permitted this a few times then decided to pick him up and take him back to the seat by the window where the obvious grandparents and mama sat talking. They boy didn't seem to agree with this but quieted down when his Mom held him.

She watched a young couple groping and kissing in such desperate passion that Emily wondered if a motel waited for them on the mainland.

And there was the energetic teen playing the car racing video game with his two friends loudly cheering him on, and a woman with a cigarette in her hand being reminded by a ferry worker that smoking was not allowed.

But mostly she found herself worrying about this date and even considered just riding back to Haven Port. However, when they docked she found her courage and was one of the first people off the boat at Coleman Dock, the main ferry terminal on the Seattle waterfront.

At the east end of the walkway, a stairway led down to the street and there, parked just to the right of the driveway where the cars were coming off the ferry, was a blue BMW convertible with the top down. Sitting in the driver's seat was Carl looking catalogue handsome. When he saw Emily approach he got out and said, "Wow. Steve didn't tell me how beautiful you were. I thought this would just be a mercy date with some ugly school teacher."

Emily smiled and said, "Are you Carl?"

"You bet baby." He came around the car and opened the door for her. She got in and he went back around to his side. When he got in he said, "Well, where should we go for dinner? I want to show you off."

Emily smiled again and said, "You pick the place. I don't know Seattle very well."

"Okay then, we're off, but you need to put your seatbelt on." He reached across and with a little fumbling that just happened to touch her neck as he pulled the buckle from the back of the seat and then just happened to drag his hand across her breast as he pulled it across to secure the buckle. Emily stiffened but he just smiled. "Don't want to lose you on the way, do we?"

Just relax, she told herself. *It was just an accident.*

They stopped at the first stop light and Carl said, "By the way, my friends call me CA. You can too."

Emily wasn't very comfortable with him yet and didn't have a clue what she should answer so she just smiled. She decided to just look at the scenery and she could face talking to him later.

They were off again and as they approached Interstate-90, he said loudly, "I'm taking you to Charlie's Place on Lake Washington. I'm sort of known there and they have good food. We can have a few drinks, watch the sun set, then have dinner. Sound good?" It wasn't really a question and she was sure he wasn't waiting to see if she approved it was just his take-charge attitude and as he glanced at her he smiled. He was delighted again with how she looked.

It seemed to her that conversation wasn't really necessary with the wind blowing so she just smiled, and she missed the leering smile on his face.

They drove across the Lake Washington Floating Bridge and soon they were at the exit that took them to the east side of the lake. In a few minutes Emily saw the marina and Charlie's Restaurant. The deck was full of laughing people and a couple of them waved as Carl parked the car. He got out and came around to open Emily's door. When she got out of the car, he moved in and stooped to kiss her on the lips. As he did he said, "I'm so happy to meet you." He took her hand and they headed up the walk to the restaurant.

Emily was glad she wasn't expected to respond. She was a little taken aback by the kiss but then thought, *He probably didn't mean any harm by it, just being friendly.* He stopped at the reservation desk and said they would be having dinner later, "...but we're headed for the bar now." It was obvious he came here often and the young man behind the desk said, "Okay Mr. Randall. I'll let you know when we have a table. Around eight, as usual?"

Carl nodded his head yes and took Emily's hand again. "Come this way. We'll go out on the deck for a drink and if it gets chilly we can always move back in." Carl said hello to several people as they went through the bar area to the patio. Again several of the people on the deck spoke to him and called his name, and a couple said to join them but Carl declined saying, "Not right now, thanks," and kept walking to a corner table.

There was an umbrella over the table and Carl adjusted it so they were sitting in a shadow. Then he took off his sunglasses and looked at her. "Are you glad to meet me too?"

It was an odd question and Emily thought for a second and said, "Yes, I think I am. The weather is wonderful for this kind of outing and I'm happy to meet any friend of Steve's."

It wasn't the exact answer Carl had hoped for but the waiter came just then. Carl ordered a double Stoly martini straight up and a vodka Gimlet for Emily. "You'll like it. It's a sort of a martini and lemonade."

"I don't usually drink martinis," Emily said. "I'd rather have a glass of white wine. Chablis, please."

Carl was not used to having his women decline any of his ideas, especially when it came to drinking and he gave her a strange look "Okay, give her what she wants." When the waiter left he said, "Why not try something new? You might like it."

"Yes I might, but I'm happy just having wine." Emily was surprised at herself. It wasn't like her to be assertive, but she had a feeling this was not the time to try drinking hard liquor. Tell me about your work. Do you like it?" Mary told her if she had trouble with conversations during a date, to always ask questions about their work. Men were always happy to talk about their work.

He started talking about the businesses he owned now and the one that was opening soon in Bellevue. He told her about the problems of staffing. "Not everyone is suited to sell cars you know. The good ones are friendly but have a knack of closing a deal. Some of the guys get into the habit of putting the screws to a customer, but that's a mistake. The hard sell just never works out. We had this one deal where the father was buying a car for his daughter, at least that's what we thought, but it turned out it was just an old guy buying a car for his honey. We thought she was the daughter because she called him 'Daddy'." He threw his head back and laughed loudly at this joke. "And we had another guy who wanted a car for his mother but he wanted us to put a speed governor on it because she was eighty-two and he thought she drove too fast." Again he threw back his head and laughed loudly.

Emily found these stories only slightly amusing but she smiled. Carl took that for encouragement and told her several more involving a woman who thought she wanted a green car because they were safer on the road, another who wanted a car big enough so she could wear a hat while driving, and another about a man who bought a car with space enough for his eight basset hounds who 'liked to go for rides'.

Carl signaled for another drink and to Emily's

surprise said, "Now little lady, tell me about your job."

"I'm really retired but I was a grade school teacher."

"Any good stories from those teaching days?"

She had lots of stories and started off with the one about a boy who thought people with red hair were evil. He'd learned about red hair from a story in the book of *Grimm's Fairy Tales.* He never asked anyone if it was true but there were twin red headed girls in his class and every time they were supposed to hold hands in a circle or be in the same reading group, he cried and got almost hysterical. Emily said it took several weeks to finally get him to tell her what was wrong and a few months of the school counselor's help to get the notion out of his head.

While Emily was telling this story, Carl was busy looking around. He waved at a couple at a distant table and when they called out, "CA, come join us" he just nodded his head yes. She finished her story but he made no comment and instead stood up and said, "Let's join my friends." He picked up their drinks and started toward the other table. Emily could do nothing but follow.

"Joyce, Jim… this is Emily. Emily these are two of my friends. How you guys doin'."

Joyce and Jim both said hello and Emily sat down in the chair Carl pulled out.

"CA said he had a date tonight but he didn't say how pretty you were." Jim was sitting next to her and he laid his hand on her thigh as he spoke. "Where you been all his life?"

Everyone laughed but Emily just smiled and shifted her weight and the errant hand moved.

"Let her alone. She belongs to CA, you know." Joyce didn't seem a bit put off by the familiarity Jim was showing. "Just tell him to buzz off if he gets too close. He's been drinking since he got off the golf course at two."

They all laughed again and Emily forced a smile.

"No kidding, though. Where did he find you?" He moved his arm up to her shoulder and then put his hand on the back of her neck. "He hasn't come up with such a good lookin' gal since Sheila. Remember her? The one with the big—"

Joyce broke into his sentence and said, "Yes, we remember Sheila, but Emily is a lady. I can tell by just looking at her she isn't like the other women he dates. Where you from?"

"I live on Haven Port." She knew she should say something else but she didn't know what.

"Haven Port, huh? That's a nice place. I've played the golf course there with Steve and Law." He moved his face closer to Emily's and said, "Do you know Steve... can't remember his last name. He lives in Haven Port too."

"I do know him and I think he still plays golf quite often. Where do you usually play?" If she could get him talking about golf then maybe he would stop focusing on her.

"We live on the golf course on Mercer Island and come over here to play sometimes. Do you play?"

Oh no, back to me. "I haven't played for many years. Maybe I'll take it up again sometime but I don't play now."

Joyce said, "Jim, I'm hungry. Let's go eat and then maybe we can catch the show at the Roxy." Then to Emily she said, "They just renovated this theater in Bellevue and it's so great. Tonight they're showing *The Producers*. Have you seen it?"

Emily smiled. "No I haven't, have you Carl?"

Both Joyce and Jim laughed.

Joyce said, "You must not know old CA very well to still call him Carl. Okay let's go eat and then think about the show. You two want to join us?"

Carl said no they would eat later, and Joyce and Jim began their weaving way to the dining room.

Emily expected Carl to apologize for Jim but not one word was said. "Well, what do you want to do after we eat?" He looked at Emily and winked, as if she knew what the plan was for the evening. He'd motioned for the waiter to being him another drink, his third double martini. Emily was still on her first glass of Chablis.

She tried to keep her voice steady but she was feeling very unsure of what he expected. "I think for tonight and this first date we should just have dinner and get to know each other." She didn't say it but she was thinking, *That's all I think I can handle.*

Carl didn't make a comment but started to look around again, no doubt hoping he could bring in someone else entertaining but most of the people had moved into the dining room. He looked at his watch and said, "Are you hungry, want to eat now?" Seeming to clutch at a straw and before she could say anything, he stood up.

She felt the same way. *Let's eat and get this evening over with.*

As they moved into the dim dining room, Carl moved up close behind her, giving her a pat on the behind. She stepped forward quickly and Carl laughed. Their table was by a window so they could watch the boats and people in the marina. They watched a man and a girl about ten-years-old take fishing poles out of a boat, both talking animatedly. "That's Henry and his kid. She's just here for the month of June then goes back to her mother. Nice kid and she sure likes to fish. How about you? Do you like to fish?"

Now they were on territory she could discuss. "Yes, I've been fishing practically my whole life." It was the only thing her mother let her do that was in the least athletic or could be called unladylike. It was only because of her father that she was allowed this activity.

Carl leaned back in his chair and laughed. "Somehow I can't picture you fishing. Did you use worms?"

"No, we tied our own flies. My dad taught us, and we learned to fly fish almost as soon as we could walk."

Carl was interested now and leaned forward. "Where do you go on the island?"

"My favorite place is down below the cliffs by East Harbor."

"What did you use for bait? Did you say you tied your own flies? Do you still do that?"

"Yes I still have all the equipment and some of the parts left. I haven't tied many lately but I use a small Sand Lance and a Chum Fry sometimes... do you know about fly fishing?"

They chatted about the bait and best locations on the island and Carl remembered his father trying to teach him too, but he'd been too busy chasing girls to care. "If I'd seen you fishing I probably would have taken more interest." He laughed loudly.

The waiter came and he ordered another drink and a steak with onions and mushrooms and a salad with Roquefort dressing. Then he said, "Wha' you goin' to have, Babe?" Emily ordered a Caesar with shrimp.

"Why don' we have a bottle of wine? Wha' kine you like? Same kine you been drinkin'?"

Emily quickly told the waiter she'd had enough wine and they didn't need a bottle. Carl just smiled looking directly at her. She wasn't sure why, but it made her uneasy. Not only the way he was looking at her but the way he sat sort of slumped and the fact that his words were starting to slur. She was becoming very uncomfortable. When the waiter brought his drink she wondered, was this his fifth or sixth double martini on the rocks?

Carl seemed to forget they were talking about fishing and Emily was almost frantically trying to make conversation when another friend stopped at the table. This friend was female and had almost white blond hair. Her well fitted jeans showed her curves, and the very tight yellow, strapless top showed everything else.

He smiled as he looked up. "Sheila."

She gave Emily a frosty look and said, "Yes, it's Sheila. I told you I'd be back today and we were supposed to meet here for drinks at eight. I guess you didn't think it was important or I got here too early."

Emily expected him to start apologizing or explaining or at least to introduce them, but he didn't. He just stood up, took Sheila by the arm and went to the end of the bar. Emily watched as the blond gestured toward her and they talked. Then Carl smiled and put his hands on her shoulders. They talked some more, a little more calmly and finally Carl leaned in and kissed her. She moved closer and put her hand on his back, continuing the deep, deep kiss. She finally stepped back, gave Emily another *drop dead* look. Carl was busy fishing car keys out of his pants pocket. He handed them to her and she went out the door smiling.

On the way back to the table he ordered another drink.

"Well, I don't know what to say." He sat down and leaned toward her giving her his best *little boy did something wrong* look.

Emily said, "I think I'll leave now. Thank you for an interesting evening."

"Oh hell, don't go. Sheila's at my apartment but I don't have to hurry back there. Let's have our dinner and a couple of drinks. Then we can talk about when we're going fishing." He was trying to make nice, like his mother always told him to do, but Emily found determination she didn't know she had and stood up and went to the front desk.

"Could you call me a taxi please?"

Carl came sauntering out with his hands in his pockets, no doubt for stability, but also thinking it was sexy. "Want me to get your salad to go?"

CHAPTER 24

And I didn't get home until almost eleven."
Mary was listening to Emily and trying to decide what to say about this fiasco.

"I'm sorry I didn't call you but... Mary, I don't think I want to go on any more of these dates. It's not easy to think of things to talk about, and I'm not sure how to handle the flirting." Emily was starting to fret. It was what her mother always said she did. 'You fuss and fret over everything.'

"Why don't we have lunch and discuss this whole thing," Mary suggested.

"Would you like to come here? I could come get you if you like."

"No, I need to walk so I'll just come there and maybe ask for a ride home, if that's all right?"

"Yes, that *is* all right."

"I'll leave here at eleven. Do you need anything from the store? I could stop on the way."

Emily said she couldn't wait to see Mary and

no, she didn't need anything from the store.

Mary did stop at Archie's Grocery store anyway. She bought one of their Key Lime Pies. Archie's wife made them once a week and they were exactly what was needed today. When Mary gave Emily the pie she said, "What a wonderful surprise and good idea. I love these pies. Should I put it in the refrigerator or leave it out?"

Mary smiled and said, "I sort of like it cold but either way will suit me. I like the taste of it frozen or thawed."

Mary decided frozen for today and put it in the freezer for later.

"Is it soup I smell?"

"I'm just heating up some corn chowder I made earlier this week. I can't seem to make a small batch so it's sort of leftovers."

"Love leftovers of this kind," said Mary. She wasn't about to hurry Emily in her telling of last night but she was anxious to hear.

It wasn't an unpleasant day outside but it was overcast with the weatherman saying a storm was moving down from Alaska. Through Emily's front window they could see the wind had started to blow and the sky was getting darker. Mary laid her jacket on a chair and went to the kitchen with Emily. She sat on a stool at the counter and looked around. The living room, dining room and kitchen were essentially one room. The kitchen was not large but set up very well. Mary loved the oak cabinets and dark blue granite countertops.

"This is such a nice place and I really like the colors. Did you get to choose them?"

"No, but they're the colors I like so I feel lucky. I

did paint some though. The walls were all white when I moved in so I painted that one dining room wall a dark red and the bedroom's a sort of soft dusty rose. And I painted the guest bathroom in happy colors. Wait until you see that."

Mary said, "I think I'll go look."

The walls were sunshine yellow and the ceiling was sherbet orange and the towels were bright blue. It was a happy room for sure. Bright blue tiles could be seen in the walk-in shower and the soap in the blue dish was red. When she'd finished washing her hands, she came out smiling.

Emily was stirring the soup and looked up at Mary. "Sort of a holdover from grade school primary colors."

The bathroom paint job was another sign Emily was not the shy introvert that everyone thought she was.

"I have iced tea or milk or hot tea or coffee. What would you like to drink with this soup?"

Mary opted for iced tea and so did Emily. She dished up the soup, took the warm bread from the oven and both Emily and Mary sat down at the small kitchen table by the windows.

They started to eat and then Emily blurted out, "After having lunch with Brad I sort of thought I'd gotten the hang of this dating thing. We didn't have trouble making conversation and we talked for hours. What did I do wrong this time?"

"Emily, you know don't you, that it was not your fault? It was his bad judgment to drink too much and to treat you like he did. He obviously likes a different class of woman than you could ever possibly be so..."

"If you look at the dates I've had you can see

I'm the common factor. First Harry ignores me and then Carl makes two dates in case ours didn't work out—and it didn't. I think I'm done dating. I think I'll be perfectly happy being just me and living here and..."

"I know how it seems and to have two rude dates is really bad. I'm so sorry you had to go through it but all men aren't all alike. Look at Paul and Mr. Chu and at Brad. Lovely men, fun to talk to and gentlemen."

Of course. All men weren't like those two but she was wondering why she should bother sifting through all the others. "Maybe there are good reasons for these men still being single."

Mary smiled then laughed. "You might have a point there but look at Dr. Pete. He'd be a catch, if he was dating."

Emily smiled with her. "Yes, and if he were I be happy. He's a man I can talk to." She got up to get some more iced tea and said, "Okay, I get it. All men aren't losers but maybe just the ones that want to date me are."

"Now you just stop it," Mary said. "Let's just brush ourselves off and get up and try again. Nothing really bad happened did it?

Emily said no.

"And you did get to wear your new white suit before it got rainy again, didn't you?"

Emily smiled and said yes.

"Well, there you go. Nothing ever happens so bad some good doesn't come out of it."

Emily laughed. "No it doesn't, and to celebrate, let's eat pie."

When the pie was properly disposed of and only two pieces returned to the freezer, Mary decided she wanted to walk home instead of the offered ride. "The extra piece of pie you know."

The sky was lighter and maybe the storm wasn't coming in after all. She hugged Emily at the door and went down in the elevator feeling better but determined to find Emily someone really, really wonderful for the next date. On the street she walked down to the rose garden and paused to inhale their rich perfume. *Mmmm, roses. The smell of romance,* thought Mary.

"Mary. Mary Murray."

She heard her name being called. It was James Pritchard, bowler hat and all walking towards her.

"Hello. I thought I recognized you. Out walking or do you have a destination?"

"Hello. I'm on the way home. Are you just out walking?"

"Well, sort of. I planned to walk down by St. Francis in hopes of stopping for coffee with Natalie. Do you know if she's in?"

Mary smiled. "I'm not sure but let's go see."

They turned and walked down Elm Street, stopping to admire flower gardens and lawn ornaments as they went.

Mary told him how much she enjoyed the dinner and his nephew on Thursday. "I certainly understand why he's in such demand on the concert circuit. How's he feeling after performing?"

"He was tired but so happy to be playing for an audience again. I think I'll have another music party soon."

They chatted and strolled and when they got to St. Francis Mary said, "Come in and we'll see if Natalie is around." They didn't have to look far. Mary was leading JP down the hall towards the dining room as

Natalie was coming out of her apartment.

"Hello," she said, looking from Mary to James, then back.

"Hello. I was on my way to see if you wanted to come out for a cup of coffee and ran into Mary."

Natalie relaxed, then smiled. "Yes a cup of coffee would be nice but why don't you come in and have a cup with me in the dining room?"

"That would be very nice too. Mary will you join us?" James smiled as he spoke but he was looking at Natalie.

"Thank you but I'm headed for my apartment," she said and started to walk down the hall.

Natalie turned away and they were already into a new conversation and headed toward the dining room. They filled their coffee cups and he said yes to a cookie. She put four oatmeal raisin cookies on a plate and they went to a table by the window. They chatted about the Thursday night dinner party and James told her he wanted to plan another one. "I want to have Bruce play again soon. It so helps his frame of mind."

"Have you thought of maybe having him play at the high school or give a program at the theatre? Maybe for charity?"

"You know I haven't, but let me talk to him about it. Would you be able to organize such an event if he says yes?"

Of course she would be able to help and even had an idea. "Why not have it at the theatre on the same weekend as the Haven Port high school reunion? That's at the end of July." She opened her notebook and started to make notes. "I'll need to know as soon as possible if he wants to do the show so I can secure the theatre and get it advertised."

James smiled. He thought Natalie was at her

best in this planning mode and listened to her with pleasure. When she stopped to take a breath he said, "Would you consider going to dinner with me sometime?"

Natalie blushed. It had been very many years since anyone had taken her out to dinner. She and her husband attended work related dinners and went out in groups, but he never invited her to go just with him. She had decided they just didn't have that kind of marriage, and he decided he had better things to do with his time. "Yes I think it would be lovely."

"In that case, how about going to dinner with me in Seattle next week? We could walk on the ferry and go to the Skyview at the Bay? It's not a very far walk from the ferry dock."

Again Natalie blushed but she smiled too and said, "Yes, I'd like that. Could we discuss the details on Monday after we see the weather report for the week?"

He agreed and it was decided he would call her Monday.

They finished their second cup of coffee and she walked with him to the side door.

"I'll see you next week for sure, maybe sooner. Have a lovely evening," he said and leaned over to kiss her forehead.

Natalie smiled. "You have a lovely evening too and I'll talk to you very soon."

He went out of the door and turned to wave. She waved back then walked back to her apartment. *It was so very nice to have a friend like James.*

Before dinner, Mary found Natalie sitting alone at her table. She told her about Emily's date. She finished with "...and she took a taxi back to the ferry and home. I think we need to have a meeting. Emily doesn't want to meet anymore of these men and can you blame her?"

Natalie was still in a good mood from her earlier conversation with James and instead of her usual exasperation at not being the one to call a meeting, she said, "Yes, I agree. Right after dinner?"

Mary went to tell her guys and Natalie went to tell Steven and Lawrence and Sarah.

The whole group was present but before Natalie could call them to order, Steve stood up and said, "I want to apologize for my candidate. He took Emily to dinner last night and made a complete ass of himself and embarrassed Emily."

"And just how do you know about the date?" Natalie was back in charge.

"He called me this afternoon to say he thought maybe Emily misunderstood him and had walked out on their dinner. After I questioned him I got the picture. He drank too much and then forgot he already had a date with another woman. She came to the restaurant and the confrontation embarrassed Emily. He said he sent Emily home in a taxi. I didn't think he would act like that. Sorry."

Natalie smiled at him. "Thank you for the information but I don't think you can be held responsible for Carl's actions. Mary, would you give us a report on Emily's feelings and progress?"

Mary cleared her throat as she stood up. "I had lunch with Emily today and she was very upset. She's had two dates and both turned out to be less than a good experience. First she went out with Harry and he ignored her most of the evening, then last night Carl drank too much and she chose to leave when it was apparent he arranged another date that he sent to his apartment to wait for him."

Paul said, "I didn't say anything before but Harry called me and said he didn't know what to say all night. He's a little shy and he said whatever he said came out wrong and he didn't want to offend her so he didn't talk to her. It wasn't the right way to treat her or to handle his problem, but he's sorry and so am I. I like the guy and thought Emily would too."

"The bad part of it is that our Emily is disappointed with this project and wants to stop meeting *any* of the other men." Mary sat down and no one said anything.

Dolly raised her hand. "Ya' all know my ex-husband's son Ronald? After seeing him in our social situation last week, Ah don't really think he's the type for Emily. Ad'd like to withdraw his name."

Natalie said, "Thank you Dolly. Is there anyone else that wants to withdraw their candidate?"

Larry raised his hand. "I still think Emily would like to know Brian."

Natalie looked around. "Is there a discussion?"

Mary took a deep breath and said, "Natalie, do you think your nephew's right for our Emily? He acted so, well, I don't know, what do you think Natalie?"

Natalie did not smile nor did she look at Mary but she said, "I think I'll withdraw his name too. I think Emily needs a more worldly man and I must admit, Patrick is so focused on his business, he doesn't really know about anything else."

Both Mary and Sarah looked at Natalie. This was so very unlike her to admit any plan of hers was not perfect.

Sarah recovered first. "Natalie, that took guts. Shall I mark him off the list along with Dolly's guy?"

Natalie just nodded her head yes and looked

down at her notebook.

Mary spoke again. "I think we should tell Larry's guy to call Emily."

Everyone said yes and Natalie seemed to recover.

"Lawrence, would you please tell your candidate he can call Emily?

Larry said yes he would and reminded Natalie once again that his name was Larry.

Natalie smiled and said, "I'm sorry, of course I know that. Thank you, Larry. Is there any more business for this meeting?"

"Do we want more men for our list?" It was George and everyone was surprised. He didn't seem as grumpy and he seemed to have heard the whole meeting. "I mean, if those guys are taken off the list, what we gonna do, set her up on the computer for dates?"

Paul smiled at him. "You got your new hearing aids, didn't you?"

"Yep. Got 'em today and I have to tell you there's a lot of unnecessary noise in this world."

The whole group laughed and George smiled.

"Well, you can let me know what happens at the rest of this meeting. I gotta go," said Paul and he left the room.

Natalie tapped her gavel and said, "Let's see how her date goes with Brian, shall we, then we can make a decision after that."

Everyone agreed and the meeting was adjourned.

Larry went immediately to his apartment and the phone. He would have a good heart to heart talk with Brian before he gave him Emily's number. Brian had better not screw this up.

Brian put the phone down and sat for a minute thinking. This broad that Law wanted him to date must be pretty special if he felt it necessary to caution him to treat her right.

He ran his hand across the top of his crew cut and stood up. Just maybe this would be the person he'd wanted to spend his life with. God knows he wasn't happy since Annie left, and he'd thought she was the one. The phone rang and he answered it.

He said hello and then had to hold the phone away from his ear. "*When are you going to come pick up your shit*?!" The female voice continued but in less forceful shrieks. "If it's not picked up by Monday when I get home from work I'll throw it in the garbage."

Of course he knew who it was and he tried to respond in a calm voice, although he was feeling anything but. "If you will remember, you are living in my condo. When are *you* moving?"

There was silence, then crying. "Aren't you ever coming back? I thought this was like last time. You'd stay in town for a few nights then come home and we'd make up." She was sobbing now, with hiccups.

"No, not this time. Could you be out by Wednesday? I've got painters coming." He hadn't even talked to the painters yet but he was hoping to hurry her departure.

The crying stopped but the words were watery. "Yes I'll be out of here tonight. I'm moving back to my mother's house in Seattle. I'm so tired of this commute."

"Good, then we'll both be happy. I'm on my way over to help you. See you in a few minutes."

All she said was "Oh." Then she heard the click on the phone.

Brian had been staying at the Mountain View Motel near the golf course and it didn't take long for him to gather up his clothes and pack. He checked out of the motel and headed for his condo on the Cliffs. It felt good, finally making a decision and going home. He'd bought his unit in The Cliff Condos before they were built and had lived there now for almost ten years. Off and on he'd had a live-in lady friend but now he would be *single* again. The prospect made him sad, when he knew he should be happy. He would really miss Annie and even if they did fight, they fitted each other so well. On the way across the island he decided to make it a whole new place, maybe new furniture too. Thinking about that made him feel hopeful there was a life for him out there. He just needed to look around, and this date with Emily was a way to start.

CHAPTER 25

Brian knew Emily came to work at four o'clock and at four-fifteen, Monday afternoon he was parking his car by the front door.

Emily looked up from her computer and saw a tall, dark haired, handsome man walking through the outside door into the business office. "Hello. May I help you?"

Brian smiled. "Yes, I think you can if you're Emily?"

"Yes?"

"My name's Brian Daniels and I'm a friend of Law's. He gave me your phone number and instead of calling, I decided to come by to meet you."

Emily was a little surprised and she blushed. She thought she'd made it clear to Mary she didn't want to date any other men but she was too much of a lady to be impolite so she said, "By Law I take it you mean Larry Williams?"

"Yes, I mean Larry. I forgot. I grew up next door

to him and we always called him Law because of his initials and because he was a lawyer." Brian chuckled. "But I'm here to find out if you would have time for a cup of coffee or a drink after work?"

"I don't get off until nine-thirty."

"Is that too late? I mean, we could have coffee or lunch or something tomorrow if it would be better for you?" It was not like Brian to be unsure of himself, but he was having a bit of trouble with this arranging part. He wondered why.

Emily smiled. "I think I'd enjoy a cup of tea tonight after I get off. Where shall we meet?"

Brian smiled back. "The only place I know that's open, except for the bars, is the Mountain View Restaurant on the west side. Do you know where it is?"

She did and they made the time to meet at nine-forty-five.

"I know this is not a conventional way to meet someone but I'm truly looking forward to knowing you. See you later."

Emily said goodbye and watched as he walked back to his car. She watched him drive away then went back to the computer, but it was hard to concentrate. She was hoping this meeting would be better than any of the others... well, except for the lunch with Brad. That had gone well and she wondered briefly if she'd ever see him again.

Brian was sitting at a table by the window when Emily arrived. She'd worn black slacks and a black blouse with the bright blue sweater today. Brian stood up and offered his hand. "Hello Emily."

Emily took his hand and said, "I'm happy to meet you again, Brian."

They laughed as they sat down at a small round table. The waitress came to take their order. Besides the tea, Brian ordered a piece of Lemon Custard Pie and Emily had a piece of Apple Crumble Cake. The waitress said she would bring the hot water and a selection of teas.

"I hope it warms up some this week," Brian said. "I'm having painters come on Wednesday."

"Where's your condo? I thought you lived in Seattle."

Brian smiled. "No I live in The Cliff Condos. I've lived there for a long time but just decided to update my stuff. First I'm painting then I'm going to do something with the floors. I never really took the time when I moved in. Just used the furniture I had when I was married but it's time to get some new stuff. Do you know much about furniture?"

Emily smiled. "Well, as the saying goes, I only know what I like." She told him about furnishing her condo and how much fun it was to go to those really expensive and exclusive furniture stores, find what she liked and to shop for a less expensive version. "I found a wardrobe that was hand carved for $18,000 and then found one almost like it at a used furniture store for $300. Of course I bought it and now it holds the TV in my bedroom. I found several things by doing that."

"Maybe it's a place to start and I'm going to have some time off because I'm switching jobs. I've built up so much overtime we decided I should just take days off to compensate me. I really like that idea."

Emily knew from Mary that Brian was a pilot and she was so determined to make this a good experience, she decided to start with a safe conversation about his job. "Aren't you still flying?"

"Yes, but I'm stopping the flights to England and Italy. That'll cut my time away to about twelve days a month. I want to have a life again." He laughed. "Not that I didn't have a life, but I would like something, well something different. Maybe a home with some horses and a big garden. I'd really like to have a garden again."

They talked about gardens. Emily told him about the flowers she'd raised at her home on the Cliffs, and he told her about his giant zucchini experiment when he was a kid, and how it got to be ritual almost to grow at least one zuke that weighed fifty pounds. "They didn't always make it, but sometimes they went over. Fun days. That's when I lived next to Law."

The conversation flowed smoothly, and all too soon it was almost midnight and Brian said, "We've talked about everything except when I'll see you again. How about dinner one night this week? When do you work again?"

She told him she worked Monday through Thursday normally but this week she was trading with someone and would be working Friday.

"Does mean you have Thursday night free?"

She said it did.

"Would you like to have dinner in Seattle? If you walk on the ferry I could meet you..." and all the while he was saying this Emily was having a flashback of the last date that started this exact same way.

"I'm sorry... say that again. I missed where we would go for dinner?"

Brian smiled. "I said, if you walk on the ferry Thursday, I could meet you and we could walk down to the Skyview by the Bay, then we could both walk on the ferry to come home. Would you want to do that?"

Emily laughed to herself and said, "Yes, Thursday. What time?"

They arranged for her to come over on the five o'clock ferry. He'd be there to meet her. By now the tea was gone and Brian said, "Would you think me over protective if I said I'd follow you home from here? Just to make sure you got there safely?"

She said it would be very nice and thanked him. They went out to their respective cars and Brian followed her home, then gave a toot of the horn and turned down Front Street towards his condo.

CHAPTER 26

W
ell, I did it again." It was Tuesday morning and Emily was talking to Mary on the phone. "I said yes to another date and would you be able to have lunch with me today at the mall so we could shop?"

They decided Emily would walk down to St. Francis and they would meet at ten on the patio.

Mary was opening the outside door when Natalie came up and said, "Hello. Going for a walk?"

Mary took a deep breath expecting that what she said would probably end in a confrontation, but when she said, "No, I'm meeting Emily to go shopping," Natalie just smiled.

"Good. She needs more new clothes, don't you think? After all you can't start a new life in an old wardrobe." Then she pushed open the door and walked out ahead of her, headed off towards the golf course.

Mary went out too and saw Emily just arriving.

She was shaking her head in wonderment and at Natalie's new attitude. What could be changing her?

Emily wanted to shop for pants suits and dresses. "...and I saw a pretty red dress with a jacket last time we were here. Do you think something like that would be right for dinner or... I guess I just need help knowing what to wear for different occasions."

Mary smiled at her. "I think you have a pretty good sense of what looks good on you, so all you need to do is go to a few of these places you talk about and see what others are wearing. I think the rule is that if you are comfortable with how you look, then you're dressed right for the occasion."

"Last Saturday at the marina I saw all kinds of outfits. Pants that fit so tight I'm surprised the girls could breathe and tops so low cut I'm surprised they didn't show their bra, but they did show their belly buttons and some had jewelry clipped in them. Ugh!"

Mary laughed. "See, you did notice the fashions."

They looked at the red dress but Emily decided not to try it on because it was so short. "I just wouldn't feel comfortable standing up all the time."

"Here's a pretty dress. It was a yellow and orange flowered print of a sheer material and it was lined with soft white cotton. The skirt was flared, the top sleeveless, and in case of cooler weather, it had a bright yellow bolero sweater. Emily tried it on and liked it as much as Mary did. The next store was called Mix-'N-Match. Here they found light blue slacks with a cropped jacket of the same material and a white top with the exact same blue piping on the scooped neck. They also found a dark red suit with a pleated skirt and a boxy button-up-the-front jacket of a heavy knit. Emily said she had a black sweater that would go with this, but wasn't it a little dark for summer? Mary agreed but Emily decided to buy it anyway, saying with a smile and a shrug of her shoulders, "Winter's coming."

By the time it was twelve o'clock they'd purchased two pairs of shoes, three blouses, four pairs of slacks... two with jackets to match, one pair of jeans, one jean jacket, three cotton shirts to go with the slacks and jeans, and a raincoat that had a plaid lining.

They went to the food court and placed their order at Teriyaki Time, then moved to a table nearby. Mary sat down while Emily got napkins and collected their food and iced teas.

"Isn't this fun?" said Emily as she sat down and Mary smiled back. She loved seeing her so happy.

"Now aren't you glad you decided to go out with Brian?"

"Yes I am. And you helped me realize that two bad experiences mean nothing. I also had a good experience with Brad. We had a good time at the dinner and then he took me to lunch and we had a good time, so I guess it's not me that's the problem. I know I'm a little too shy and inexperienced, but it's not me that's a bore." She laughed. "At least it's what I keep saying to myself."

"Good. Just keep it up. And, you had a date with Brian already and it went well, so you can expect it to go well again, can't you?"

"It wasn't really a date but yes, it went okay. We talked and laughed and I enjoyed his company. He grew up here at Haven Port and went to school here too but he's three years older... just enough ahead of me so I didn't know him."

"Good. You have the same base, anyway. Is he going to the all-school reunion in July?"

"I don't know. I don't even know if I'm going. But I might." Emily laughed. "You know I didn't even consider it when I saw the announcement in the paper, but now..."

"Now that life has started to renew itself?"

Emily laughed again. "Yes, now that life is renewing itself. I like that phrase."

They ate their lunch and chatted about Brian and Brad and about the other dates.

"How many more are on the list?"

Mary was surprised. "I thought you didn't want to do the list any more?"

"I know what I said, but I thought it over. How else am I going to meet anyone?"

"Well, you could go down to Poker night at Jake's, or hang out at the golf course, or at Mickey's? There's a number of places."

"Right. Plenty of places." Both women were smiling at the prospect of Emily hanging out at bars.

They finished their lunch and got up to leave.

Emily said, "Would you mind shopping just a little longer? I want some underthings and I think I'd like to get some jewelry. Are you too tired?"

Mary said that lunch had been rejuvenating so off they went again. They returned to the same store and the same woman who had helped Emily find the burgundy bra, she showed the ladies the same style in several colors. Emily picked one in beige, a white, and a pale blue, and when the purchases were wrapped they headed for the jewelry store. The same nice man in the jewelry store helped them again. She bought some pearl stud earrings, a single drop-pearl on a chain, and a pearl bracelet.

"May I suggest you try this? It would look so lovely next to your skin." The jeweler held up a pair of stones mounted as drop earrings that were iridescent and, depending on the light, went from a lovely rose color to a blue, then back again as the stone moved.

Emily smiled. "Yes I like them, but aren't they expensive?"

The jeweler smiled. "For you I could make a very nice deal. My wife truly liked you and it would make me happy for you to have them." He told her the price and it was affordable.

"I just couldn't take these for that price. I think you must have paid much more for this than..."

He cut her off. "No, as a matter of fact I got a very good price on these stones and on another set. I had my wife in mind when I bought them. She chose the others, and I think these would be perfect for you."

Mary smiled at Emily and nodded yes. It was a good price and they were lovely. "Thank you," Emily said. "I do like them."

As he wrapped her purchases he said, "Where is your other friend? The one you were with last time. Is she here somewhere?" He looked to see if Natalie was sitting on the bench in the corridor.

"She's not with us today," Mary said, and smiled. *My, my.* She would for sure tell Natalie she had been asked about.

Finally they were finished and Emily and Mary walked out the back door of the mall and across the street, parting ways at the back patio of St. Francis. "Thank you for going with me. Maybe next time I can shop by myself," Emily said.

Mary smiled at this lovely woman who was truly coming out of her shell. "It's my pleasure to go with you any time. Please don't hesitate to ask me."

Emily hugged her and said, "See you later." and started the walk back to her condo.

She had gone only a few steps when a car pulled up beside her.

"Going somewhere I can take you?"

It was Brad.

CHAPTER 27

"Hello, Emily."

"Hello Natalie. How're you this evening?" It was after dinner and Natalie came into the office and sat down by the desk. "Did you get some pretty new clothes today?"

"Yes I did. Did Mary tell you about them?"

"No I haven't seen Mary since this morning. Tell me about your purchases."

Emily told her about the flowered dress and the pale blue pantsuit and the new earrings. "And... remember the jeweler who said his wife taught with me? He asked about you today."

Natalie looked at her and said, "What? Who asked about me?"

"You know the jewelry store where I got the gold chains?"

Natalie nodded her head.

"He's the one who asked if you were with us and was disappointed you weren't. Do you remember him?"

Natalie was pleased but that flustered her a little, and she was not easily flustered. She said, "Well, now isn't that nice," and she got up and left, forgetting why she had come to see Emily.

It was almost eight o'clock and Emily thought she would like to have a cup of coffee instead of her usual tea. She picked up her cup, put the BACK IN A MINUTE sign on the counter and headed out of her office, going towards to the dining room.

Mary and Paul were sitting at a table by the window. Emily got her coffee and stopped by their table. "Hello."

Mary smiled at Emily and said, "Hello back. Did you get home safely this afternoon?"

"Yes I did and I had help carrying in my packages. It was Brad. The nice guy from the dinner party."

"Yes I saw who it was. Is he back in town?"

"Sort of." Emily sat down. "He's gone again until this weekend. We have a date to go see the high school baseball game on Saturday. Want to come?"

Mary looked at Paul, smiled at Emily and said, "Let us talk it over and I'll let you know, okay?"

Emily said okay but before she left she said, "Mary, thank you again for going with me today." She smiled and not waiting for an answer, left the dining room to go back to her office. In the hall she met Larry.

"Hi," he said.

"Hello Larry. Did your friend Brian tell you he called me?"

Larry smiled. This was exactly what he wanted to know. "No, I haven't talked to him since Sunday.

Are you going out?"

"Yes we are, on Thursday. Want to join us?"

"Oh no. This is supposed to be a date not a *baby sit an old fart* night. Where you goin'?"

"I'm going to meet him in Seattle and we'll walk down to the Skyview on the Bay. Have you been there?"

"Oh yeah. They have a foxy lady manager. If you run into Barb say hello from Law. She'll know who you mean."

"Okay, if I see her." Emily smiled and went into her office only to find Dr. Pete waiting.

Emily thought she was seeing more people tonight just getting coffee than she ever saw in the office.

"Well, what have I been hearing about you and your social life?"

Emily laughed. "Well, it has picked up some. What have you heard?"

Dr. Pete laughed with her and sat down in the chair that Natalie had just vacated. "So you *are* aware of the dating service we now have running at St. Francis? I understand Natalie Greene is in charge and she has committees and everything."

Emily laughed again. "Oh yes, I am very aware. I've even participated in a couple of those set ups."

"And where have you gone and with whom? I feel responsible for bringing you into this retirement home situation and..." but he didn't finish because he was starting to laugh with Emily.

"How much do you know?"

"Sister Nora tells me there's a committee called Procurement to get potential dates for you. That's pretty much all I know. How many of these potentials have they procured?"

Emily filled him in about Harry and being ignored, about Carl and being embarrassed, about Brian and the Thursday night dinner. She ended by telling him about Brad, the man she met at the Reinhold party. "He sat next to me and was so charming and we had lunch the next day and we're going to the highs school baseball game on Saturday. He's very nice."

"What do you know about him?" Dr. Pete told himself he was taking on his fatherly role now, but he was also very curious. "Where's he from?"

"I don't know all that much, but he works for the U and his office is here at the Satellite school. He has something to do with studying earthquakes and has to go where there is action at a moments notice so he's not always available for dates."

Dr. Pete made a mental note to check this Brad person out.

"What's his last name?"

Emily thought for a moment and said, "I don't know. If he told me, I can't remember."

"Well, I'll be here for a few more hours, and then I'm going home. Want a ride?

"Thank you. I'd like that."

Dr. Pete came out of Emily's office deep in thoughts of his own. With all this changing Emily was going through, she was still the same sweet woman he'd known for so many years and this made him happy. He went back to his office smiling.

CHAPTER 28

Wednesday morning Paul was up early, as usual, but it wasn't a usual day. He'd had his bran cereal with a banana and the one cup of coffee he allowed himself at breakfast and was waiting when Dr. Pete pulled up to the front door. Sister Nora was there to see them off and wished Paul good luck. "Does she know about my problem too?" he asked as he got into the car. He was feeling a little embarrassed.

"Paul, as much I would like to tell you that this problem was only known to you and me, almost everyone knows because you have to excuse yourself so many times during every function. Did you think it was a secret?"

"No I guess not, but I think I was hoping."

"Well, don't worry. Help's on the way. We're going to see a fellow I went to school with. His name's Paul too and he's the best at this kind of thing. Thanks for letting me go with you so I can see him again."

Paul wasn't fooled by the *letting me go with*

you ploy but went along with it and it was certainly easier to have someone else drive, especially in the Seattle traffic. As soon as they were on the ferry Paul took a trip to the men's room. Not so much as he had to go but he wasn't sure when his next opportunity would be. He refused coffee but Dr. Pete got a cup and they met back at the car.

"Are you in on this dating thing for Emily?"

"Yes. I thought it was a good idea and I still think it is, don't you? She's certainly perked up since we started."

Dr. Pete had to admit she had. He had hoped working there would help, and maybe it did, but this seemed to help more.

"And when Mary and Emily cut their hair and then when Emily got some new clothes... she looked happier I think."

Dr. Pete had to admit he thought so too.

Soon they arrived at the Seattle ferry dock and it was only about a twenty minute drive to the University. They chatted about how Seattle streets seemed always to be under construction and how many new buildings were in downtown area now, and soon Dr. Pete pulled into the University of Washington garage and into the space for visiting doctors. They located the elevator and went up to the fifth floor to the Department of Urology.

Dr. Paul Parker was at the reception desk when the elevator doors opened. "Hey Pete. How you doin'?" The doctors shook hands and both were smiling. "Is this the friend you wanted me to meet?"

"Paul Engles, meet my buddy Paul Parker." They shook hands too.

"Nice to meet you. Let's go to my office." They started down the hall and Dr. Parker leaned towards

Paul and said, "The men's room is right here if you want to make a stop. We're right across from it."

Paul smiled in appreciation and stopped at the door marked with a male figure. "Stress makes the urgency worse," Dr. Parker said, as he and Pete entered the office and sat down.

Dr. Pete smiled. He knew he'd picked the right guy to help Paul and now it was reinforced by the kindness he saw his friend still possessed. They made small talk- "how's your golf game?" and "how's things since your wife died Pete?" and "how's your wife Marge?"

Paul joined the doctors and Dr. Parker said, "Paul, this meeting's a type of stress, and stress makes this situation worse so anytime you need to have a break, just stand up and we'll know to wait for a few minutes. Okay?"

Paul said thanks and sat down on the small sofa next to Dr. Pete.

"Okay, let's get down to business. Pete sent me your physical records and I don't see any reason to do more testing except, if you don't mind, I would like to take a sample of urine for analysis as part of a study we're doing."

Paul looked at Dr. Pete and said, "I don't think I'd mind if you took a kidney if that would help solve my problem."

All three laughed.

"I don't think we'd require that of you but I'll make a note for another time. I talked it over with Pete before your visit and I think you're a prime candidate for this medication that comes in patch form. You renew the patch every other day and it should help the problem... well, stop the problem really. If we put on a patch today, could you use them for the rest of the week and come back next Wednesday for a follow-up urine sample... then every month for awhile?"

"Of course, I can do that but are there any side effects?"

"I'll give you a paper that lists them but most common are dry mouth, constipation, drowsiness, and sometimes a headache. In general, if you have anything going on differently in your body, like flu symptoms or anything, tell Dr. Pete and he'll know if it's a side effect or not. Most of my patients have found that the dry mouth is the most they experience. They keep mints or lemon drops handy to help with this, and don't forget to drink water too. You'll still need to hydrate your body." He smiled at Paul. "Any more questions?"

Paul shook his head no and looked at Dr. Pete again. "Is there something I'm forgetting to ask?"

Pete said, "How about bathing with the patch?"

"Just try not to rub it off when you shower or get in the tub, otherwise there's no special care. And, as I said, you're pretty healthy and a good candidate for this patch so I don't think you'll have any side effects or problems."

"I'm sure I'll have some more questions when I'm away from here. Does this affect my blood pressure?" Again Paul looked at Dr. Pete.

"No I already told Paul about the BP meds you take and they're compatible."

Dr. Parker waited a moment then said, "Well, if there's no more questions, ready for the patch?"

Paul smiled. He was ready to be finished with this problem and to have control again.

Dr. Parker stood up and went around to his desk. He pulled a box out of the drawer and said, "Paul, would you please stand up?"

He did and so did Dr. Pete.

"Would you please undo your pants? This works best if we put it on the hip."

Paul undid his belt and pants and Dr. Parker peeled off the back of the small patch and affixed it by Paul's right hip. "Now all we have to do is wait. It should be taking effect as we speak and be fully doing its job in about twelve hours. Do you feel anything?"

Paul shook his head as he buckled his belt. He was so close to tears he didn't want to speak and he was praying this would really work.

Dr. Pete put his hand on his friends arm and said, "Thank you."

Paul held out his hand. "I don't know how to thank you." He moved in and gave Dr. Parker a hug. He stepped back and was embarrassed but Dr. Parker was smiling. He patted Paul on the shoulder and said, "Good luck and see you next week."

"Don't forget to stop by the receptionist desk and she'll direct you to the place to give the urine sample. See you soon and see you too Pete. And by the way Pete, going to the Summer Frat Dinner Dance?"

"I don't' know. When is it again?"

Dr. Parker laughed. "You know when it is. It's the same day every year. The Saturday after the Fourth of July. Why don't you come even if you can't find a date or call me and I'll see if I can fix you up, just like old times?"

All three men laughed. Dr. Parker handed the box of patches to Dr. Pete, and Paul headed for the receptionist desk to finish the paperwork.

Pete said, "Thanks Paul and I'll get back to you about that date business. "

It was after one o'clock when they got back in the car and Dr. Pete said, "How about stopping for lunch somewhere?"

Paul thought it was a good idea and said so. They drove out of the parking lot and Dr. Pete headed toward downtown Seattle. "Let's treat ourselves to lunch at one of my old stomping grounds." He turned left and drove over the Alaskan Way Viaduct, then to the West Seattle Bridge and Salty's Restaurant on the water. When they walked in the door Dr. Pete was greeted by name and then when they were seated, several more people stopped to say hello and ask if he'd moved back?

"How long ago did you live here?" Paul wasn't surprised people liked Dr. Pete but he'd never really thought of where he'd been before Haven Port.

"We lived here in West Seattle on Beach Drive for many years and had our place in Haven Port as a getaway, but when Kathryn died I decided to just move to the island and cut down on the work load."

"And aren't we glad. I've known you about four years, when did you move over?"

"Let's see. Had a place in Haven Port for twenty-three years but decided to sell it and I moved to the condo when I took the job at St. Francis. It's been a little over five years."

The waiter came and Paul ordered a bowl of split pea soup and Dr. Pete had a bowl of bouillabaisse. They chatted about St. Francis and Dr. Pete asked again about Emily. Paul told him everything up to and including the meeting to take some of the applicants off the list. "Our poor Emily had to suffer through those dates but you know what I think? I think that as long as she didn't get hurt it made her stronger. More aware that there are all types of guys out there and some are rats."

Dr. Pete laughed. "Yes, some certainly are not

nice guys for sure. Maybe she'll meet someone... if it's in the cards. Was Mary in charge of her makeover?"

"Yes, it was Mary's idea to update her looks. It's like a new person's come to St. Francis. Our same sweet Emily, but a whole new look." Paul smiled. "She's so beautiful, inside and out."

"That she is," said Dr. Pete and as their food was served he added, "...and, she deserves to be happy."

They chatted while they ate and when they were finished with the soup, they each ordered a piece of black berry pie with vanilla ice cream. Suddenly Paul took a sharp intake of breath. "I just realized we've been here over an hour and I haven't had to go."

Dr. Pete smiled. "I hoped it would work this fast."

"Do you know I feel like I've lost a hundred pound weight off my shoulders? I think I'll have another cup of coffee with the pie." He smiled then laughed. "I never get to have a second cup of coffee."

They drove into St. Francis parking lot a little after four o'clock and Paul hurried off to find Mary. He couldn't wait to tell her about his day and to tell her he thought they could go to the baseball game on Saturday.

Dr. Pete headed in to find Sister Nora to give her a report but as he passed the office he saw Emily at her desk. "Hello," he said. "How are you today?"

Emily smiled and stood up. The counter was between them but Dr. Pete could see she was wearing a skirt.

He thought, *Nice legs she's been hiding.*

"Hi. How're you? Just coming home from Seattle with Paul? How'd it go? I saw him hurry in, but he's always hurrying to the restroom. Did he get to see the specialist?"

"Yes, we're just back. It went well, and yes he hurried in but not to the restroom. He got some meds and I think they might be helping already. He went to find Mary to share the news."

Emily smiled. "I guess that was a lot of questions all at once, wasn't it, but I'm so happy for Paul. If it does work, it would be so wonderful for him, and for Mary."

Dr. Pete was happy too. Here was Emily laughing and talking animatedly, and she seemed to be out of her depression. He congratulated himself on suggesting she come to work here and then realized he needed to thank Natalie too. She was the real architect of this Emily transformation. He told Emily he'd see her later and headed down the hall. He found Natalie in the library reading the newspaper. "Any good news?"

"Well I think it depends on your interpretation," Natalie said. She took off her reading glasses and smiled at Dr. Pete. "How are you today?"

"I've had a good day... and I came to thank you for your Emily plan."

Natalie was a little flustered. How did he know about her plans?

"Our Emily came here as a plain woman with very low self esteem and look at her now. I think your plan to get her back into the dating game has really done her a good turn."

Natalie still didn't know quite what to say. "Well," she began.

"No need to say anything. I just wanted you to know I think it was a very nice thing to do... helping Emily."

She found her voice and said, "Thank you but I don't deserve all the credit. There were others involved and our work's not quite done."

"I know, but you were the head of it." He smiled at her again and left to find Sister Nora.

Natalie just sat there. It was nice to have someone recognize her hard work and she was very happy with her life at the moment too. James had called to arrange their dinner date for Thursday, and she was excited. A real date with a handsome man. She mustn't forget her hair appointment tomorrow and she wondered if perhaps she could get a manicure too. She stood and headed for her apartment and the telephone. She still might be able to get an appointment.

CHAPTER 29

Mary and Emily had another confab on Wednesday night about what would be appropriate attire for the dinner date the next day. The temperature was expected to be in the low eighties, just like today, so they decided the flowered dress with the yellow sweater would be right. She could wear the white heels and some of the new fun jewelry. Mary also thought Emily should have a manicure and a pedicure since her toes would be showing.

"Oh, I don't know. Isn't that a little, well, a little self indulgent?" Emily was hearing her mother's admonitions in her head.

"Don't be silly. It'll only add to your fun tonight. It's a part of the shopping and everything else to look nice."

"What if I do all of this preparation and the date turns out to be another dud?"

Mary laughed. "Look at it this way... you're

doing this for yourself so you'll feel good and if he thinks you look good too, that's just a bonus."

Emily agreed, even if there was some reluctance, and Mary said she'd make the appointment. "Want me to go with you?"

"You can if you want to but I'm okay to go alone." Emily was starting to get into the spirit of this thing. Yes she would do this for herself. Why not?

Thursday at noon she was seated at Suzie's Nails at the Mall, station number one. The nail polish company that supplied this shop had fun names for their shades of polish and Emily and Suzie settled on Orange You Happy Today. It was a bright coral and definitely in the orange family of colors. Suzie had already finished the pedicure and was applying the top coat to Emily's fingernails when Natalie came into the shop. Both Emily and Natalie were surprised.

"Well," Natalie said.

Emily recovered first and said, "Hello."

Natalie sat down beside Emily and said, "What a pretty color. Are you getting ready for something special?"

Emily smiled. "Yes, I have a date tonight for dinner in Seattle and I thought I'd just splurge a little."

"I'm also going to Seattle tonight... to the Skyview. Where are you going and with whom?"

"Larry Williams' friend Brian asked me to dinner and we're also going to the Skyview. Isn't this a coincidence?"

And it was so amusing, Natalie actually laughed. "We're taking the five o'clock ferry. You?"

Emily laughed too. "Same ferry. Do you think there was some higher power that planned this so just in case it didn't work out on my part? So I wouldn't be alone?"

Natalie shifted back into her Chairwoman mode. "Well, certainly we would be available in case of any unpleasantness, but do you expect this date might not go well? If so...."

Emily hurried to reassure Natalie that she *did not* feel a failure coming on, and that she was only making conversation. "I thought I was being funny, but I guess I have to work on that part of my small talk."

Natalie smiled. "I think you're doing just fine. Small steps make for big changes, you know."

Emily didn't really understand what this meant but she was certainly going through changes and they didn't seem small. As she prepared to leave she said, "See you on the ferry."

Natalie smiled and said, "Yes, you will."

Thursday had turned out to be a sunny and warm, just as the weather predictors had promised. Emily felt happy with the prospects of the coming evening and kept reassuring herself that this would be very different from her last dinner date. She'd already met Brian and they could talk easily, and she liked him. She drove back to the condo humming *Chances Are*, the old Johnny Mathis song and when she walked in her door she saw the phone message light blinking she thought, *Oh no. Is he canceling?*

There were two messages. The first one was from Brad. He was asking for a rain check for the Saturday game. He found out he wouldn't be able to get back as he'd planned but could he see her when he did return next week? He'd try to call her again later tonight." Emily was disappointed but understood. She wondered where earthquakes were happening now and speculated on how difficult it must be for him to always have indefinite work hours. *Oh well,* she thought, *it will all get straightened out later.*

The second message was from Brian. He was confirming their date for tonight and left his phone number in case she needed it, but hoped she wouldn't. He added he'd be there to meet the ferry in Seattle at five-thirty. She made a note of the number then picked up the phone and dialed.

"Mr. Daniels' office. This is Patricia. May I help you?"

"Yes, you can. I'd like to speak to Mr. Daniels please. This is Emily Barnes." There was a short burst of elevator music and then Brian's voice came on the line.

"Oh, Emily. You don't have bad news for me, do you?"

Emily laughed. "No I don't think so. I was just letting you know that yes we are still on for tonight and to tell you that a couple from St. Francis is also going to be on that ferry but we don't have to have dinner with them if you don't want to."

Brian let out his breath audibly. "Oh good. Who is it and do you want them to join us?"

"It's Natalie Greene and... well, I don't' know who she's going with, she didn't say, but I thought you should know so you wouldn't be confused about dinner."

"Well, whoever it is, we'll just play it by ear."

Emily was pleased with the answer. She wouldn't want Natalie offended nor would she want to horn in on their plans, so it was a good solution.

"Okay, see you later then." He said good-by and they both hung up.

As the ferry pulled into Seattle, Emily could see the commuters lined up in the waiting room, ready to take the boat back to their evening destinations. The ride from Haven Port to Seattle had been pleasant and she wasn't really surprised when Natalie's date turned out to be James Reinhold. He was fun and his observations of life kept both Natalie and Emily laughing. They walked up the corridor from the boat and as they came onto the open passageway, Emily saw Brian. Then he saw her and broke into a very happy smile. Natalie and James saw the smile too and as they approached him James said, "Do you think he's that happy to see us too?"

Introductions were made and they headed for the stairs that would take them down to street level. "Do you know that boy?" asked James. He and Natalie were walking a little behind Emily and Brian.

"Well, only because he's an old neighbor of Larry Williams. Do you know him?"

"I think he was in the group of boys who played baseball when I used to coach the summer league."

"We could certainly ask him," said Natalie thinking again that after all, they lived on an island and if you'd lived there for very long, you probably knew everyone else that lived there too.

Brian and Emily reached the restaurant entrance first and waited until James and Natalie caught up. Skyview on the Bay was located on the top floor of an office building and as they entered the foyer the elevator doors opened and a couple came out, obviously arguing. "I don't care what *you* call it, I call it flirting." The man was livid and the woman seemed in a hurry to get out of the elevator, out the door and perhaps away from him."

The two couples got on the elevator and James

pushed the button marked Restaurant then turned and said, "Hope the rest of their evening gets better."

Everyone laughed.

CHAPTER 30

As it turned out Natalie and James were meeting two other couples, and they were already at a table waiting, so there was no decision to be made. Brian suggested that he and Emily go to the bar and wait for their table. He'd made their reservation for six-thirty.

Barbara Scott, the manager came into the bar and said hello to Brian. He introduced Emily to her and she said, "Welcome to the Skyview. I hope you enjoy yourself this evening."

Emily said thank you and as Barb moved away to speak to other guests, Brian smiled and said, "Barb's an old friend but she's not going to be here at the Skyview much longer because they made her a General Manager of several of the restaurants in this group. Spokane and here and Portland I think she said."

"She's so pretty and seems the perfect type for running a restaurant. Do you come here often?"

"Almost every day I'm in town. My office is just up on Second. It's a nice walk down to the waterfront and a good break in the day."

Brian asked Emily what she would like to drink and suggested a Cosmopolitan. "It's sort of like a martini but has cranberry juice in it and it's a little sweeter."

Emily was about to say no, she'd have wine but changed her mind. This was a night of adventure so why not try something new. "Okay, I'd like to try it. Thank you for the suggestion."

Brian ordered one for each of them and said, "What do you usually drink?"

Emily laughed. "I'm not much of a drinker, but I do like wine sometimes."

They talked about what wines she knew, and he told her about the French wines he liked. He'd been flying into France for many years and had even gotten to know a few of the vineyard owners. He was telling her how beautiful the vineyards were just before harvest time with the grapes hanging of the vines, and at that moment Barb came to tell them their table was ready.

As they passed the table where James and Natalie, they both smiled. Emily said hello to the other couple, Flo and Ed, longtime residents of Haven Port, and Brian said hello to a very nice looking man with dark curly hair. When they were seated he said, "That was Jerry Billings I said hello to. Do you know him? He directs and plays in the Seattle Symphony. He lived in Haven Port for a while as a young kid. I think that lady with him did too but I can't remember her name. She's a lot younger than I am and so I didn't know her very well."

Emily looked at the table and said, "I think I

recognize her. She's the niece of Flo, the other lady I spoke to. And yes, she's a lot younger than we are... by ten years probably."

The waiter came to ask if they wanted another cocktail before ordering and they did. Emily liked the taste of this new drink and felt a little sophisticated, at least more than she usually felt. They looked at the menu and Brian decided on Beef Burgundy and Emily said it sounded good to her too. To go with it Brian ordered a bottle of Merlot from the winery he'd told her about. Their table was in the corner by the window and they watched the ferries coming and going, watched a cruise ship come into dock, and talked about the sailboats they could see. They sipped their drinks and when the food came and their wine was poured Brian made a toast. "Here's to a long friendship." Emily raised her glass and smiled at Brian. She clinked his glass and said she was hoping for the same thing.

Dinner was pleasant and they laughed and talked and ended the dinner by sharing a piece of three-layered chocolate mocha cake and port. When the waiter cleared away their places, Emily excused herself and went to the ladies room where she found Natalie and the girl from her table.

"Oh Emily, are you having a good time?"

"Yes I really am. Brian's a very nice man."

Natalie smiled. "I'm so happy to hear that." She turned to the woman beside her and said, Toni, do you know Emily Barnes? Emily this is Antoinette Nygaard. She's engaged to Jerry Billings, the concert violinist."

The woman smiled and said, "My friends call me Toni. I'm happy to meet you. You probably know my Aunt, Flo Janson."

"Oh yes, I know her and I remember you too as

a girl. Do you ever come back to Haven Port?"

"I visit but not as much as I'd like. I'm planning to go to the school reunion at the end of July though, so I'll be there for a few days."

Emily smiled. "I think I'm going too. I love the fact that they have an all-school reunion every year and honor the graduates who're celebrating their twenty-fifth reunion. A fun way to honor the class."

Toni laughed. "This is my year to be honored. It's my twenty-fifth already."

They chatted a few minutes longer about the reunion then Toni and Natalie started out the door to return to their table but Natalie paused and said to Emily, "Are you alright to go home?"

Emily knew that meant *do you want to go home with us,* but she assured Natalie that everything was fine and she was very comfortable with her date.

Emily returned to the table and Brian asked if she'd like another drink. "No, I think I've had enough for tonight. But if you want..."

Brian stopped her by putting his hand on her arm. "No, I've had enough too. Let's stroll down to ferry and see how long we have to wait."

Emily looked over at Natalie's table and saw her watching them. As she stood up she mouthed, "See you later," and walked with Brian to the elevator door.

They exited the elevator into a warm summer night full of people slowly walking and laughing, and many of them eating ice cream in cones. "If I wasn't so full, I'd like some ice cream too," Brian said.

Emily smiled as he took her hand and they talked, laughed, window shopped, and indeed, strolled in the moonlight towards the ferry terminal.

CHAPTER 31

Mary's walk on this beautiful Friday morning just happened to take her up to Emily's condo and when Emily heard her voice on the intercom, she was happy.

Emily opened the door as Mary came off the elevator. "I hope I'm not calling too early after your late night."

Emily laughed. "It wasn't so late and I have to work today so I'm up and around as usual."

Mary could hear the clothes dryer going and saw that Emily had the vacuum in the middle of the floor. "I'm sorry to interrupt your routine, but I was excited to tell you Paul and I are going to the baseball game tomorrow too."

"Sit down and have a cup of coffee or would you rather have tea?

"No, I'll just have a glass of water. I'm trying to keep up with my quota of eight glasses a day."

Emily filled a glass from the refrigerator

dispenser and sat down at the table too.

"Dr. Pete did some tests on Paul and then they went to Seattle and saw a specialist. He gave Paul something to help with his problem... do you know about his problem?"

Emily nodded her head.

"It's so wonderful. The difference it's making in Paul's confidence. He even talked about going dancing at Micky's Restaurant. Did you even know they danced there? I knew they used to but...." Mary stopped and smiled. "I'm just rattling on and on. And I really came here to hear about your date last night. Did he turn out to be good or, well, like the last one?"

Emily told her from start to finish how much fun it was and about Natalie and James on the ferry.

"JP is funny and Natalie's a different person when she's with him. She laughs and is relaxed and she's a fun person to be around. They had plans to meet some people there, so we sat by ourselves and had a good time. We watched the ferries and other boats and a cruise ship came in. Brian even mentioned he would like to take a cruise and was asking me if I'd ever been and, well, I think he might ask me to take a trip with him. I probably won't because it wouldn't look right, but..." she trailed off.

Mary smiled. Here was that plain-Jane Emily, talking animatedly about *should she go on a cruise*, and looking like she could be the cruise activity director. "Why don't you just cross that bridge when you come to it?"

Emily blushed. "Yes, I guess I'm a little bit ahead of myself. But he's nice and I like him. No butterflies when I see him but he's fun."

Mary stood up. "Well, back to my walk and see you later." She went to the door and opened it then turned, "Emily do you realize just how far you've come out of your shell?"

Emily smiled and moved to give Mary a hug. "Yes, I guess I have changed, and it's all due to the committee Natalie started. I guess I should thank her."

Mary left and Emily went back to the vacuum cleaner, humming *Mairzy Doats and Dozy Doats*, an old tune her father used to sing when they were fishing. *Yes she was well on her way to a new life.*

It was almost four o'clock and Dr. Pete was standing in his office door. He watched as Emily came in from the parking lot, then he watched as she put her purse and sweater in the locker, and when she turned, he smiled. He crossed over to her office and said. "You look lovely today."

She was wearing tan slacks, an apricot cotton blouse that she'd left untucked, and the paisley sandals. "Hi, Dr. Pete. Thank you for the compliment. How are you today?"

"I'm fine and I hear you went out on another date last night. Is he going to be someone special?"

Emily's look was questioning. *Someone special?* "Well he's very nice, and I like him, and we had a good time. Yes, I guess you could say he was special."

Dr. Pete just said. "You deserve someone like that in you life," and he turned to leave.

As he walked back to the clinic, Emily felt sorry for him. She was thinking *You deserve someone special in your life too.*

Soon after Dr. Pete left, Natalie was at the office door. "Do you have a moment?"

Emily had been expecting to see her. It was report time and as Natalie sat down in the chair by the desk, Emily sat down too. This report was more of an interrogation. Natalie asked pointed questions. "Did he try to hold your hand, did he try to kiss you, and did he get fresh?" She whispered the last part.

She might have been upset but she was beginning to understand Natalie and knew this was her chairwoman mode so she answered the questions with, "He did hold my hand, and he kissed my cheek when we said good-night, and no there were no problems. He was a perfect gentleman."

Natalie relaxed and switched to her *I'm your friend* tone of voice. "I liked him too, the little I saw of him. Will you be seeing him again?"

"I think so. He's redecorating his condo and asked me to help pick out furniture. He's going to call and we'll pick a time. Did you and JP have a good time last night?"

Natalie smiled, and still in her *I'm your friend* voice said, "Yes, we did. James is so entertaining and then the people we met for dinner were lovely too. Jerry Billings and his fiancée Antoinette, oh I must remember to call her Toni, are coming to the school reunion. Didn't she mention that when you met? Well, they'll be staying at Flo Janson's house and Flo's planning to have a cocktail party so they can meet some of her friends. James is planning something too, to introduce Jerry to his nephew since they're in the same business, more or less. And speaking of the nephew, James has asked me to organize a concert during the week of the reunion. Let me see, it's the last weekend of July, so I'm hoping it could be on Friday night." She paused then said, "Do you know who's organizing the evening activities?" Emily shook her head no. "Well, back to you, did you have other gentlemen call you to go on dates?"

Emily smiled. "If you mean have other men from your committee called to arrange a date, the answer's no. If you mean do I expect to have more dates, the answer is yes. Brad, the man who sat next to me at the dinner party has asked me out, and Brian and I have plans for next week. Is that what you meant?"

That was exactly what Natalie meant and as she got up to leave she said, "Well, Emily, I'm happy you had a good experience and I'll chat with you later."

Dr. Pete was coming out of the clinic just as Natalie was leaving. "Hello Natalie. How is everything with you?" He expected her to just say 'fine' but what she said was, "You know, I've been meaning to talk to you," and she took his arm and guided him back into the clinic.

CHAPTER 32

At dinner that night, Natalie spoke first to Mary then to Steve. A meeting was needed.

The committee members thought this was probably for a wrap-up, and after everyone was seated Dolly was the first to speak. "Ah hear our dear sweet Emily had a lovely date last night. Is that right Natalie?" Her southern accent was in full swing and dripping with honey.

Natalie smiled. "Yes, I was privileged to see Emily and Larry's friend Brian have dinner last night, and Emily reported it was a lovely experience with another date to follow next week."

"Well finally. A good guy after those too bozos upset her." To everyone's surprise, George was speaking up. "Good job, Larry, I mean finding a decent guy for her finally." It was the most words anyone had heard George speak in a very long time, but now that he could hear again, he felt comfortable contributing to conversations.

"Thank you George. Any other comments?" Natalie smiled at him but took charge again after only a short pause. "Steven, you have a comment?"

"I talked to Brian this afternoon and he said they had a good time too and he liked Emily. Does everyone know I told him before the date that Emily was a lady and he better treat her that way?"

Natalie and everyone else smiled. No names were spoken but they all knew he was trying to make up for Paul's recommendation and Steven's too-aggressive golfing friend.

There were no more comments so Natalie said, "Well, I think we've handled this project well, and I have another one to propose, since we were so successful with Emily."

The room got quiet and the air expectant when Natalie said, "What would you think of finding someone for Dr. Pete?"

After a moment of silence everyone spoke at once.

"Does he want to be fixed up?" from George and Paul almost in unison.

"I think it's a lovely idea," from Dolly.

"I don't know any dames," Steve said scowling.

"Phooey." Sarah thought they had interfered enough.

"Hmmm," Larry said.

"Well, shall we have a discussion?" Natalie asked.

"I don't like it. We can't keep messing with people's lives. We were just lucky that Emily went along with this and I think it turned out good but what if this doesn't?" Sarah was adamant.

Natalie gave Sarah her best *I'll permit your comments but really!* look. To everyone else she said,

"What do you committee members think?"

No one spoke.

"Please speak up. If you don't agree I'd like to hear that too."

Sarah and Mary both looked at Natalie. This was another new wrinkle in her personality. She wanted to hear about disagreements too?

Mary finally said, "Dr. Pete knows lots of people. Don't you think he would already be dating if he wanted to? And we don't know much about his life away from St. Francis, do we?"

Paul raised his hand. "I think you all know that Dr. Pete took me to see Dr. Parker last week and he turned out to be one of Dr. Pete's friends from school. He mentioned that their Frat Dinner dance was coming up and Dr. Parker even joked that he could help Dr. Pete find a date if he couldn't find one of his own. Maybe we could do our part and help him."

The committee was listening attentively. Some were now smiling.

"If we ask him first, I think it would be fun." Dolly was thinking of her friend Lila Lane. She laughed a little loud sometimes but she was fun.

"There's Edith Ann from the kitchen... she's single. I heard her talking about going to Jake's sometimes." George smiled. This was another new thing from George. First communicating, then joining in, and now smiling.

"I talked to Dr. Pete this afternoon and he said we did such a good job for Emily he would be willing to try our suggestions, but he wasn't going to cut his hair shorter or get a new wardrobe." Natalie and the whole group laughed and every single member looked pleased. Just when they thought it was back to their mundane everyday life, another project was presented.

By now Natalie was beaming. She had picked this group and they had turned out to be very productive and cooperative. "Is it all right with everyone to keep the same committees?"

As a group they all nodded and some said yes.

"All right, Procurement Committee, let's get started. We can have a meeting tomorrow morning after breakfast to get suggestions or names of prospective dates. Does this give you enough time?"

Steve said, "I think I'd like everyone to participate in this getting dates process. I don't know many single women who would be good enough for Dr. Pete. Could everyone help on this?"

The group shook their heads... all except Sarah. "I don't want to be involved. I'll just take the minutes. Like before."

"Thank you, Sarah. We would like you to continue doing this job you do so well. Any other discussion? Can we start a list tomorrow?" Natalie was pleased everyone wanted to help. Well not so much Sarah, but everyone else.

Again there were nods and Paul raised his hand. "Do you think we should have another coffee hour and invite these ladies to come?" Once more nods and agreement from the group.

"Let's do this. Everyone talk to your lady friends and invite them to tea on Sunday. I'll check to see if we can have the room and get cookies and we'll all report back here tomorrow."

The group was standing and starting to leave when Sarah spoke up and said, "Meeting after breakfast?"

"Yes," Natalie said, and as Sarah left, she smiled. Maybe Sarah was interested in this new project after all.

CHAPTER 33

Larry was feeling pretty happy with himself. Not only had Brian turned out to be a good match for Emily but he was the one who came up with this fix up. It had been a long time since he'd done something so right and it felt good. This AA making amends thing was working well for him even though he hadn't thought it would at the beginning. He'd started his *sorry list* as he called it, from the beginning of when he thought things had gotten out of control, and now he was starting to see the end of this reparation part. Neither of his ex-wives wanted to talk to him. The first one hung up when she heard his voice, and the second never returned the messages he left. After a little thought he decided that getting out of the rut of just thinking about himself sure was proving to be good. Maybe there *was* going to be life after booze. He was smiling as he went to the patio for a smoke and found Paul.

"Hi Larry. Want some coffee?"

Larry was surprised. Paul was not only drinking decafe coffee but sitting down with an almost full pot on the table. "I'll go get a cup."

"I brought out three mugs just in case someone stopped by." He poured the coffee and gave it to Larry. "Isn't it a nice night?"

"Yea... it is. I think the moon is coming up too. Nice romantic night if I was about twenty years younger." Larry laughed. "Maybe we could be next on the fix-up list."

Paul laughed too but said, "I don't think I'm interested. I already have my sweetheart picked out."

Larry thought for a minute then said, "Are you and Mary a couple?"

"I'm not sure but I think we're definitely very good friends and I'm going to make that more and more friendly if I can."

Larry smiled. It would be nice for both of them and he knew there was a bigger apartment for couples open on the second floor. He'd talked to the painters yesterday and they said they'd be done *refreshing the paint* by the middle of next week. He'd heard there would be new carpet installed too.

"We're going to the baseball game tomorrow at the high school. Want to come?" Paul was pouring another cup of coffee.

"Hey, I just realized you're drinking coffee and not rushing off. Whatever they did to you in Seattle must be working, huh?"

"Definitely working and what a relief. Dr. Pete sure is such a good guy. I hope we can help him out."

Larry agreed. Dr. Pete was really a good guy but he was a little uneasy about this fixing-up thing for him.

Emily was turning off her computer and putting away files, ready to leave for the night. She went to turn off the light and saw Dr. Pete was still in his office. She stepped across the hall and as she knocked on the door-frame she said, "Working late?"

He looked up and smiled. "Catching up on my reading. How late is it?" He looked at his watch and said, "Nine-thirty already?"

"Yes it is. I'm on the way home. How about you?"

Dr. Pete looked tired. "These journals seem to multiply after they're delivered. Are you walking tonight?"

"Yes. Are you?"

Dr. Pete laughed. "No, I need my car in case of emergencies. Want a ride?"

"It's such a beautiful night. The moon is coming up and I thought—"

He interrupted her and said, "Let me give you a ride and we'll stop at Mickey's and have a drink on the deck, if it's still warm enough."

She smiled. "I think it is and I have a sweater for just in case. Thank you, I'd like to. Let me finish closing the office and I'll be right back." She went across the hall and turned off the lights, got her sweater and purse and was back in the hall as Dr. Pete closed his door

They walked out to his car and Emily said, "Did you get a new car?"

"No. I've had it a few years. Bought it after the kids left." He patted the top of the dark green XK8 Jaguar that had tan leather seats and a tan soft-top and said, "Shall we put the top down?"

Emily said yes and he opened the door for her to get in and went around to the driver side. With a few releases of levers and a flick of a switch the top was down and they were off in the moonlight.

Mickey's Restaurant was almost next door to Dr. Pete's and Emily's condo building. Directly east of the condos was the marina boat launch then the North Side Boat Repair and Storage, then Mickey's. Dr. Pete parked at the condo and they walked to the restaurant. When they entered they were greeted by Gus, the bartender. "You two been out strolling in the moon light?" He laughed and so did the guys at the bar. Emily was blushing but she and Dr. Pete laughed with them.

"Guess we have. Can we have our drinks on the deck?"

Gus said yes and took their orders. Beer for Dr. Pete and a glass of Chardonnay for Emily. They went out the door onto the deck and it was just as bright as being indoors. They picked a table and almost immediately Gus brought out their drinks. "Now I want you to know we can't see you from inside but if you want to neck, go ahead."

Now Emily blushed again and was glad no one noticed.

Dr. Pete laughed. "Well I'm not sure you can see us from inside, but there probably won't be a show for you tonight."

Gus grinned and said, "Oh, you don't think so, huh?" He went back through the door saying, "No show tonight. The guy's been here before." The guys at the bar laughed and turned back to their drinks.

"I hope that didn't embarrass you," Dr. Pete said.

"Well, a little but I'm over it now."

"It's a wonderful evening. Don't get very many of these in June."

Emily and Dr. Pete chatted and watched as the ferry came in and disgorged fourteen cars and they wondered anyone they knew in them. They chatted about how smooth the water in the bay looked. Then Dr. Pete said, "What do you have planned for tomorrow? It's probably going to be as nice as it was today."

"I'm gong to the baseball game at the high school for one thing."

"Going with anyone?"

Emily was surprised at the question. "No. I had a date but he had to cancel."

"How about I take you then we do something afterwards, like dinner?"

She was surprised again. "Well, yes, Dr. Pete. It sounds fun. I'm meeting Mary and Paul there for the game but we didn't make any other plans."

"And while we're at it, will you just call me Pete? I think we've been friends long enough so you could use my first name and no titles, don't you?"

Emily smiled. "Yes, I think I can do that, but I'm so used to saying Dr. Pete I might forget."

"I'll remind you if need be."

They ordered a second drink and talked some more. When it was finished they walked back to the condo. Pete swiped his security card and they went through the elevators. Emily turned to go left and Pete only hesitated for a moment. She lived on the top floor of this six plex in number 3-A, and he lived on the lower level in 1-B. Opposite corners. She pushed the elevator button and the doors opened. "Good night Pete and thank you for a lovely drink and ride home."

He smiled. "I thank you. What time is the game tomorrow? I haven't been to a game or really anywhere for so long. I'm looking forward to it very much."

Emily smiled and said, "So am I. I'll take a blanket in case we need to sit on the grass. See you tomorrow about twelve? Game starts at one I think."

"Twelve it is—I'll bring a cooler. Might be hot you know." He smiled as the elevator doors closed, then turned to go to the other side of the building. He was humming. It was tuneless but still a happy sound.

CHAPTER 34

Saturday was as warm and as beautiful as predicted. Earlier this morning the weather report said it would get to the high eighties and Pete was humming the same tuneless song of last night when he knocked on Emily's door.

"Hi," she said. "Right on time." She was wearing a navy blue and white print cotton dress and sandals. The skirt was full and fitted at the waist and the top had short sleeves and a scooped neck. It made her look younger than her years and her step had a youthful spring to it, adding to the allusion.

"Want to come in or shall we go?"

"I'm ready if you are." Pete was smiling at Emily. He knew what a nice person she was, and he had followed her makeover and thought that was nice too, but today she was enchanting.

She handed him the blanket and picnic basket and picked up her sweater and purse. "I'm ready, too." She pulled the door shut and turned to smile at Pete.

He was standing very close and could have leaned down and kissed her but he didn't. He didn't know which of them wasn't ready for that, but he was pretty sure one of them wasn't.

He stowed the blanket in the truck of the car with the cooler, put the basket in the back seat and opened the door for Emily. He liked the couple feel of the situation. Maybe Natalie was right. Maybe it was time for him to have a woman in his life.

Mary and Paul were already at the ball park sitting in folding chairs. They brought four chairs and Pete and Emily sat with them. Pete opened the cooler and passed around bottled iced tea and then Mary leaned over and spoke quietly to Emily. "I didn't think you had a date today. I thought Brad was out of town. We brought the extra chair in case Steve showed up."

"If he does come we can sit on the ground. We brought a blanket." And Emily hoped Steve would join them. The more the merrier.

The Players were warming up and Dr. Pete said, "See the boy on the left, the tallest one?"

Emily and Mary and Paul all looked.

"I wasn't practicing on the island then, but we were here for the weekend and his mother was expecting him any minute. I happened to see her at the grocery store and she complained he better be a good boy because he was sure giving her an uncomfortable nine months. I wondered how he turned out."

Emily smiled at him. "Well, I had him in my class when he was seven, and he was a hard worker and very polite. And his mother was very nice too and volunteered in the classroom quite a bit. She must have forgiven him."

"I had him in a class too. In the summers we, or should I say they, since I don't work there any more, gave classes on sea life at the University Satellite Campus. He wanted to be a deep sea diver at that time as I recall. However, he was only twelve then. I liked Jack. Smart kid."

"Oh, she named him Jack, huh? He was number four in the family. Do you know if there were more kids after that?" Dr. Pete looked at his friends.

"Well, here's something that might interest you. He's part of twins. He has a beautiful sister too. Maybe that's why his mother was so uncomfortable." Emily was smiling.

They all laughed and Dr. Pete said, "I have little doubt that's what it was."

They watched as Jack stepped up to the plate, waited for the pitch and swung the bat. The ball went over the fence and into the soccer field that was thankfully empty at the moment. A home run.

"Wow! What a hit." Dr. Pete was standing and cheering along with Jack's team and everyone in the bleachers. "I'm thinking pro-baseball instead of deep sea diving."

Jack ran the bases and Paul said, "Too bad he was the first hitter. Maybe he could have pulled in three runs."

From then on the game was exciting and Dr. Pete and Paul took turns cheering the team and muttering about the umpires. The teams were evenly matched and needed to play two extra innings to finally see who would win. It turned out to be Haven Port High.

They'd munched on the chips and dip and sandwiches Emily had packed all through the game, but now that it was over Pete and Emily helped Paul and Mary take the chairs back to the car and load them into the trunk, then they went back and folded the blanket, picked up the cooler and basket and headed to their car. "Did you know that Paul is going to ask Mary to marry him?"

Emily stopped walking. "No I didn't. Did he tell you?"

"Not exactly. He asked Sister Nora if the upstairs couple's apartment was vacant and she asked him why... that's how she found out."

Emily smiled and blinked back a tear. "That is so beautiful. I hope they can work it out. No one should live alone unless they want to."

Pete agreed. Alone should only be by choice.

Once the blanket and cooler were in the trunk and basket in the back seat again he said, "Would you be okay with taking the ferry and going for a drive before having dinner somewhere?"

It was still warm, the top was still down on the car, and Emily thought it was an excellent idea. They drove off with Pete mentioning he was glad no birds had found the open car and with Emily saying she better remember to check the seat before she got in the next time.

The ferry was just pulling into Haven Port and after the two cars drove off, Pete and the other three cars drove on. The ferry was going to the Kitsap Peninsula on this trip and when they arrived Pete said, "Any preference as to what direction we go?" Emily said no so he headed north to the Olympic Peninsula.

In this part of Washington one can find some of the most spectacular scenery in the world. Water and trees and mountains and wonderfully interesting people make tourists return year after year, and it makes for very happy residents. Pete thought maybe they would end up in Port Angeles for dinner and decided on the scenic route through Quilcene, a little town famous for its oysters. They decided to make a stop at the Ah Shucks Oyster Bar for a drink and a sample.

As they entered they saw the FOR SALE sign. They sat at the end of the long bar and after they ordered, they listened to the conversation of the six people already occupying the other stools. They were discussing the latest *lookers* from Wisconsin.

" n like oysters and talked about curtains on the windows. Tell me it ain't true," said a burly man dressed in wide suspenders holding up dirty jeans, a blue tee shirt with the word TROUBLE on the front, rubber boots, and the requisite knit seaman's cap.

The man sitting next to him said, "...and they said they would have milkshakes too. Now no respectable oyster eater washes them down with ice cream." That brought laughs from the whole crowd, tables, bar and all.

"Don't worry Henry. I won't sell to no ice cream, curtain hanging people." Again laughter, with Emily and Pete joining in. After they tasted barbequed oysters and washed them down with a beer, they got off their stools to leave. The bartender called from the other end of the bar and said, "You two come back anytime. We have a nice hotel too." The whole bar was laughing.

Pete smiled and said," Okay, next time we come this way we'll think about the hotel." Pete was smiling and Emily was blushing but by the time they got into the car they were giggling.

The sun was warm and pleasant even though it was almost seven o'clock. They were almost to Sequim when they saw a sign for a lavender farm. "It's a little early for the festival but I'm sure there's lavender already growing," Pete said and turned at the sign. Soon they could smell the flowers and see the variant shades of purple from almost white to the darkest, almost black purple. Pete stopped at a roadside kiosk and bought a bouquet for Emily.

She held it to her face and took a deep breath. "Heaven." She looked at Pete and smiled. He was smiling too. They returned to the main road and Pete said, "Want to try a restaurant here? She did and they drove only a short distance when they saw the Claw House. The sign said, Crabs, Shrimp and Other Delights. They both agreed this sounded like the right place to eat.

There hadn't been much conversation in the open car while they traveled. The wind and the traffic noise made it hard to hear so they'd mostly just looked at the view and held their own thoughts. As soon as they entered the restaurant, Emily and Pete both went to wash their hands, and after they were seated by a window Pete looked at Emily and smiled. "I've missed taking little impromptu trips like this. My wife and I did this often before she got sick. Are you enjoying the sun and the day as much as I am?"

She smiled back. "It's been a wonderful day." Her husband had never wanted to do anything spontaneous. It took weeks of planning just to visit the kids at college in Oregon. Sometimes she'd taken the boys on outings to the festivals around the area but never with him.

"When did you lose your wife? I remember seeing her in the wheelchair sometimes at the store and a few times at the beach but I only met her that once at Christmas."

The waiter came at that moment to take their

orders and when he left, Pete said, "Kathryn had a stroke when she was just about fifty-two and never quite recovered. She had a leg injury in a bike accident and they think a blood clot came from there and caused it. From that accident she also got an infection that eventually caused her to lose her leg. Almost seven years ago she went into a coma and after six months she just slipped away. I miss her."

Emily reached across the table and laid her hand on his. "I know about losing a spouse. I miss Sam too."

They sat there for a few minutes looking out the window, then Pete said, "Well, enough of the looking back, let's look ahead. What shall we have for dessert?"

That broke the melancholy mood and they were talking about the Seahawks when their food arrived. Crab Cakes for Emily and Clam Strips and Shrimp for Pete. It was good food, well prepared and they talked little while they ate.

"Now I think for dessert we want to have some Lemon Sherbet with a wafer cone, don't you think?" The waiter left to get their cones and when he returned with the bill, Emily held both cones while Pete paid.

They took their ice cream and walked down the street looking in windows and commenting on the displays.

"Thank you for the bouquet. I can't remember when I was last given flowers. And I've never been given lavender before."

Pete took her free hand and squeezed it. "You are so welcome. You've made this day good for me too."

Back at the car they decided it was time to put the top up and they started the drive home, going along the water, talking about the scenery until they had to cut across to take the Hood Canal Bridge. When they were on the ferry going back to Haven Port, he said, "I have a party to go to the week after the 4th. Will you go with me? It's a sort of reunion type of gathering we have every year since we graduated from med school at the U."

"I think I would like to go but let me check my calendar. My twins are coming home sometime at the end of the month and I'm not sure exactly when or how long they'll stay. Can I let you know tomorrow?"

Pete smiled. "It has been a lot of years since I asked anyone to go somewhere with me and I've been practicing it in my head this whole day." Then he laughed and took Emily's hand. "Hope I didn't scare you away from spending more time with me."

Emily smiled. "Pete, you couldn't be scary if you tried." They laughed together and Pete gave her hand another squeeze. "Well I've asked you now I'll just wait patiently."

Emily looked at him and was still smiling. This dating thing was still pretty new for her too and she totally understood his feelings.

The ferry ride from the Kitsap Peninsula to Haven Port was short and as they drove off the ferry and the short distance to their condos he said, "Thank you for helping me have a wonderful day."

She smile and said, "I thank you too."

He drove into his parking spot in the garage and then got out and opened her door. She got out and they went towards the elevator. It had been a good day and she was happier than she'd been in a very long time, and so was he.

CHAPTER 35

Emily was up early on Sunday and walking down the sidewalk headed for seven o'clock mass at St. Mary's. The day was a duplicate of yesterday and she walked with long strides, smiling to herself as she relived her time with Pete. She was happy and she had a plan. Next time she saw Dr. Pete... *oh I must remember to call him Pete...* well, next time she saw him she was going to ask him to dinner. Her mind wasn't paying attention to the traffic so when a car stopped and someone called her name she was startled, but only for a moment. It was Brian.

"Where you going so early? You're too dressed up for jogging." He stepped out of the car and joined her on the sidewalk.

"I'm on my way to church. Want to join me?"

"Am I dressed okay for church?" He was wearing jeans and a pale green golf shirt with tennis shoes. "I was on my way to play golf. Why don't you come with me?"

She smiled. "Why don't you come with me first then I'll go with you?"

It was fun to banter and Emily was enjoying it. She realized it was something she hadn't done since her children were home and memories came flooding back of Sundays on the way to church with them. Sam never went to church so it had been their time alone. "We'll pretend you're a tourist and then dress doesn't matter. Come on, you'll enjoy it."

Brian smiled. "I used to go to St. Mary's when I was a kid." There was a pause then he said, "Okay, I'll go and then you'll go golfing with me, right?"

"Yes, okay but I'll have to go home and change."

It was a deal and she got into his BMW. They drove down Front Street then along the water on Willow. As he was parking he said, "I hope the church doesn't fall down."

When they came out of St. Mary's Brian said, "I enjoyed that. Maybe I'll start going regularly again."

"Good idea."

They got into the car and were driving back to Emily's condo when he said, "How long will it take you to change and do you have clubs?"

"Just a few minutes, and no I don't have clubs any more, why?"

Brian smiled. "I'm going to drop you off then go get a set for you. I bought them for my mom but she never used them and she was just about your height."

Emily went up to her condo and changed to white slacks, a navy cotton tee and tennis shoes, and took a sweatshirt just in case. The golf course was located on the water and sometimes the wind could be chilly. She put some money and a lipstick in her pocket along with her keys and headed for the door, but before she could leave, the phone rang.

"Hi. Are you missing me?" It was Brad.

Emily smiled and said, "Well..."

"Not even a little?"

"I really haven't had a chance. You only left a few days ago. Are you home?"

Brad laughed. "No, not quite but maybe by Wednesday. Could we have dinner?"

Emily sighed. "I can't. I'm working on Wednesday. Could it be lunch instead?"

There was static and then the phone went dead. *Darn cell phones,* Emily thought and hung up. Now the Security phone was ringing. Brian was back.

Emily told him she'd be right down, went out the door and hurried to the elevator. She didn't hear her phone ringing again.

When they got to the club house, Brian took both sets of clubs out of his trunk and carried them over to the golf carts. "I think we better take a cart today for your return appearance." He secured the bags to the back of the cart and they went inside to register. This golf course allowed its members four rounds of golf a month and two passes for guests. Brian had a pass for Emily in his hand.

"Hey Brian, haven't seen you for awhile. Where you been?" The young man behind the counter seemed delighted to see him and Brian seemed happy too.

He collected a score card and took a pencil from the box. "Been busy in Seattle but I'll be spending more time here now. How's school?"

"Just graduated and I'm off to Annapolis in a few weeks. Can't wait."

"Hey, I'm impressed. You must be smarter than you look." They both laughed. "Bet you're grandma is happy for you too. Wasn't your grandpa in the Navy?"

"He was an admiral and Gram is very happy. I'm picking her up later to have dinner with us. I'll tell her I saw you."

"Thanks. I'll have to go see her again soon. Tell her I said I'm still in love with her, will you?"

Donny laughed. "I will. You can tee off when you're ready."

Brian said, "Thanks," and they went out the door.

"Do you know Ima Stump at the retirement home?"

Emily smiled. "If she heard you she'd be fluttering all around correcting you."

"What? She's still married isn't she?"

Emily explained the situation and that Dolly was not Ima anymore nor was she a Stump. She was Dolly McBride now. "How do you know her?"

"She was a friend of my Mother. They were in the same Bridge club and several other volunteer things and they were good friends. I like the old dear even with her funny accent."

Emily laughed at that. She'd never thought of Dolly as having a *funny* accent, only as *that's Dolly*. "Come and have lunch or dinner with her sometime. Just let me know and I'll make the arrangements."

He liked the idea and said he would call soon.

They got into the golf cart and Brian drove to the driving range. "How much have you played? Do you need instructions?"

"I haven't played for several years but let me give it a try and then when I'm the laughing stock of the course, you can help me." Emily put on the golf glove Brian handed her and took the Number Three wood from the bag. "I'll start with an easy club."

She stepped up and planted the tee, balanced the ball on it and stepped back. "Here goes something." She planted her feet, took a practice swing and then moved up to address the ball. The club swung back and then down and connected with the ball, sending it up and out.

"And you haven't played for how long?" Brian was happy she had the fundamentals down at least and looked forward to the round. She hit a few more while Brian warmed up next to her. "Ready to play?"

"As ready as I can be." Emily like playing this game but was remembering the reason she'd stopped. Sam didn't want to play golf with her and had discouraged her from being on the course when he was. It didn't seem fun to play with strangers so she just gave up.

The first hole was a dog-leg to the right and a par three. They approached the tee and Emily hit first. It went sailing out and landed about halfway to the green. "Good shot," he said. He hit and the ball landed on the edge of the green. They got into the cart and drove to Emily's ball first. "Do you know your clubs? Can I help?"

Emily pulled out the Four Iron and said, "I know what should be used and we'll see what I can do." She hit a little behind the ball and the divot went almost as far as the ball. "Oops."

Brian just laughed and waited as she walked up to the ball and hit it again. They played around to the ninth hole with Emily alternating good and not so good shots. "Shall we play the next nine or are you tired? I don't want to wear you out your first time back."

She wasn't tired. In fact she was happy and full of energy. They played the next nine holes then went to the club house for a drink. They ordered rum and cokes and rehashed the game. Their conversation was easy and enjoyable with a great deal of laughing, and they were about to leave when Steve and Larry showed up.

"Well, look who's here. Been playin' or just drinkin'?" Larry was laughing and truly happy to see Brian and Emily together.

"Hey Emily. Do you need saving or what? I'm here if you need me to stand up for you."
Steve was smiling too. One of his favorite girls was out and having fun.

"Hello fellows," Brian said. "I don't think this fair damsel needs saving but I'll buy you a drink if you have time."

"No thanks, we're just going to finish playing our round, but I saw you through the window and had to say hello."

"Glad you did Law. I'm always going to be happy to see you now that you introduced me to Emily." The two men smiled at each other knowing that the past was definitely healed.

"Everything seems okay here. Let's go, Larry." Steve headed out the door and Larry followed. "See you kids later."

Brian looked at Emily and said, "I really meant that. I'm so glad Law introduced us or made it possible for me to know you. I haven't felt so relaxed with a friend or had this kind of fun for so long I didn't even know I missed it."

Emily smiled and patted his hand. "Me too."

CHAPTER 36

Monday was almost as normal a day as any other day at St. Francis.

George was busy talking to Dr. Chu about tonight's travelogue, and Mary and Paul were holding hands as they walked toward the dining room, and Dolly was having a guest for lunch. It was as normal as Natalie busy making phone calls trying to find the person in charge of the Reunion Activities, and Larry busy congratulating himself and telling the other committee members that he was the one that found Brian for Emily, and Steve being Steve... winking and making suggestive remarks to any female who would listen. The only person who was not being himself was Dr. Pete.

"Are you okay today?" Sister Nora was concerned. "Didn't you have a good weekend?"

Dr. Pete said he was fine, just a little tired and went back to the clinic but he was not really feeling fine. After spending Saturday with Emily he thought they would spend Sunday together as well, but when he called her no one answered. Then later he saw her come home with a man. He hadn't stopped to consider she might be on a date. Somehow he'd gotten the idea the committee dates were over and that she'd met all the guys they had to present. He didn't know why he felt like this. They'd had a wonderful day together, but it didn't mean..., well anything. *I should stop assuming she had as good a time as I did* and that *she felt as comfortable with me as I wanted her to*. They'd been friends since their kids played on the same summer teams together, seeing each other at swim meets and baseball games. *I'm probably assuming too much.* That was it. He was hurrying her. He'd slow down and see how things went. This made him feel a little better.

The health clinic office hours at St. Francis were scheduled from seven until eleven on Monday and Thursday mornings. Afterwards, Dr. Pete usually had lunch with Sister Nora in the dining room before going to his office in the Doctor's Building. Today after they went through the food line and they were about to sit down to eat, Dr. Pete's cell phone rang. It was an emergency and he had to go. He left his tray and on the way out the door he almost knocked Emily down.

"Hello and good-bye," he said. "I'm on the way to my office. I'll talk to you later."

Emily thought, *Okay*, and wondered why he would be coming back. She hurried to the dining room and found Dolly waiting by the door.

"Is he here yet?" Emily knew who Dolly was waiting for.

Dolly smiled her sweet smile and said, "No, not yet. But he said he'd come and he will. The boy never promised his mother anything he didn't do and I just know he wouldn't disappoint me either."

At that moment, Brian came in the door and his smile was as wide as Dolly's.

"I hope I'm not late. I got busy pulling up carpet and time got away from me." He took her hand and said, "Now where do we go? I haven't been here before so you lead." He smiled at Emily and winked.

"Come this way young man. We'll just go through the food line and then Ah'll show you where our table is." Her drawl made it a slow speech and they were in line before she finished. Today's lunch menu was tomato soup and sandwiches you made yourself. First Dolly placed a glass of ice tea on her tray then she took one piece of rye bread and spread it with Thousand Island dressing. Next she laid on two thin slices of corned beef and a slice of Swiss cheese and had Edith the cook cut it in half. That looked so good that Brian did the same except with two pieces of bread and a few more slices of meat. Then they got the soup, a cup for Dolly and a bowl for Brian, and headed for a table. A special *guest table* was available at each meal for just such occasions. If there were no guests, it was left empty but today Dolly was pleased to have everyone see her with this handsome young man.

Emily was only there to make sure Dolly and her date met up and she was leaving when Natalie came into the dining room.

"Hello, aren't you a little early for work today?"

Emily smiled and said she was just leaving. "I'll be back at four. See you then."

Natalie smiled. Emily was her success story. Just look at her in her trim jeans, red tee shirt and sandals. Quite a transformation and the dating was still going well too. Steve told her about yesterday.

After lunch Larry chatted a few minutes with

Brian and said, "Come back again and have lunch with me sometime or you could have lunch with both of us. We're friendly."

Dolly said, "Yes, do come back and we'll invite Larry to join us. Want to set a date now?"

"I'd like to but my schedule is never fixed for me until I go to the office on Tuesdays. I'll give you a call, okay?"

He left after shaking hands all around and giving Dolly a kiss on the cheek. Larry said, "You know I thought he was an okay kid but he turned out to be one hell of a man."

Dolly smiled at him and said, "Yes, he did. His mother would be so proud."

They left the dining room and parted company with Dolly heading for her apartment and Larry heading for the patio and a cigarette.

As was her custom, Emily came into the office that afternoon at three-forty-five. She was wearing dark green slacks, a pale green cotton sweater set, and tan sandals with a wedge heel. When she left St. Francis after lunch, she'd walked down by the golf course and then home. She was feeling good. Her face had a healthy glow from the sun she'd gotten over the weekend and her energy level was high.

She put her purse in the locker and decided today she would finish going through the box that held the pictures. Every month they posted pictures on the bulletin board on the wall just outside the office door. The pictures came from the residents or from Sister Nora's camera. There were snapshots in the box of Dr. Chu's travelogue group intently watching the slide screen, of people having coffee in the dining room, of guests coming and going with their families and friends, and several of grandchildren. At the end of the month the pictures were replaced with new ones and the old snaps put into this box. Emily had been sorting and giving the pictures away. She'd started the project last week and had folders full of group photos, one for people she didn't know and one for those she did. She picked up several photos and looked at the top one. It was taken just before Christmas this last year and Emily was standing with several others in front of the Christmas tree in the dining room. There was Sister Nora, Dr. Pete, Edith Ann Taylor from the kitchen staff and Anita from the office. Emily could hardly recognize the woman with her long black skirt, long-sleeved sweater that hung almost down to her knees, and those glasses with the dark rims that were as big as her face. She put the picture in the group photo pile. The next picture was of Dr. Pete and his boys and their wives and his three young grandsons. It had been taken at Christmas in front of the same tree when they were here visiting for the holidays. Emily knew the boys from years ago when they were younger and loved meeting them again as grown men. Seeing this picture started her thinking about her own boys. If they didn't make it up here this month, she definitely was going to go visit them. She made a mental note to call them tomorrow.

It was almost eight o'clock when Pete came in the side door of St. Francis and into Emily's office. She wasn't there. He scowled and went across the hall to his clinic. He'd left so abruptly today he hadn't had time to put his files in order and clean off his desk. Emily found him there on her way back from the dining room with a cup of coffee.

"Hi. Want some coffee?"

He looked up and smiled. "Oh yes I would like

that. Just let me finish here and I'll join you."

"I'll get the coffee. Decaf?" He nodded and she went back to the dining room.

He was finished in just a few minutes and as he closed up the office she was coming back with his cup. They went into her office and he said, "Have you seen Sister Nora lately?"

"Yes, she's in the dining room talking to Dr. Chu and Marilyn."

He smiled at her again and said, "I'll be right back."

He was back in less than five minutes and sat down. "Now for coffee." He picked it up and sipped. It was sweet, just the way he liked it. "How did you know I take sugar in my coffee?"

Emily smiled. "I think it's part of my job to know the little things that will make life happy for you and the residents here. That and the fact that I've been behind you in the dining room a number of times when we were getting coffee and I've watched you add a half spoon of sugar."

He laughed. "Well, I know you like a little milk in your coffee. How's that for observant?"

She laughed. "Do you know how Sister takes hers?"

"Black but she prefers tea... no milk, no sugar."

They were both smiling.

Dr. Pete wanted to say something to Emily about Sunday but he didn't know how to start. He was about to say something he hoped would be brilliant and on the subject when the phone rang and saved him. Emily answered by saying, "St. Francis Retirement Center" and then said, "Just a moment." She handed him the phone and said, "It's for you."

He took the phone and said, "Pete Laferty." He

listened then said, "How long?" He listened some more. "Okay, I'll be there in about fifteen minutes. Are you at home?" A pause then, "Okay. I'm on the way." He handed the phone back to Emily. "Well, I thought we could have a chat but now I have to go. If I'm done in time, I'll call you before you go home, is that okay?"

Emily said it would be and smiled at him. "Something bad?"

"No, it's just Thelma Stewart. She's having problems carrying this baby and I told her to call me if she had any labor pains. She's had them twice and it was indigestion the first time and a then false labor. This is her third baby and you'd think she'd know the difference but she doesn't. See you later maybe." And he took his car keys out of his pocket and left, only having had a sip of coffee.

Emily put his cup on the small table by the door and went back to her computer. She thought when he called she'd ask him if he wanted the pictures from Christmas.

At nine-fifteen the phone rang. It was Brian calling. "Are you about to get off work?"

"Yes I am."

"Did you drive today?"

"Yes, why? Do you need a ride?"

Brian laughed. "No but I wanted you to see what I've done so far at the condo. Can you come by? I'll give you a beer."

"Well that's an offer I can't refuse. Sure. Be there shortly after nine-thirty."

She finished typing, saved her document on the computer and turned it off then put away the file she was working from. She gathered up the picture folders and put them in the drawer, turned off the lights, locked the office door and went to see

Brian's accomplishments.

At nine-thirty-five the phone rang and Sister Nora answered. It surprised Dr. Pete but he asked if Emily was still there and was told she'd gone. He hung up and decided to call her at home and beg a cup of coffee to replace the one he'd had to leave. He dialed and got her answering machine. "Hi, it's Pete. I'll try you again in a few minutes." He was on the south side of the island when he'd called, so in a few minutes he drove up to his condo and parked. He called Emily again from his cell phone as he came out of the garage. She still wasn't home and he didn't leave a message this time. *Was she out on a date on Monday? He should have asked when he saw her if she was free tonight* but he was tired and decided he would see her tomorrow and get things straightened out. As he walked into his condo he resisted the urge to call her again.

CHAPTER 37

Brian's condo was located on the Cliffs, the part of Haven Port that faces east. The view was of Seattle and the Puget Sound's shipping lanes and tonight the Seattle lights were sparkling in spite of the drizzle. Emily was glad there was a covered area where she could park. He buzzed her in and she took the elevator to the third floor where she found Brian waiting at his front door. His jeans and shirt were paint spattered with various colors.

"Wait until you see what I did." He was excited and Emily was excited too. He led the way into the condo and said, "Surprise!"

The first room was a living room with the walls painted a very pale gray. The wall facing the water was all windows, and on one wall was a white and gray stone fireplace with book cases on both sides. The walls had a white crown molding around the top about eight inches down from the high white ceilings. His large, dark brown leather sofa faced the windows and the floors were of a beautiful gleaming hardwood. The only other thing in the room was an area rug in front of the sofa. In spite of the sparse furnishings, the room was warm and beautiful.

"Come see the rest." Brian was like a kid showing off his accomplishments "This is the den." Here he had dark green walls, a large roll top desk, his computer and printer on a table, and several filing cabinets. The floors were the same hardwood and in this room he'd put down a geometric print area rug of bright red, green, yellow and dark blue. The windows were covered with bamboo roll up shades and the drapes were made of heavy corduroy, the same color as the walls. "This is the only room that has all the furniture I need."

As Emily was exclaiming over the colors and the fun rug he was pulling her toward the kitchen. It was a pale yellow with red counter tops and black stove and refrigerator. There was room for stools at the counter and also room for a kitchen table but he had neither.

Next he was showing her the dining room with the walls painted a soft green. The only furniture was a buffet side-table that was obviously an antique. "My mother got this as a wedding present from her mother who got it from her mother." It was hand carved and stood on high, heavy legs. There were doors on the sides and three deep drawers in the middle.

"I'm thinking of putting a chair rail in here, what do you think?"

They discussed the need and look of chair rails in a dining room and what color they should be and Emily admired the hardwood floors in here too.

"I started pulling up the carpet and got as far as re-doing the floors in the den, the dining room, the kitchen and front room but I still have to do the bedrooms. I haven't painted them yet either."

"How many do you have?"

"Two. I used one and Annie used the master for the last few months." As he said this he was realizing how much he missed having Annie here to share the fun. "I'm still sleeping in the little one until she finishes picking up her furniture." He made a mental note to call her and to make the arrangements, but what he really wanted to do was tell her about the condo and, well, just talk to her.

Emily was curious about Annie but didn't ask. "Do you have colors picked out?"

"No, not yet and after this weekend, I'm pretty tired. Can't wait to get back to work to rest up."

They both laughed.

He went to the refrigerator and said, "I have Miller Lite or a German beer I brought back a few trips ago. I suggest the lager."

"Okay, I'll try that."

He poured each of them a glass and said, "Let's sit in the living room. There's only the sofa but it's comfortable."

When they were seated he said, "Did you mean it when you said you'd help me pick out furniture? I need everything. Even a new bed."

"Sure I meant it. I even have some catalogues left from my own decorating adventures. We can start there. I'll bring them by."

"I'm a visual kind of guy so I'll need to see the actual furniture and sit in it before I buy. Will that be a problem?"

"Of course not. We'll look at the catalogues, see what styles appeal to you and then go to the stores that carry that style. You can shop and try sitting until your heart says buy it. Is that a good plan?"

Brian laughed. "Perfect. I have to work tomorrow and then Wednesday I fly out so I'll call you and we can maybe make shopping plans for the weekend."

"I'll need to check my calendar but I think I'm free. Call me when you get back. Did you say you have a place in Seattle too?"

"I do but it's just a studio and close to downtown. Just up on Capital Hill. A place to crash when I get in late. All I need there is a TV and a bed and microwave."

She laughed and said, "Well, you call me when you're ready and we'll go spend your money."

They talked another half hour but Emily could see Brian's eyes were starting to droop. "I'm going home now and you get some sleep. How early do you have to leave the island?"

"I don't have to be at work until nine so I'm good to sleep in and take the eight o'clock ferry. Can I follow you home? Will you be okay?"

"No you stay here and I'll bet you'll be asleep before I get in my door."

He smiled, put his arm around her shoulders and hugged her. "I'm so lucky to find a friend like you."

Emily liked the fact that they were friends too but she hoped that was all he was feeling. For her there didn't seem to be any *sparks*, just a feeling of warm friendly togetherness.

He walked her down to the car and she was home in twenty minutes. As she readied for bed she thought about Pete. She wondered if the baby actually came or if it was another false alarm.

CHAPTER 38

Tuesday afternoon, Emily picked up her keys and purse and was ready to leave for work when the phone rang.

"Hello, how're you today?" It was Brad.

Emily smiled. She was happy to hear from him. "I'm fine. How're you?"

"I'd be better if we were having dinner together."

"I have to work. In fact I was just leaving. Where are you?"

"I'm just getting on the ferry to come home. How about a drink after work?"

"Okay, where shall I meet you?"

"Want to meet a Jake's? Do you know where that is?"

Emily laughed. "You forget I've lived here all my life and I know where everything is. Yes, Jake's will be fine. A little after nine-thirty?"

"Yes. I can't wait to see you." And he was gone.

The day was misty and not exactly warm. Emily was wearing navy slacks, the red and navy flowered blouse and a navy cotton cardigan. She loved her new clothes and how they made her feel. Almost like a different person.

Mary came into Emily's office to say hello and to tell her the news. "We've decided to get married."

Emily hugged her. It was not a surprise but she was so happy. "I'm so excited for you. When will this happen?"

"We've made arrangements to go to St. Mary's on Friday but it'll just be a small group, just Paul and me and I'm hoping you will come and be my witness or maid-of-honor or whatever it's called."

Emily went around the desk and hugged her. "Of course I will and I'm thinking we need to have a reception for you. To announce this to the world and to celebrate, don't you think? I would love to plan something for Friday afternoon or evening, whichever you say."

Mary smiled. "Well, maybe a little cake and punch in the church afterwards would be nice. The ceremony is set for two o'clock."

"I'll call the church right now and get it started. Oh Mary, I'm so happy for you and Paul." They hugged again.

Mary said she would check in before going to dinner because they wanted to make an announcement tonight about the wedding, and "it would be nice to tell everyone about the reception too."

Emily dialed the church and got Thelma Faulkner on the phone. Everyone in town knew Thelma. She was a retired nun and ran the St. Mark's

Catholic Church office like a military unit. Emily made arrangements for the recreation room and Thelma said she would ask the Alter Society to decorate it a bit and to set up tables and chairs.

Next Emily called Archie's Grocery store to see if Mrs. Archie would make a cake for them and also make the punch. Emily smiled to herself and wondered again what Archie's wife's name was. They'd been at this store for thirty years or more and when she was introduced with her husband as a couple, it was always this is Archie McGregor and his wife Mrs. Archie.

Mrs. Archie said she would enjoy making the cake and she'd take care of getting the cake and the punch there along with punch bowl and cups, and wouldn't it be nice to have a few mints and nuts? Emily agreed and next she called the stationary shop in the mall. They did have suitable napkins and Emily said she'd be in to pick them up tomorrow.

Mary came back on her way to the dining room and said, "I forgot to tell you we'll be moving."

Emily must have looked both surprised and sad because Mary hastened to say, "We're moving upstairs to the bigger couples unit, the one that looks out the front and has a deck. Paul is giving his furniture to the Thrift Shop and we're going to Seattle tomorrow to get a new bedroom suite. Would you like to come with us on this adventure?"

"Yes I would but I have to work. Wait... are you going in the morning?"

"Yes. I knew you had to work and we plan to take the three o'clock ferry home so that would leave you plenty of time, wouldn't it? We want to go to the Sears Warehouse Store and we know just what we want so it won't take too long. Sears will bring it here on Thursday. It's their day for island deliveries so we have to go on Wednesday. Oh Emily, isn't this exciting. I just can't wait to start being Mrs. Paul Engles."

"Do you think you'll take a little honeymoon trip?"

"Oh my. I forgot to tell you that too. Paul is taking me to Florida. I've never been anywhere outside of Washington and Oregon... well once we went to Idaho. Anyway, he's going to show me his favorite places. He worked in Florida for many years and... I'm rattling now." She laughed. "Can you tell I'm a little nervous?"

Emily smiled. "I don't think you need to be very nervous. He's a lovely man and you love each other and now that he has his problem under control, travel shouldn't be a problem either."

"That's what we thought. We're no spring chickens but with a little care we can still travel and I'm so looking forward to that part and the part where I have someone special to love. Oh Emily. I hope you find that too."

They hugged again and then Emily filled her in about the arrangements for the reception. Mary was pleased and hugged Emily again, then she was off to find Paul and tell him.

At nine-thirty that night Emily turned off the lights and locked the office door. She was happy to be seeing Brad and having a glass of wine or maybe a beer like she'd had at Brian's.

She parked in front of the door and went into Jake's. Once in the entry way she could turn right and she would be in the dining room, and if she turned left she could go into the bar. She turned left and as she sat down, she could hear the poker game in the back room was in full swing. Brad could be heard saying, "No really, I have a date. I have to leave to see a beautiful woman." The other men were saying he should *come back* when the date was over, and then he appeared at the door. He was wearing a tan, long-sleeved, knit shirt with the sleeves pushed up, and brown slacks. He looked as handsome as she remembered.

She smiled and said, "Were you winning or losing?"

"Winning. That's why they want me back. I think I'm up twenty-seven bucks." He laughed and leaned across the table to kiss her softly on the lips. "I've really been looking forward to that."

Emily liked it too but it made her blush. She was sitting at the table for two by the window and he sat across from her. When the bartender came for their order, he said, "Hi, Emily. How you doin'? What will you have tonight?"

"Hello Sam. Do you carry any German lagers?"

"Yes we have Dortmunder and Bitburger. Do you know them?" Sam smiled because this was not only unusual to see Emily here but with a guy.

"Not really, but I'll try the Dortmunder."

"Good choice. How about you Brad?"

Brad was impressed. "I'll have one too."

Sam left to get the beers and Brad said, "I didn't know you liked German beer. Come to think of it, I don't really know much about your likes. I know you like children and old people and wine and now German beer, but what else? Do you like me?"

Emily smiled and to her surprise, didn't blush. "Yes I do like children and old people and yes I do like you. Tell me where you've been."

"Oh, here and there. I was in New Orleans for a few days and Texas and then in Canada."

"What do you do again? I thought you said it was something to do with seismic activity. Isn't that earthquake related?"

Brad smiled and said, "Yes it is earthquake related and yes that's what I do. I've been commissioned to try to predict earthquakes so we can save lives."

"So what was in New Orleans and Texas?"

"Well, it was a board meeting and—"

"Was it an extra board meeting that made you get called away or did you just forget about it and had to hurry to get there?" Emily thought she was teasing but Brad was very serious.

He didn't smile when he said, "No, it was a planned event and that's where I was. Now let's talk about you and what you've been doing without me."

She realized that his work wasn't something he took lightly and thought, *That's okay. I can appreciate that.*

Trying to change the subject she told him she played golf on Sunday and started to tell him how badly she played but he interrupted and wanted to know who with? She told him.

Then she told him about going to Sequim for dinner on Saturday and he did it again, wanting to know who with again, and she told him that too.

"Well, I guess my not being here didn't matter too much. Did you have a good time in Sequim and golfing?" He was getting too serious and sarcastic and it made Emily uncomfortable.

With courage she didn't know she had she said, "Why does it matter? You were busy on Saturday and we had no plans for Sunday."

Brad tried to relax and he did smile but it was tight. "It's really none of my business but I like you and I think I'm a little jealous of not being able to be with you more. I'm sorry for the inquisition. Do you forgive me?"

The beer came and Emily relaxed. She took a sip and it tasted as good as the one last night with Brian. "Yes, I forgive you." She smiled back at him and realized she really did want to be friends and this was just a little bump. It was nice to have someone care where she was."

They drank the beer and chatted and then ordered another. Emily told him about the excitement at St. Francis and the upcoming wedding and ended by saying, "They're so happy. To think of finding someone that special twice in your life."

Brad looked pensive. "I'd just like to find someone special for now. Are you available?" His gaze turned intense and there was no hint of teasing or banter. This was a serious question.

She was a little surprised. They'd only just met and hadn't really spent any time together. "Well, I'm available but I think I'd like for us to know each other better before I really commit."

"I can live with that, thank you." He seemed to relax a little. "Now, speaking of getting to know each other, let's talk about lunch tomorrow. The more we see each other, the more we'll find out and—"

Emily laughed. "That's true but I can't tomorrow."

Brad stopped smiling and said, "Why not? Do you have another date?"

Emily didn't smile this time. "I have plans."

He leaned forward and said, "Is it another man?"

Emily was getting uncomfortable again and didn't like his manner towards her, so she decided she would end this evening.

"No, it's not. I'm going to Seattle to help a friend pick out furniture." She picked up her purse and stood up. "Thank you for the beer."

"I'm sorry. I get a little intense sometimes. I was just worried—"

She didn't let him finish. "Yes you are a little intense sometimes. Good night." She walked out the door to her car. She could see him still sitting at the table with his head hanging down and she felt sorry for him, but Mary told her if any situation felt uncomfortable she should leave it, and Brad had made her uncomfortable twice tonight with his questions about other men and where she was going and what she was doing.

Shortly after she left Jake's, the poker game broke up and the men came out of the back room. Steve and Larry said good night and went out the door but Pete and the others sat at the bar and ordered. Murph saw Brad alone and said, "Hey, where's the beautiful woman?"

"She's gone and I'm ready for another beer." He moved to the bar stool and Sam said, "Want another lager?"

"Yes. Maybe it'll drown my sorrows."

Pete was sitting next to him and said, "We all have women problems now and then. Things will be better tomorrow after a good nights sleep."

"Well, maybe," Brad said and took a big drink of his new beer.

Pete took a drink of his coffee and not having a clue about Brad's problem thought, *And I think my woman problem is maybe getting better.*

CHAPTER 39

The clouds from last night were gone, leaving this Wednesday morning pleasant and sunny with the promise of a warm afternoon. Emily volunteered to drive them on this adventure and when she pulled up at the front door she saw Mary and Paul talking to Dr. Pete. As she got out of the car she thought, *Why is he here when it's not clinic day?*

"Here's our driver now." Paul was full of good cheer and it was catching. "We asked Dr. Pete to come too. Now we have our Best Man and our Best Woman with us."

Oh, thought Emily. "Well, if we go now we can catch the nine-thirty ferry." They agreed and hurried to get settled in the car with Paul and Mary in the back and Dr. Pete in front with Emily. As they were fastening their seat belts he said, "And from now on could I be Pete and not a doctor for today?"

They all laughed and Emily reached over and patted his hand. "Sure Pete." They all laughed again.

Emily had ferry passes that covered the trip to Seattle. Once parked on the ferry Pete and Paul went to get coffee and Mary said, "Oh Emily isn't this fun?"

"Yes it is and very I'm happy but surprised that Pete joined us. Shouldn't he be working today?"

"We were a little surprised too but he called Paul last night to say he'd be happy to be the Best Man or witness or whatever on Friday and Paul told him about this shopping trip. He sort of invited himself. He said he needed some time away from work and Paul said this would make it more fun for us too. Do you mind?"

Emily smiled. "I certainly don't mind. He's so sweet and fun to be with, it couldn't help but make the day even better."

They were both smiling broadly but when the guys came back to the car they were suddenly silent. "Want to share this happiness with us?" asked Pete.

Mary looked at Emily and they broke out in laughter that was almost giggles. Mary said, "We were indulging in a little girl talk and you both know we can't possibly share that."

Paul looked at Pete and said, "Don't you just love being with women that are happy?"

Pete nodded but he didn't say out loud that he really did like being with happy people and with happy women and particularly with Emily.

As they drove off the ferry Paul said, "Do you need directions?"

"I don't think so. Aren't we going to the furniture warehouse by the South End Shopping Mall?"

"That's the one," said Paul as Emily got on the freeway and headed south. She drove into the parking lot just about fifteen minutes later but near to the door parking spaces didn't seem to exist.

"Why don't you all get out here at the door and I'll park and meet you inside?" Emily stopped by the big double doors.

This was one the super warehouse type store that covered an acre or so.

"I'll stay with Emily," said Pete. "How about we meet you two in the bedroom department?" and it was decided. Paul and Mary got out of the car.

As they walked to the mega store, Mary said, "I'm glad I wore my walking shoes."

Paul took her hand and said, "Me too. Let's get started. Do you have the list?" She did and they walked hand in hand through the front doors.

Emily found a space about a block from the door. "They need a shuttle service from the parking lot when parking is this far away."

Pete laughed. "The walk will do me good but you look in shape. I see you walking all the time. That probably accounts for you robust, good health."

"That's probably part of it but good company also helps." She smiled at him and thought, *Pete is really good company. I'm glad he's here.*

They walked into the store and found themselves in the bathroom department." We could wander around for hours and never see them again." Pete was smiling. He was relaxed and happy and that hadn't happened to him since—well, since Saturday.

"We're supposed to meet in the bedroom department. Wonder where that is?" said Peter.

They finally found a directory on the wall and turned left, heading where the arrow pointed.

"I like shopping for furniture," said Emily and she stopped and stroked the back of a chair covered in silk brocade.

Pete smiled at her. "I don't think I've ever done this kind of shopping thing before." He felt the covering on a foot stool. "Is this silk?"

"It's a brocade but probably not silk at this price. Synthetics looked so very real sometimes that you really can't easily tell the difference." Then she pointed out the linen cover on another chair and a corded material. "All made to look like expensive materials but if you read the tags you'll see they're mostly cotton and polyester.

He pointed to a bench and said, "That's leather, right? I'm not completely stupid."

"No, not completely," she said and they both laughed.

Pete and Emily were having fun. They walked on bantering back and forth with Pete asking questions and Emily trying to keep a straight face when she answered.

They passed the kitchen cabinet department and exclaimed over all the choices of wood and the other finishes available. Next they came to the counter tops: marble, granite, wood block and more. Pete said, "There are too many decision to make. When we built our house in '65 we had standard counter tops of Formica, and the cabinets were just painted particle board and linoleum floors were everywhere except the living room. I know Kathryn updated the flooring and we did get new windows and siding, but I feel a little out of it to not be even able to recognize any of these materials that are in homes now. What's wrong with me?"

"I suspect Kathryn did everything connected with the home and didn't want to bother you with the details. The old wives-takes-care-of-the-home and the husband-works thing. I know that's the way it was in my family too. I don't think my husband knew what wood was in the flooring or that we kept the floors in good condition by stripping them every five years and having them redone. Men don't see those things as long as everything runs smoothly." Emily smiled. "The young people marrying now are really more partners than we were. My boys change diapers and baby-sit while my daughter-in-laws go out for a day or a girl's weekend. I don't think our generation even thought about it. Men did men things and women did women things. Now they seem to share more. I like it and wish I'd had it."

Pete smiled. "Yes my kids seem to have happy marriages too. And they do enjoy each others company a lot. More than I seemed to have time for when I was a young husband. If I get the chance again, I want a marriage like that."

Emily smiled at him and thought, *Me too. I want a marriage of talking and sharing and just wanting to be happy when you are together."* That made her remember the picture she found yesterday. "I found a picture of you and your children from a past Christmas. I meant to ask you if you would like to have it."

"Yes, I would. Thank you. Pictures and stuff like that I left in Kathryn's hands too. I left too much for her to do."

"Do you miss her? I know I miss my husband but that doesn't mean I'm unhappy. I've started a new life and that was the old one. I miss the happy parts but I think I'm happy now, just as I am."

"I do miss her and I agree I miss the happy parts most. However I know I need to be happy in this part of my life too." He reached for her hand and said,

"And being with you makes me happy."

Paul spotted them just at this moment and waved.

"I'd like to continue this conversation later." Pete was smiling and he squeezed Emily's hand again as he looked into her eyes.

Emily was smiling too, and squeezed back. "It's a date."

It was the first time she'd let her feelings out into the light and had expressed the fact that she *was* happy. She missed her boys but that could be remedied, and she was looking forward to more long talks with Pete, and spending more time with him. A lot more time.

Mary and Paul watched them from across the room and Paul said, "Do you think they might become a couple too?"

Mary said, "I hope so" and she looked directly at Paul as she took his hand. "I hope they can find the same happiness we're feeling." Paul raised her hand to his lips and kissed the back of her fingers.

Pete and Emily made their way across the room and Emily was thinking, "*This friendship is so very nice, and I have real feelings for him. I don't want to ever let him out of my life.*

Pete was thinking *I hope I can make Emily realize how much I care for her, no... love her.*

And they were both thinking how lucky they were to find each other and to be here together.

The shopping went well and the purchases were completed with only a few questions from Pete and answers from one of the other three. They picked out one bed with mattress and springs, one large dresser both in a dark walnut, and two chairs for the living room, and a wooden kitchen table with four chairs of a lighter wood that Pete proudly identified as oak. They were now on their way to have lunch when Paul said, "Emily thank you for coming with us and thank you too Pete. You made this day special."

Pete looked at Emily then at the couple in the back seat and said, "Yes it *has* been a special day and we owe it all to you two."

Emily smiled because she knew exactly what he meant. It had become a very special day indeed, because she too realized she had already found the one she could love forever... from this day forward.

Mary and Paul were also smiling as they held hands and looked at their happy friends.

Two new beginnings...
...and not even close to an ending.